ENTANGLEMENT

CASS LENNOX

RIPTIDE
PUBLISHING

Riptide Publishing
PO Box 1537
Burnsville, NC 28714
www.riptidepublishing.com

Entanglement

Cover art: L.C. Chase, lcchase.com
Editor: Grace Stack
Layout: L.C. Chase, lcchase.com

ISBN: 978-1-62649-962-1

First edition
May, 2022

Also available in ebook:
ISBN: 978-1-62649-961-4

ENTANGLEMENT

CASS LENNOX

For Matúš and Martina: in honour of our beautiful friendship.

TABLE OF
CONTENTS

CHAPTER
ONE

The universal clock in the terminal ticked with frankly disrespectful verve, increasing the Parliament member's lateness—and, more importantly, Renée's hunger—with every second. The terminal was quiet, the public temporarily barred. Ticket-holders for the portals had been relegated to a waiting room, and stars *above* that wasn't an exercise Renée wished to repeat anytime soon.

She eyed a nearby bench, wishing she'd sat down ten minutes ago. Not that it would help for long; another ten minutes and she would no doubt drop dead from low blood sugar. Things like that happened all the time and there was no reason it couldn't happen to her, if only once. Even worse, her saviour and redeemer—the pork bun she'd bought on her way to work—sat forgotten on her desk, in her office, in the police station, in the centre of the city. Not here in her hands, before the Arden portal gate, in the terminal, on the edge of the city.

"Has he arrived yet?" Atkins crackled in her ear. "Over."

She scoffed into the microphone in her collar. "As though Parliament members could do anything on time. No. Any updates? Over."

"Yes. Keller is gathering the leeches, and we're reviewing the hotel footage now. If we find anything, I'll report back immediately. Over."

"Good. Over and out."

Food stalls weren't allowed in the terminal for reasons she couldn't remember, but were probably illogical. How were passengers and people waiting for passengers supposed to cope? Her blood sugar could handle the drive back to her office, maybe. But that wasn't a prospect, as no one could drive her anywhere, because they had to *wait*, all because some *connard* of a bureaucrat couldn't activate a matter displacer *on time—*

Violet light seared through the skylight in the ceiling and the portal gate in front of her glowed, announcing his successful arrival. Finally.

She murmured into her mouthpiece, and her colleagues straightened as Janus Parliament Member Richard Elleul appeared in the gate. When the transfer completed, the status light turned green and he stepped out of the portal, through the barrier, and into the waiting area. Average height and heavyset, he moved with the swagger of someone powerful and wore the expression of someone who'd bitten into a mouldy sandwich.

According to the Intelligence database, he was an outspoken devotee of the party line, climbing high in Parliament, and—notably—the minister responsible for the latest restrictions against enhanced beings. He was here supposedly to investigate the recent murder of a courier, but Renée didn't believe that for a moment.

She glanced him up and down, feeling . . . what was the word? Disappointed? Disapproving? Somehow the man responsible for bringing so much business to her little outpost here on the edge of the system seemed a little short. Very ordinary looking. Someone who'd implemented the kind of policies he had should be more striking. Intense eyes, perhaps, or a wide smirk, or a full head of hair. This man looked like the thieves who chased after the refugees in her city's streets: self-important and underwhelming. The only difference was the quality of clothing.

Oh well. C'est la vie. The pork bun was close now.

Renée bit back a grin as she saluted him. "Neutral space welcomes you to Pann, Member Elleul."

Elleul took in her and her colleagues and sniffed before saluting in return. "I wish I were here on more pleasurable business, Prefect Bellevue."

"Don't we all, monsieur." She introduced him to her colleagues, then began walking him through the terminal building. She waited for him to appreciate the old Haitian architecture dating back to the initial days of terraforming and building, when this had been the original entry point to the Janus system for pioneers and explorers from Orion, but he ignored the mosaic on the floor and didn't even look up at the magnificent skylight in the ceiling. *Tch*. It was the original glass. Some people had no appreciation for history.

Nonetheless, she had to be professional. "I was hoping you could elaborate on Parliament's interest in this unfortunate incident."

The report had appeared on her dash that morning: a courier from the core planets had been found dead in her hotel, room and luggage stripped clean. Nothing unusual about that—people died and their things were redistributed all the time in Pann—until Renée had received a notification from the core planets, stating Member Elleul was coming to personally look into the matter that same day. Naturally she'd bumped the incident up in prioritisation level on her officers' dashes.

Elleul shook his head. "It's simple. The courier was actually a diplomat with a missive for the government of Fides."

Well. A *diplomat*. How *interesting*.

Renée didn't consider herself prone to dramatics, but this raised her hackles ever so slightly. While this region of the habitable zone had been designated neutral space to allow diplomacy and trade to occur between systems, Janus's Parliament was vocal about refusing to formally negotiate with enhancement-sympathisers. Fides was the closest system to Janus, and welcoming of enhanced beings, which meant it was where all the refugees fled.

But neither system's government had told Renée the diplomat would be passing through Pann—which meant that this "diplomat" was meant to have slipped over without any notice.

Most interesting was that the missive of said courier/diplomat and her gold standard, iron-clad, irrefutable ticket for the portal trip to Caeliton in Fides were now somewhere in Pann's black market. Elleul would wish those recovered, though the missive was probably long subsumed into the local resistance cell. They enjoyed any scrap of information they could get.

Renée supposed she'd have to spare an officer to waste their time looking for it on whatever channels the Tech division could access. The ticket might still be possible to retrieve. It would be less easy to hide and too much of an opportunity to destroy.

Now that she wasn't in the portal area with its huge skylight, she couldn't glance up towards the star that marked the Fides system, but she could picture its gentle twinkle. The people she'd had shuffled into spare waiting rooms might be picturing it too, because they watched her and Member Elleul walk through the building with silent glares. She ignored them. After all, they'd paid, received their own tickets, and would shortly no longer be her problem.

"I see," she said, injecting the right amount of surprise into her voice.

"You and your mayor weren't informed because of classified reasons."

Classified reasons. Renée knew exactly what *classified reasons* meant. "Seems a little strange someone so important would travel with something so important without protection of some kind while in Pann. I keep order as best I can, but, as you may have noticed, unfortunate incidents still occur."

Elleul made a face. "That reason is also classified."

"I understand completely. You are here to ensure justice for the unfortunate diplomat?"

"Of course."

"You have my force at your disposal, monsieur. I have them rounding up likely suspects as we speak, but I'll ensure we have at least twice the usual number on this occasion."

"Your help is much appreciated, Prefect." He glanced her over, eyes flickering to spots on her face, joints, and limbs for signs of enhancement. "I know this is a neutral territory, but I'm glad to see that the leader of law enforcement here doesn't feel the need to pollute her body with foreign objects."

Au contraire, there was a pork bun she was desperate to pollute herself with. Also, he had to know she was a Janus citizen. The prefect always was. Renée smiled at him. "I don't require much to fulfil my duties beyond coffee, data feeds and good people." And timely lunches.

The receiver in her ear gently buzzed to life. "Prefect! We have reviewed the camera feeds. It's Fentiman. Over."

Putain. Fentiman was a minor but stubborn leech who'd only lasted as long as he had in Pann due to his sole talent of being in the right place at the right time. He'd always been so polite whenever her force had arrested him. She was going to miss puzzling over his airtight alibis and prodigious upselling.

Still, he was nothing if not predictable, which made her job *much* easier.

She angled the microphone in her collar closer to her mouth and responded, "Excellent work, Atkins. I'm with the member now and will inform him. Over and out." She turned to Elleul. "We have discovered our murderer."

"Already?" He beamed. "Prefect, this is superb. Do you have them in custody?"

She waved dismissively. "Oh no. Plenty of time for that. Have you had lunch yet?" Perhaps she could swing a meal on Parliament expenses; failing that, Neutral Zone Committee expenses.

Elleul looked aghast. "This is a matter of utmost importance!"

"Relax, monsieur. He'll be at Lane's Salon tonight, we'll pick him up there." When Elleul's expression didn't change, she patted his arm. "Trust me, he'll be there. Everyone goes to Lane's."

His arm twitched away. "What are you talking about?"

Only one of the most popular video salons in the city, where the games were good and the booze was cheap. It didn't hurt that Lane didn't give a shit if people traded on her premises, meaning the leeches and thieves came in droves. Renée was particular to the virtual poker console there.

And particular to Lane herself. Ah, Lane. Renée could almost forget how hungry she was at the thought of seeing her.

"It's the main salon where Fentiman conducts his sales," she explained.

Elleul frowned. "Sales? What would he be selling?" His face cleared. "The missive!"

Renée resisted the urge to laugh. "No, Member. That is likely long gone. I mean, of course, the diplomat's portal ticket."

They stepped outside the terminal into the busy thoroughfare. A clear day meant the sun beamed down weakly on her city, bringing welcome warmth and light. Clusters of people hung around the building, eager to watch ships come and go from the airfield behind it, and to latch on to newcomers before they could get their bearings.

Some lingered to watch the purple light of the intersystem portal shoot through the sky, gazes hungry.

That portal was the conduit between their system, Janus, and their system neighbour, Fides. Portals also connected Salus to the core and other Janus planets. When their star wasn't in the way, they could also connect to the home solar system in Orion, but it was out of range this time of year. Thankfully. The last thing anyone in Janus needed was Earth's opinion on events here.

Portal journeys were quick but expensive. Most in demand and most expensive of all was the connection to Fides. Trips were few a day, tickets were extortionate, and slots were booked out for months in advance. The people in Pann had to wait—for a ticket, for a cancelled slot, for the money to purchase a scalped ticket, for months to use their advanced booking, for hackers to open and charge the portal when her force was looking the other way. And while they waited, they watched others leave and arrive and tried to make a living.

Renée noticed the usual scalpers and pickpockets slinking into the crowd at the sight of her and her team, but the regular people—the refugees, the enhanced, the locals, the plethora of beings from other systems—stayed in their clusters, smoking and chatting and waiting.

Elleul's nose wrinkled as he scanned the area. Renée wondered what it must be like seeing all the people his policies had chased out of the core planets to the very limits of the Janus system. Most rarely thought about this tiny rock on the edge of nowhere and everywhere, let alone visited it. Two years of his policies and Salus's cities were struggling to support the people fleeing the Parliament. His timing was either dreadfully off or darkly perfect; she couldn't decide which.

Since her own voluntary expulsion here, she'd come to appreciate Salus for its dubious merits. Most did; most had to. Perhaps he would too. Pann made up for what it lacked in elegance and civility by its sheer amount of entertainment and business—including food.

Speaking of food.

She indicated the car they'd cleaned up especially for Elleul. "Get in. We can discuss more details of your visit over lunch."

Elleul moved to the car with hilarious speed. "An excellent plan. Of course, it's not just the murderer we're concerned about."

She paused in opening her door.

"There's someone who'll be arriving in Pann shortly—two someones, in fact." Elleul glowered at her over the roof. "It's very important these two people don't leave Pann."

More enemies of the government, perhaps, like the ones surrounding them. These two would be special if this Parliamentary member was here to confront them. Related to those classified reasons? She nodded. "I'm sure that can be arranged, monsieur."

He smiled at her for the first time. "If it can, you can count on a promotion."

As though Renée could be swayed by something so tawdry. Well, she could, but that depended on the nature of the promotion. After all, the last time she'd been "promoted," she'd ended up out here. The location left something to be desired, but she was literally prefect of the Pann police force.

"A promotion? *Here*?" she said casually. "How incentivising." The next person up the chain was the mayor, and Renée was very happy to avoid *that* kind of promotion. Responsibility like that aged people terribly.

He made a gruff, unimpressed noise. "I think we can find you something more appropriate back home."

Home. Well, thank goodness. Not that she was eligible for mayor in the first place, as she didn't fulfil the fundamental requirement of being Fides-born, but apparently Elleul thought Janus would welcome her back.

Returning to the core: quite the prospect.

Bah, merde. He was a politician. He could mean running the local police office in one of the desert research stations, typical population of several dozen. He could mean nothing at all. She had to focus.

As she took the seat next to him, Renée considered the rest of the day. Lunch, details of these mysterious visitors and whatever diplomatic missive was so important it required the presence of Elleul, perhaps une petite sieste to recover from all this activity while Elleul checked into his hotel, organising her people to scoop up Fentiman at Lane's Salon, then executing said scooping.

How unusually busy for her.

Maybe she should message Lane and give her a small warning beforehand. It would only be polite. But it was always so much nicer delivering the message in person.

Elleul was staring at his tablet. "Lane's Salon. Are you totally certain the murderer will be there tonight?"

"Completely."

"Who is Lane?"

"Lane Kovacs. She runs the salon."

Oh, Lane. How could Renée begin to describe her? Lane was like every other refugee who'd fled to Salus and never quite managed to leave, yet to consider Lane as similar to anyone else in the universe would be insulting. She was incomparable. Intelligent, fierce, sarcastic. She was a demon straight out of Renée's dreams. She was—

"Ah, I see," Elleul said. "I look forward to speaking with her." His gaze was fixed on his tablet, and Renée angled a glance at the screen. The Intelligence file on Lane Kovacs shone back in the familiar wide font.

Renée realised she was holding her breath and let it go. Then she dragged in another before turning to look out the window. The people-choked streets around the terminal rolled by, gradually giving way to clearer roads and fewer shops. Soon the government buildings would appear.

Most of the city's population had to be in the Intelligence database, Renée included. Of course Lane had a file. Renée hadn't read it; she rarely read anyone's Intelligence files. What was the point? They were all the same. Enhanced or suspected of colluding with the enhanced resistance. Family left behind. Fides ticket request submitted. Payment forthcoming. There was only so much boredom Renée could take.

Now it seemed she'd have to read Lane's file. Elleul had. Perhaps Renée shouldn't have flagged the salon to him and thus brought her to his attention, but it was too late now. Something about this wasn't, as the expression went, sitting well. Something about Elleul, supposedly a high-level pencil-pusher, having such easy access to the Intelligence files very much didn't sit well with her.

Lunch might help things sit better.

She'd decided: it would be much more pleasant to speak with Lane in person this evening.

Lane wasn't sure whether it was the air in Pann turning smoky and gasoline-raw in the evenings, or if she was so used to having two fingers of whisky on hand that it had imprinted on her sinuses, but evenings lately tasted like the stuff. It wasn't a bad thing. Not necessarily. Even if one of her bartenders had muttered something about placing a new order *already* while opening a fresh bottle for her.

Psh. Like it mattered.

She sipped her drink as she scanned the bar area. The low lights were on, making the place inviting and homey. It was early; just those who wanted to drink or trade in peace were there so far. Most people walking through the door headed straight for the games area through the door in the far wall. She could take in everyone with one sweep.

Several cyborgs entered, followed by a group of humans noticeably lacking tech, enough to mark them as neoluds. They made faces when they saw the cyborgs, but no one said anything. Good. The door policy was clear: people were here to play, sell, buy, or drink. No fighting.

Helen stopped in front of her table, and Lane looked up. Helen raised an eyebrow. Dramatic, but well-executed. "Serge just told me that's the third bottle of Event Horizon we've gone through this week."

Lane wrapped her hand around the base of the bottle. "Serge has a big mouth."

"At least his isn't bottomless." Helen picked up the bottle, easily pulling it from her. "Keep your lips off the top shelf."

Lane narrowed her eyes. "Who owns this place again?"

"You, and I want to keep it that way." Helen's face was smooth, her voice low and even, but Lane could imagine her original sincerity very easily. "You can't run it from the grave, Lane."

"Not with that attitude."

Helen flicked Lane's forehead, which stung.

Lane grunted. "Rein it in."

Helen sniffed. "You're welcome for the concern, darling sister of mine." She walked off, taking the bottle with her. Lane watched it go with a sinking feeling, then checked her glass. Oh good, she'd topped it off in time.

It was a slow evening. One of the games glitched, requiring a manual reboot, and Rakesh needed help kicking out a recalcitrant human who'd overstayed her welcome in one of the VR decks, but otherwise Lane was left in peace.

Then Fentiman came through the door. Lane was scanning through the latest news from the core on internal view, her glass down to its dregs, when he sat opposite her. Like every time she saw him, he was dressed to the nines—brushed suit, slicked-back hair, latest in fashionable kicks. Well, latest in what counted for fashion in Pann.

He flashed his greasy salesman grin at her. "Bon soir, Lane."

"Fentiman." He couldn't see the lights flashing on her tech as she read? Wow, people forgot the basics quick out here.

"You know, Lane, there's something I've always liked about you. You're so direct."

"Pity I can't say the same about you."

"That I'm direct or that you like me?"

She was trying to *read*. "Either."

He chuckled self-consciously. "How silly of me to say anything at all. What's the latest from the core?"

She switched off the headlines and closed internal view to study him more closely. Fentiman's rat-like face shone and he wore a new shirt; someone was in a good mood tonight. "Since when do you care about the core?"

"Did I say I cared?" He gestured at one of the servers, who came over and took his order of a glass of champagne. When he gestured at her glass, she nodded. The server left.

"What's the celebration?" she asked.

Fentiman grinned. "It's a little preemptive. You see, I'm finally leaving Pann. I'm leaving Salus entirely."

Oh. There had to be a story behind that, but looking at his delighted features and relaxed posture, Lane could guess. "Congratulations."

"We've had a great relationship, Lane."

"We have?"

The server set down the champagne for him and another whisky for her—and really, it wouldn't kill her to listen to his rambling for once.

"You've never kicked me out of here," he elaborated. "I'm so grateful. I thought you should know I'm doing one last sale, then it's au revoir, Pann; au revoir, Salus; au revoir, Janus; bonjour, Caeliton;

bonjour, Fides; bonjour, freedom." He raised his glass to her, then drank.

One last sale. *Right.*

"I take it you're doing well out of this final leeching of yours."

He made a shocked face and pressed one hand to his chest. "Lane. I'm hurt. You know my business. I give these poor people"—he indicated the people in the bar with a lazy wave—"a way off this forsaken rock. A chance at a better life. And for considerably less money than some of the other brokers out there."

"Uh-huh." He was definitely doing well out of whatever deal had dropped his way.

He smiled at her. "I know you disapprove of what I do."

She shrugged. "I run my business, and you run yours."

"Rightly so. The thing is, I've finally reached the payoff. I've got my hands on something that no one, including you, Lane, could obtain, not from any contacts or from your Prefect Bellevue."

That grated a little. Renée wasn't *her* anything.

Fentiman pulled out a ticket. At first glance it looked like any other portal ticket, but then he pointed out the holograms and invited her to scan them. "Offline," he added. Like Lane ever had her tech connected to the main net these days. She kept her gaze still to scan it, and when the ticket information and authorisation played out across the internal view on her optical nerve, she sucked in a breath.

This ticket had been generated by Parliament and granted the holder immediate transport to the Fides system. No expiry date. Couldn't be rescinded or overruled or faked. A person with this ticket could walk up to the portal, demand it be opened and charged for them, and step through. Easy as that. Not even Renée would be able to stop them. In fact, Renée would be obliged to help them if requested.

"You see, Lane"—Fentiman covered the ticket with his palm—"I'll be selling this for a very good price to some lucky people tonight, and with the proceeds, I'll buy my own way out. That's my last sale. Go on, you can tell me how impressed you are by me now."

Gobsmacked was more like it. "I'm impressed you're selling it."

He shifted weight in his chair. "I would prefer a more, ah, obscure departure for myself."

One of the headlines had read *Diplomat killed on Salus*.

She deleted the scan from her archive and cache.

Something about her expression made him shift a little in his chair. He cleared his throat. "The thing is, I have to wait for my clients to arrive, and your games have always been so useful as a distraction. Could I leave this with you while I play? To keep it secure?"

He wanted to hide in one of the games until his customers arrived, and he didn't want the ticket on him until he made the sale. Given the police's motivation at following up black market sales could be described as *whimsical*, at best, this level of caution made her nervous. Lane frowned. "Why me?"

Fentiman finished his glass. "You hate me. It makes me trust you implicitly."

"You don't want to keep it on you?"

"No, not when I'll be deep online. Besides, what if the games somehow scanned it? Far better you hold onto it for me."

She couldn't begrudge him that. Her firewalls weren't good—on purpose; no one expected a salon game to have iron-clad security—so it was a given that there was a hacker or three monitoring game inputs at any moment. And if it helped him leave permanently . . . "I don't want it here overnight."

He shook his head. "No, no, of course not. An hour or two at most, I swear." He slid it across the table to her with one hand as he used the other to wave exuberantly for another drink.

She picked it up and palmed it into her shirt's inner pocket.

"Thank you." He finished his glass. "I greatly appreciate it."

"Don't mention it. Really, don't. You know I don't do favours."

He tilted his head to the side. "You always say that, Lane, but I'm not so sure."

Lane crossed her arms and sat back in her chair, glaring at him. Fentiman stood quickly. "Then again," he said with an obsequious bow, "who can be sure about anything these days?"

The server brought over his glass. Fentiman took it, raised it to Lane, then went to the games room.

That games room. Lane hadn't realised, back when she talked herself into including it, quite how much work it would entail. The original plan had been a bar, a pleasant place where people could escape their problems one drink at a time without being disturbed. The games had been a fun afterthought, a good way to generate money because everyone loved virtual reality and the chance of winning money from games.

The joke was on her: both the bar and games room became spaces for leeches and traders to do business. The games room let people hide for a few hours if they needed to, trade or gamble under dim lighting, or simply let loose—but mostly people spilled food and drink. Sometimes the machines broke down. The maintenance was momentous.

Not that it wasn't nice putting things together again. Fixing problems. Using her hands.

She picked up her whisky and took a large sip.

At the bar, one of the neoluds sat next to one of the cyborgs and was showing him a magic trick with a coin. *Cyborg* was a bit excessive for him—only one arm and one leg as tech—but it was a term Lane found difficult to drop. *Modified* seemed too clinical, and it wasn't enough to describe the people who had only a few organs' worth of organic human left. *Mod* was a bit better, but still sounded weird to her when describing a person, and besides, its meaning had changed with the rise of the resistance.

Mod was still way ahead of *enhanced being*. Awful.

Despite their differences, the neolud and cyborg seemed to be getting along. Lane stood with her glass, intending to sequester herself in her office before anyone else asked her for a dubious favour.

A body flew in front of her and landed hard on the floor, sliding until he met the stools at the bar. He swore a blue streak and rolled onto his knees. The place went silent, and Lane spun around. One of the cyborgs—the label was more appropriate for this one; she was so kitted out the only organic parts Lane could identify were her head and one shoulder—strode after him, fury on her face.

Lane whipped out her electric wand and pointed it at the cyborg. "Oi." Held down a button and the wand lit up. Electricity crackled, and a minor magnetic field generated, sending strange pulses along her arm.

The cyborg kept going.

Lane swung the wand into the cyborg's knees. She went down hard, legs going dead as the electricity and field fucked with the circuitry. On the floor, twitching, she swore as much as the guy she'd thrown. Lane eyed her warily, but she stayed down.

Lane gestured at her bouncers, then at the cyborg and the guy she'd hurled across the room. "These two, out. Add them to the blacklist." She took in the other people in their groups, who'd frozen. The neolud girl and cyborg guy at the bar looked deeply uncomfortable. "You lot are free to keep drinking, but any more shenanigans and you're out like these two." She circled in one place and raised her voice to address the rest of the bar. "I'm sorry for the disturbance, everyone. Everything's okay. Please keep having a good time."

First thing: rescue her drink. Second thing: help the bouncers escort the troublemakers out. Both of them tried to make excuses at the door, but Lane didn't care enough to hear them. She watched them limp away from the salon—the cyborg arm-crawling to a nearby alley to wait out her reboot—and turned off the wand. Her glass still had a few drops in it. Lucky. She drained it, taking in the view from the façade of her place.

The salon was on a hill, looking out over the rooftops towards the centre of Pann and to the terminal on the outskirts. A river snaked throughout the city, disappearing for a short stretch in the splash of red where the park was. Pann wasn't a large city, but a dense one. High-rise construction sites lined the edge of the original town, but supply didn't keep up with demand. People crammed in wherever they could fit. No one had built over her small view yet, but it was a matter of time.

Beyond the city limits was rocky terrain that melted into the darkness of the encroaching night. Behind her, a brilliant flare of orange marked the sunset. A streak of violet erupted from the terminal in a straight line, shooting deep into the twilight above, past Salus's ring, towards the blocky star that marked the Fides system. Several long seconds later, it disappeared. Another lucky escapee.

It hadn't been easy getting here, but life had fallen into a manageable pattern. People ebbed and flowed through her business. Fights were minimal. So far, she hadn't been approached or recognised by anyone from the time before her flight. The neutrality of Salus and the resultant dog-eat-dog atmosphere of its cities was a balm compared to the tense pressure in the core planets.

The Neutral Zone Committee liked to wax lyrical about its mix of representatives—namely that they were all either Janus- or Fides-born—to the point it was obnoxious, but the policy worked at keeping Janus's and Fides's interests more or less balanced. Mostly. Maybe she'd finally descended into full-on pessimism, but that neutrality seemed to be disappearing in places, the politics from the core bleeding into life here.

The headline about the diplomat bugged her. People died in Pann all the time, but usually a diplomat came with some protection and fanfare. A secret diplomat made zero sense. Killing one made less than zero sense. Parliament always took an opportunity to promote themselves as open, benevolent, communicative, and would investigate such a high-level incident. Whatever was happening there, it felt like the end of neutrality and the beginning of something else.

Of course, plenty kept saying the resistance would take back the core planets and return things to a semblance of sanity, of—ironically enough—humanity. Lane didn't know about that, or care.

She needed more whisky. She sighed and tried to relax into the moment. This was a nice evening, as far as evenings went on Salus. The sky was clear and the sunset bright. The ring circling Salus always reflected light, regardless of the planet's tilt, but Pann was angled nicely tonight—the very outer rim of the ring caught the sun, cutting the night sky in half with a thin bright line. Lane would be able to see more stars than normal.

Despite the filth and busyness of this place, and the circumstances of coming here, she did like the play of light between the sun, the ring, Salus's moon, and the terraformed landscape of Salus's surface. Salus was famous for being the only habited planet in all human-populated systems with its own ring. She could seek its beauty out more. Spending all her time inside didn't do her any favours.

"Just the woman I wanted to see!"

Lane turned. The prefect of Pann's police force, Renée Bellevue, approached up the hill, as charming, radiant, and corrupt as a fallen angel. Her dark hair bobbed around her chin and her lean arms swung freely as she walked towards the salon. Usually she showed up in casualwear, intent on scamming as much money as possible from Lane's virtual poker tables while flirting outrageously with Lane and her staff.

Tonight she looked calm and relaxed, but professional in her uniform. The badge on her belt stood out starkly in the play of lights. Six goons trailed her, meaning this wasn't a social visit. Lane tightened her grip on her glass, then forced herself to relax. Business visits weren't ever aimed at her, though she pitied whatever moron had Renée's attention tonight.

"Good evening, Renée," she called.

Renée came right up to her, smiling widely. "Always a pleasure, my darling Lane."

Business visits meant less flirting than usual, not none.

"If you came for the brawl, you're too late."

Renée arched an eyebrow. "A brawl? What makes you think I care about a brawl?" She gestured at her goons, who went inside. Lane hoped they wouldn't disrupt the atmosphere too much. It couldn't be another raid; their friendship didn't exempt Lane from the usual bribes to keep things peaceful and running, and Lane *had* paid.

Renée stayed with her. "Enjoying your evening?"

"In a manner of speaking."

Renée turned to face the same direction as Lane. "Ah, it *is* lovely. If you ever decided to do something other than tinker with your machines one evening, we could take a stroll across the river. Or there's a wonderful view from Parc Rouge."

"So you keep mentioning."

"And you keep dodging the invitation."

Lane couldn't help smiling. "Well, if you stopped ignoring your tab—"

Renée tutted. "Must it always come down to money? Lane, my darling, my sweet, I thought you were above that."

"I adapt to the company around me."

Renée pressed a hand to her chest in mock outrage. She was wearing a nicely fitted uniform shirt today. It suited her.

"Besides," Lane pointed out, "you're here every evening. Why would I take the night off?"

"Not *every* evening." Renée gently bumped Lane's shoulder with her own, then resumed their usual metre or so of distance. "Tonight would have been a good one to spend away from work. I'm very sorry to say that this isn't entirely a social call. You see, we have a special visitor in Pann—Monsieur Richard Elleul, High Member of Parliament."

Stars. That was an unexpectedly familiar name.

Renée missed nothing. "You've heard of him."

"It would be hard not to; he's the reason most of my—and your—clientele are here."

"Mm. You heard about the diplomat, oui? The news leaked fast. He wants the murderer caught, and I know for a fact said murderer is in your salon."

So Parliament sent *him*? Directly? Seemed a little weird. "Is that so?"

"Prepare yourself: it's Fentiman. The idiot finally slipped up."

Looked like today wasn't such a lucky day for him—

Oh *fuck*. The ticket. The ticket that had to be that diplomat's ticket. It was in Lane's pocket.

She *knew* she shouldn't have trusted the shit. This was exactly why she shouldn't do favours. What would it take for the lesson to sink in?

Lane tried to keep her expression calm. It seemed to have worked, as Renée blithely continued. "Such a shame. I know you don't like him, but I've always had a soft spot for him. Elleul will turn up in a few minutes, and once he's settled with a drink, we're going to make the arrest. Be a friend and don't make a fuss when we do."

Lane was going to need more booze for this. "Renée, when have I ever *made a fuss* about anyone you've arrested?"

"I meant don't stop us or interfere. I know what you're like." Renée pointedly leaned past her. "Oh my, is that an enhanced human lying in that alley?"

"I couldn't say."

"It's unusual to see one with both legs jammed like that. Remarkable."

Lane pushed the now-collapsed stun wand deeper into her trouser pocket. "So you're here to show off to this core prick." She glanced down at her glass: sadly still empty. "Not my business."

She wondered if she could alert Fentiman somehow, then decided it wouldn't matter. There wasn't time to get him out, and the goons were already inside; it was a lost cause.

"I know, but I wanted to give you the warning." Renée moved a little closer to her. "I like you, Lane. I know you've personally never sold portal tickets or participated in the black market. It's why your salon remains open."

Lane shifted weight, Renée's proximity intense in that way Lane still struggled to articulate. "Pretty sure I'm still open because I gave you the cheat codes for the virtual poker table. And I never call in your tab. Plus the bribes—"

"The thing is, Member Elleul isn't only here to ensure this murderer pays for his crime." Renée rested against the wall and crossed her ankles. "There are two people coming to Pann tonight, two very important people in the enhanced human movement. Like everyone else, they'll need tickets to Fides. It's very important they don't receive them."

Lane eyed her. "And this concerns my salon because . . . ?"

"They'll end up here. Everyone does at some point. I wanted you to know the situation."

Lane shrugged. "I don't get involved. You know that."

Renée had a strange expression on her face. "Mm-hmm. These two people happen to be special cases. They're quite high-profile. Tori and Ayumu Kusanagi."

Oh. *Oh.* "Wow."

Renée did a double take and reached for her pocket. "Quoi? Is that *respect* I see on your face? Stay still a second, I must take a picture."

Lane batted away her tablet. "I've heard of them too, that's all."

Renée fixed her with another one of those unreadable expressions. "Oh really? That's interesting. I wouldn't think they were that well-known outside of resistance circles."

Lane couldn't tag her as she didn't have integrated tech. "Unlock your tablet and bring up the Arden headlines." Renée did so, and Lane pointed out one from a few days ago: KILLER KUSANAGI STILL AT LARGE.

"Ah."

"'Killer' is a little excessive." Lane watched her put the tablet away. "All she did was block some transports and break people out of that detention camp and publish videos and protest those sterilisation laws—"

"Some of those things got people killed," Renée pointed out.

"But not by her. She never directly killed anyone."

"Killing indirectly is still murder."

Why was Renée arguing this? They rarely brought up politics, and when it did come up, Renée batted it away or Lane started another topic. Well, while they were here . . . "Of course, but then responsibility falls into a grey area. Is it really her fault if destruction happened while she was freeing people who shouldn't have been locked up in the first place?"

Renée narrowed her eyes. "Yes. She didn't have to use explosives for that. There are other methods that don't involve widespread damage. I do, however, see your point." She sagged further against the wall and sighed dramatically. "My darling Lane, I'm maybe a little jealous—you know so much about this woman's movements."

And back on familiar footing. She had to fight the smile. "I just see the headlines like everyone else."

"If I didn't know better, I'd actually believe that. I can't remember the last time you looked so interested in someone."

Lane held up her now-smudged glass for something else to focus on. "She's practically a celebrity. Funny thing is, for a celebrity, she's kept anonymous crazy well. No one's come close to catching her, or taken a clear picture of her or her husband."

"Probably glitch clothing."

"Probably."

Renée sniffed. "It won't help her here."

"No." Lane couldn't stop the smile now. "Your keen eyes see past such low tricks."

"And in sheer coincidence, our surveillance software is so old it isn't affected." Renée suddenly grinned. "Oh my. We will have pictures of the infamous Tori Kusanagi! Imagine what the core networks will pay for them. I can finally get a new carpet in my office."

A car stopped in front of the salon and a tall man with the doughiness of an office worker stepped out. Renée snapped to attention and went to meet him. Clearly this was Member Richard Elleul, here to see Fentiman arrested.

Damn. Lane had to lose the ticket. If—when—Fentiman spilled his guts, she'd be in galaxies of trouble.

She went back into the salon and surveyed the place again—all quiet, no obvious tension between the neoluds and the cyborgs. Then she headed for the music centre. It was tucked behind the bar, inaccessible to patrons; a clunky piece of crap that ran hot after three hours and lost the network connection every three and a half hours, meaning someone had to restart it when songs stopped to buffer for a nonexistent data feed.

She'd loved it as soon as she'd seen it, because it had tinny retro speakers, an inability to be accessed by personal tech, and the mechanics to play older technology. Like, say, plastic discs. She crouched down in front of it and changed the song, slipping the ticket out of her pocket and sliding it into the disc drive before clicking it shut.

That done, she swiped a mid-shelf bottle of core blend and poured herself another three fingers.

Heh. Three fingers.

Stars. She was too drunk, not drunk enough, or Renée was getting to her.

Renée and Elleul stepped inside. Renée directed him to the comfiest sofa in the place while the goons positioned themselves in a way that Lane guessed was strategic. Lane rounded the bar and took a large gulp of her drink.

Helen stopped next to her, a tray of empties in her hands. "Lane, is that Richard Elleul? *Parliament Member* Elleul?"

"Yup."

"What the hell is he doing in Pann?"

Lane didn't respond; she'd download the answer quicker.

Helen swore softly. "Seriously? A *diplomat*?" Her voice lowered. "I want that asshole out."

"You know I can't do that if he's just sitting there."

"You kick out people all the time. He's in Pann now. He's got no political sway—and we *know* he's not modified. You could do it."

"Renée wouldn't cover for me if I did."

"Yes, she would."

Lane wanted to shake her. Instead, she sipped at her whisky, not missing the way Helen's eyes darted to it. "It's more trouble than it's worth."

"I owe it to myself to kick him out."

Lane glared at her, refusing to play along. "You feel that strongly about it, do it. Then put up a sign out front telling all neoluds to stay out and enjoy your new job as a bouncer enforcing our new door policy. Oh, and hope I have the bail money for when Renée arrests you."

Helen couldn't cry anymore, but the glistening effect she now implemented in her eyes still did the intended job of jabbing Lane right in the guts. "You know, if my sister is still somewhere in that boozed pathetic excuse of a meatsuit, she's welcome back anytime."

Lane scowled, ready to tell Helen where she could shove those empties, then noticed two of Renée's goons heading for the games room. "Get behind the bar. There's a spill by the music centre."

Helen scanned the room. "Renée's arresting someone? Again? For *fuck's* sake." She moved away, muttering darkly.

Lane put her glass down on the bar counter, remembered she'd sent Helen behind it, and hastily picked the glass back up.

Over at Elleul's table, Renée watched with a content smile as a server poured wine into two glasses. Elleul sat with crossed arms, clearly unhappy about being in a bar with mods and visible cyborgs. A few of the patrons, mod and neolud alike, had spotted him and were looking a little twitchy.

Fentiman strolled out of the games room, hands in his pockets and a rictus grin on his face. He made for the front door, only to have two goons block it. He instantly turned around and headed towards the back exit, the one hidden by the toilets. Halfway across the bar, two others stepped in his way. Lane watched him pause, grin still in place, before streaking past them. They gave chase.

She frowned and looked back at the front door, which was still guarded by two officers. There was a shimmer in the air before them.

Ah.

It seemed that Fentiman *could* do things that impressed her.

The goons in the game room burst out. One of them pointed at the front door. "He's there!"

The guards pulled out their electric batons and swept the immediate area. Fentiman blinked into life and the projection—which had drawn most of the attention to one side of the room—disappeared.

Fentiman pulled out a gun—an honest-to-goodness *firearm*—and shot one goon point-blank, sending her down. Screams and shouts erupted as people dove under tables. The other officer lunged at him, and he sprang back to avoid him, then aimed for the bar. He hopped onto the counter and ran along it towards the toilets, avoiding the trajectories of the other officers. Lane took a step back and sipped her drink.

He reached the end of the bar counter and jumped off, stumbling into a headlong rush for the back exit. One goon threw something that hit his shoulder, sending him shuddering and jerking to the floor. Neurastim weapons. Nonlethal but effective, and typical of Renée. The chase was over. Two others went to collect him.

Fentiman's leeching days were done.

As the goons dragged him past Lane, he lunged for her. The neural scattering still fucked his system; his hands shook violently as they grabbed her ankles, his grip slimy and weak.

"Lane!" Big eyes pleaded desperately up at her. "Help me! *Please*, Lane!"

What did he expect *her* to do? "Don't be an idiot, Fentiman." It was tough to resist reaching down for him. "Spin things, you know you can—"

"*Help me!*"

The officers yanked him off her, his hands and legs shaking too much for him to coordinate his strength. They continued dragging him, his anguished cries of "Lane! *Lane!*" following him like so much waste smoke until he was out the door.

Lane winced.

She glanced over at Renée and Elleul. Both looked pleased with themselves, though as Lane watched, Renée tapped her chin thoughtfully with one hand, something like concern or pity crossing her face.

Then Lane looked to Serge and Helen. Serge was wide-eyed and wiping an already dry glass. Helen leaned in the shadow of a pillar, separating the whiskies from the rums, face calm and considering.

Serge narrowed his eyes at Lane. "If they ever decide to arrest me for something, I hope you'll be more helpful."

Lane scowled. "What am I, your mother?"

"Thankfully *not.*"

Most of the patrons were still crouched under tables and beside chairs, eyes wide and faces ashen. Lane waved for attention. "Sorry for the disturbance. Again. Please, stay and have another drink on me, folks." There. See if Serge wanted to make another crack about *being helpful.*

As people went to the bar, Renée caught her eye and beckoned her over. Lane sipped her whisky and deliberately turned away to walk to her office. She wouldn't kick Elleul out, but under no circumstances would she speak to him. And if Helen hadn't found the bottle stashed in the fake drawer in Lane's desk, then odds were good Lane wouldn't talk to anyone else tonight.

CHAPTER
TWO

Mornings in Pann were an awful, raucous affair, and Renée avoided them whenever possible. Despite vehicle taxes, the roads were always jammed; people rushed about in constant panic; the air was dense with noise; and there was always some overnight incident that required paperwork or processing or *something*. Such an endless fuss. It was all very inconvenient. During her six years in this post, she'd carefully built up a schedule that suited her; namely, only being in the office when absolutely necessary, never before eleven o'clock, and always after two coffees.

Of course, Elleul expected otherwise, which was how she found herself wearing clothes and upright *and* at work at nine in the morning. She deserved a medal for that alone. Instead she poured herself a second espresso and watched as Elleul worked himself into the ideal state for a stroke.

"What do you *mean*," he blithered at Renée's unfortunate lieutenant, "that Fentiman didn't have any documents on him?"

Lieutenant Atkins shifted his weight. "I meant, monsieur, that no documents were found on his person."

Renée drained the cup and set it aside. She picked up her tablet and scanned the reports filed last night. The usual litany of thefts, black market sales, fights, traffic incidents and so on. Just one murder, which was nice. She tapped the few reports she was interested in to gather them for perusal on her dash. A quick glance up revealed Elleul's face turning a unique shade of purple.

"No missive. No ticket. Not even a fucking ID?"

"The only things in his pockets were three credits for the video games in Lane's Salon, ten francs, a hach cigarette, and a coupon for a free calzone from Gustav's Pizzeria."

Given this was Fentiman, Renée wasn't surprised by the lack of evidence. She pulled up his arrest report to double-check everything. The evidence photos depicted the credits and money, but the hach cigarette mysteriously looked like a normal tabac one, and the coupon had been replaced by a receipt for a pizza order from the Gustav branch near the station.

Well, that was all accounted for, and it was useless anyway. Fentiman would have been there to sell something—almost definitely the ticket. He'd had it on him. Now he didn't. So where was it?

La logique said in the salon.

Fingers dancing over the tablet, she chose five people at random, copied them into an official order, told them they were searching Lane's Salon for the ticket that morning (to be finished by lunch, naturally), and added the order to the case.

Then she switched over to the messaging application and typed a message to Lane: *Are you free this morning?* Given the way Lane had beelined to her office last night, it would be a minor miracle if she was awake and coherent this morning, but Renée wanted to try. Nights spent in the office always resulted in an especially grumpy Lane.

Unless Renée was with her. Then they drank and chatted and played cards, and Lane didn't fall into her darker moods. Renée would love to attribute that to her own charming company, but realistically, it was because Lane didn't drink as much when they were together.

Renée had wanted to follow her last night. She liked Lane's office. It had shelves with pictures and books—actual *books*—and machine parts, a wide solid desk, several chairs, and a very comfortable sofa. Even though they just drank and played games, it was the kind of room that offered many other possibilities, nearly all of which had gone through Renée's mind so many times she could've acted them out blindfolded and gloved.

Yes, a far preferable location to sitting at a table with Elleul. Still, watching him silently judge the enhanced people in the bar had been entertaining too.

In front of her, Elleul was gesturing angrily. "You literally have him on camera doing it. How can he have the gall to say he didn't?"

"Criminals tend to do that, monsieur," Atkins replied.

"This isn't a joke, Lieutenant!"

"Member Elleul," Renée interjected, "we're taking this very seriously."

He turned to her. "If this is what you call 'serious,' I'm amazed arrests happen at all on this godforsaken planet."

And to think she'd been prepared to round up twice the number of usual suspects for him.

"We'll search the salon this morning," she said. "If the ticket is there, we'll find it."

"I want to be present for the search. And what about the missive?"

She shrugged. "We have contacts searching the right channels. It will surface eventually." She was fairly sure she'd made that order already.

Elleul's eyes went amusingly wide. "*Eventually*?"

"Monsieur, I said this yesterday. In Pann, your diplomat's ticket will be much more valuable than whatever was in the missive. Everyone will want it." She took in his alarmed expression. "If recovery of the ticket is so important, why not request its deletion? If the ticket information and validity is removed from our various systems, no one would be able to use it."

Elleul shook his head. "Not a possibility, Prefect. The dispensation required to authorise it in the first place is nonnegotiable and not rescindable."

"Surely, given the circumstances—"

"Classified, Prefect."

Politics, then. Had to be. Parliament wouldn't be that stupid about technology for anything less. Even her family, which had been against any kind of enhancements, had thought the insistence on certain processes being analogue was beyond stupid.

She turned back to her tablet and closed down the Fentiman report. The next report was surveillance on the Kusanagis. Like everyone who couldn't afford the portal jump from core to outer edge, they'd arrived by ship at the terminal in the early hours of the morning. There were several pictures, including one of them in their taxi stopped outside a closed Lane's Salon.

"There are also those who would be eager to take advantage of the situation, given the Kusanagis are now on planet," she added, more for herself than for Elleul.

Atkins cleared his throat. "We suspect Fentiman was going to sell it to the Kusanagis."

"Really? Why?" He was a leech; if he didn't want to use it himself, his plan would have been to sell it to *someone*, but that was a step too far. The Kusanagis had arrived too late to buy from him. And besides . . . "There's two of them and the ticket only allows passage for one. They'd have to purchase another." Catching Elleul's eye, she added, "Which they won't be able to do, of course."

"*Guaranteed* passage for one, Prefect," Atkins said. "It's still very useful. When we searched Fentiman's lodgings, we didn't find the ticket or the missive, but we did find materials sympathetic to the enhanced being movement as well as residue from cheap tranqs. The diplomat's body also had traces of tranqs, but we're waiting for confirmation of a match. Given his, er, line of work and his alleged connections, we put the pieces together. It's speculation, but he really didn't like it when we speculated in front of him."

Renée nodded. "Excellent speculation." She held up her tablet. "The Kusanagis arrived this morning and have checked into a hotel down the street from Lane's Salon. According to my officers, they went directly to the salon from the terminal, found it closed, then went to their hotel in the early hours of the morning."

Elleul took an unnecessarily deep breath. "And what relevance does that have?"

A man who needed things spelled out for him was truly pitiful. "They planned to meet someone there. Perhaps not at that hour. Apparently their particular ship was delayed by several hours due to—" she checked the report "—ah. An unexpected cargo search and two passport checks by government officials at the Neutral Zone border." Naturally, Janus government officials, but she didn't need to state the obvious.

The member's colour was looking better.

She swiped on the screen to display the clearest photo. Everyone immediately leaned in.

"Good-looking," Atkins remarked.

Elleul snorted. "Which one?"

"Both of them, monsieur."

Renée examined them. They seemed quite young. It was difficult to tell their age from the picture. They wore glitch clothing: Tori in an oversized hoodie, hood up, and black jeans; her husband in an asymmetric jacket, baggy trousers, and blocky headphones on his head. The headphones had to be for show, nearly every enhanced being had auditory implants. Strands of black hair spiked from under Tori's hood, while Ayumu had a bleach job pulled into a bun. Tech dotted the usual places: behind the ears, on the wrists, at the neck, by one eye. They looked like students.

And Atkins was right: they *were* good-looking.

"Younger than I would've guessed," Elleul remarked. "When will they be arrested?"

"When they commit a crime in Pann," Renée said.

The purple began seeping back in. "Crimes against the core government surely suffice as a crime on Salus."

Renée flicked to the next report. "You *would* think so, but alas. All this neutral territory business, you understand."

"They broke curfew," he pointed out.

She shrugged. "They'll be sent a fine notice."

"Prefect Bellevue, you *will* arrest the Kusanagis."

She smiled up at him. "Of course, Member Elleul. The second they do something illegal here, I'll have them arrested before you can say 'notre procédure juridictionelle.'"

He narrowed his eyes at her. It didn't help his expression. "Perhaps we could pay them a visit. A friendly one."

"Now, that is certainly something I can arrange."

"Excellent. The sooner the better. This morning."

"Before or after the search at the salon?"

Atkins smirked, then hid it behind his hand as he noticed something apparently more interesting on the wall.

Elleul glanced at his tablet. Renée checked hers too—it was close to ten, and her people were still on their way to the salon.

"After. Perhaps in the afternoon." Elleul sounded strained.

She tapped it into her schedule. "After the search."

A message came in from Lane: *?? why are you awake?*

Renée resisted smiling. She didn't want to explain to the member why a message from Lane Kovacs made her smile.

Renée: *I ask myself this question every morning.*
Renée: *Are you free for coffee?*
Lane: *When?*
Renée: *In thirty minutes.*
Renée: *The usual place.*
Lane: *You buying?*

She couldn't help it: she laughed.

"If there is something funny about this situation," Elleul ground out, "I beg you share it with the rest of us. I would relish a joke that isn't this department."

Renée looked up and saw the purple colour was in full bloom. Atkins had taken a step back and was watching the two of them carefully. She waved a hand. "Only Lane Kovacs. We're meeting this morning."

Elleul frowned. "While her business is searched. Ah, Fentiman clearly knew her, and the Kusanagis went to her salon . . . I'm glad we're on the same page, Prefect. If you could keep her a while, I would like a word too." He tapped at his tablet. "I had our Intelligence Department send over the entirety of what they have on Lane Kovacs. It turned out to be substantial."

Was this man set on ruining *every* moment of fun for her?

Renée could only nod though. "I see. I hope her file isn't bigger than mine. She might get precious about it."

A muscle in Elleul's jaw jumped. "I'm a little alarmed that you appear on such close terms with her. She isn't just an everyday citizen; she is at the very minimum a known sympathiser with enhanced beings."

Which made her the same as every suspicious person in the Intelligence Department's large database. Supposedly. Alas, if only that mattered in the Neutral Zone as much as it did in the core.

Nonetheless, Renée was duty-bound to carry out a murder investigation—the committee and mayor had made that *very* clear—and this was a lead into the recovery of stolen government materials related to said murder investigation. "If you wish to speak with her, I'll keep the conversation flowing until you arrive."

"Good."

Renée stood. "If that's settled, Lieutenant Atkins will take you to the salon. I will be with Lane at a café called the Red Canary. It is in the area—Atkins can direct you."

Atkins smoothed over a displeased frown while Elleul nodded. "Until later, Prefect."

Renée left the meeting room and made her way out of the building to the street, where she hailed a taxi. Once en route to the café, she checked her tablet. Elleul had sent her Lane's file. Renée opened it, but when she saw the introductory stats and photo, she turned the screen off.

This felt very strange. Renée wasn't used to feeling strange about looking at people's private information. She needed to sit with this for a minute.

She'd known Lane for, oh, five years now? Something like that. Lane had arrived like most others—on a ship from elsewhere in the system, with luggage, a family member, and a bleak story in tow. Unlike most of the people who ended up here, Lane and Helen Kovacs hadn't shared their bleak story while earning money for tickets to Fides. They'd simply bought a rundown store and turned it into a popular business. Not a single hint of a desire for tickets.

Renée had never asked, or truly wanted to know, but a few things had emerged over the years. Helen hid it well, but she was synth, which was rare and cost money, and businesses were expensive to start, even in Pann.

Lane had let the odd thing slip: mentions of university, work at some kind of research lab, a misty expression on her face as she remembered past jobs that seemed to hold better memories for her than the salon did. There was a deep and abundant cynicism in both that was probably motivated by politics—given the bits of tech in Lane and the fact Helen *was* all tech—but could be simple caution. It was hard to tell, what with their somewhat chaotic door policy and Lane's continual dodging of the topic.

Here, it hardly mattered anyway. Renée just liked being able to guess their backstory. So much more fun than having it whined at her by some beggar desperate enough to think it entitled them to free tickets.

Having the concrete details in the palm of her hand was different. Renée wasn't sure she cared to know. After all, she rarely gave out certain details of her own history, and Lane hadn't pressed. Did she want to know? Somehow she didn't strike Renée as someone who would welcome reminisces of a childhood spent in the Newportian countryside or anecdotes from training.

The taxi stopped outside the café. Renée glanced at her tablet once more, then slipped it into her pocket and paid the driver. Inside the café was warm with the body heat of multiple strangers and loud with the chatter of multiple languages. She chose a place in a bright corner; the sun was out today, and she wanted to feel it on her face.

Moon and stars, she missed proper seasons. Newport summers were hot and humid, the atmosphere so heavy it felt like being wrapped in a blanket the instant she stepped outside. Long hot days, perfect for syruped ices and barbecues with family and diving with her cousins into the lakes outside the city. Cold wines with her mother and hikes with her father.

The humidity built and built over days until the skies unleashed furious storms, forcing the family indoors for games and movies. Here, on Salus, the summer was what she considered autumn, all gentle breezes and tepid sunshine with one or two days of drizzle. There weren't nearby lakes to swim in, but if there were, they'd be too cold. Some lunatics liked to swim in the river, which tested belief. What she wouldn't give for real, genuine *heat*.

While she waited, she pulled out her tablet and checked for Newport headlines. Naturally she had a subscription to Newport, and to the core planet Arden in general, but she really did have to stop looking all the time. It was pointless. These tablets facilitated terrible habits. She didn't know how Lane could concentrate while having information available on her optic nerve with a mere thought.

Lane finally came in, looking wretched, yet somehow more gorgeous for it. She wore that blue jacket which suited her so well and trousers that traced the curves of her legs. Her hair was twisted back, showing the angles of her sharp face and her frankly magical jawline. Ah, Renée did love that jawline. Despite the many evenings they'd spent in each other's company, she needed infinite more to properly memorise its exact curvature and angle. It was the kind of feature that inspired poetry and sculpture.

Lane gave a small smile as she sat opposite Renée. "I'm not sure I've ever seen you outdoors before eleven."

Renée sighed and signalled for the waiter. "Parliament members have no compassion for alternative work schedules. Very inconvenient."

"I'll bet."

"You, however, look beautiful as always, Lane."

Lane rolled her eyes. "I'm here so your team can search my place in peace, like you wanted. Get to the point."

Had the team assembled that quickly? "You saw them coming?"

"No. I know you." Lane pointed at her tablet with the day's news on it. *DIPLOMAT KILLER ARRESTED*. Renée tapped through: there was an entire paragraph on the arrest in the salon and another on how the diplomat's precious documents hadn't been found. "I joined the dots."

How nice to be anticipated. "Elleul wasn't very happy about Fentiman not having any documents on him. No missive, no ticket. We assume he stashed both in your salon."

"In your position, I would assume that too." Lane leaned back in her chair.

Renée tried to read Lane for any tells. Lane gazed back with a perfected expression of bland nonchalance. How often had they done this? Perhaps Renée could've given her less opportunity to practise the cover-up act.

She still had to try. "You wouldn't know anything about them? Most especially the portal ticket?"

"Me? Why would I? Fentiman and I weren't friends."

The waiter came over and took their order. When he was gone, Renée rested her elbows on the table and leaned forward. "The thing is, you two not being friends makes me wonder why he asked you for help last night." She mimed her hands gripping something.

"For fuck's sake, Renée, your goons were dragging him out, and he was desperate. He latched on to the first person he knew." A small pause passed before Lane said, "Far as I could tell, he was drinking and gaming like everyone else."

"You know what his business was."

"He can conduct business where he chooses."

"Did you see him sell anything before we arrived?"

"No. I don't watch people, I tend to leave that to you."

Renée relished these exchanges. Lane's eyes were lit up with interest and a smile seemed to be gathering force behind her calm. She truly was lovely, despite never answering the damn question. Perhaps because of it. Pinning her down was impossible, but Renée enjoyed attempting too much to stop. "Oh, Lane. I hope we don't find that ticket stashed in the games room. I would hate to arrest you on suspicion of accessory to a crime."

"Please don't start doing your job on my account."

"Believe me, I'm very irritated that Elleul is demanding results from me." Renée sat back. "We'll see what the team finds. To be honest, it would be in everyone's best interests to get that ticket back. It's the kind of thing which could cause many problems here in Pann."

Lane did smile at that, perhaps a little mockingly. "Paperwork is such a pain, I know."

She was right. There were previous incidents where the paperwork had been unconscionable. Being a public official in Renée's position wasn't as glamorous or powerful as people thought it was. Having the NZC and the mayor demanding reports about every major crime was profoundly inane and if there was an opportunity to avoid paperwork, of course Renée took it.

The server returned. A cup of coffee was plunked in front of Lane, a fruit smoothie and some water for Renée. Renée picked up her glass and took a long swallow while deciding if she minded the blatant deflection enough to not warn her about Elleul. "Headaches induced by overbearing bureaucrats certainly are. By the way, he's interested in you."

Lane raised her eyebrows. "What a shame. Tell him I don't swing his way."

"Politically or sexually?"

"Either."

Ah! This was something concrete. Despite all their chats, Renée had never quite fixed on where Lane's interests lay. It had been infuriating. "Are you saying you prefer women? Please say you are. I need something to go right this morning."

Lane shifted in her seat. Her fingers—strong, limber, callused—picked up the teaspoon sitting in the table's sucrose bowl and began fidgeting with it. "I'm saying I prefer people who aren't fascist despots."

"Still keeping certain information classified, I see."

Lane smiled again. "When in Rome."

Was that a happy smile? It seemed to be. In any case, this was more than she'd revealed before. It was enough. "This is so pleasant. We should see each other more," Renée said. "Drinks tonight? Coffee again tomorrow? I promise I won't even search your place this time."

"We go for coffee all the time."

Renée couldn't tear her eyes from Lane's hand. "Lane. I mean on a date."

The teaspoon stilled, and Lane stared at her, eyes suddenly wide. "You're serious?"

Well, of course. Elleul was on the prowl, and Renée wanted her close, but while she was on this streak of honesty, her brain was done with the possibilities marching an ingrained track through it. Lane wasn't adverse to the idea of being with women; this was an opportunity, and she must take it. Orion's eye, imagine having this woman's attention and focus for more than insults and crime details. "Absolument."

Lane still gripped the teaspoon. Renée wanted to reach over and take it out of Lane's hand, then catch Lane's hand in hers, run her fingers across Lane's knuckles and feel how her bones mapped to the little cushions of muscle under her skin. She wished to trace the tendons into her wrist, find the pulse in the soft skin at the base of the palm, and press it to her lips.

She resisted going that far, but she did bump her knee against Lane's under the table.

Lane had the strangest expression on her face. She finally put the teaspoon down and sipped her coffee. It spilled on her hand, the section between thumb and index. She cursed and jerked her hand to her mouth, and Renée watched avidly. Oh, to do that, to put her mouth on her and lick the coffee off, and feel the texture under her tongue and taste the bitter richness combined with her skin . . . Instead she asked, "Are you all right?"

Lane met her gaze, then lowered her hand. "Renée, you should know—"

"Prefect. Madame Kovacs."

Behind Lane was Elleul, glancing between the two of them.

Putain! Renée wondered if it was possible the Parliament would accept their member back in tiny pieces with a curt note on the very serious matter of *not interrupting people.*

Lane twisted in her chair and saw Richard Elleul. *Oh, for fuck's sake.* Did the guy know what he'd walked into? She turned back to Renée and watched her smooth over her annoyance a little too well.

"Member Elleul," Renée said calmly. "Do join us."

Was this a fucking set-up?

Well, yes, obviously, it had been from the start, but this was a whole other level if Renée knew he'd been coming too. First the search, then the come on, now this. Just one big reminder of why Renée couldn't be totally trusted, though Lane doubted his presence was her idea.

And Lane had been about to tell her . . . what? Her mind was blank. Renée liked to flirt, always had, but that sincerity was new. Different. They made convenient excuses to see each other and danced around those excuses; that's how things worked for them. What was she thinking? And with a member of Parliament lurking around; had she lost her mind? She should be watching her back around him, not asking Lane out. Talk about inviting suspicion.

Lane was too hungover for this. She should've drunk a quick something before rushing out here, keep the brain fog at bay. And of all the places for Renée to display her deeply hidden serious side: the Red Canary was Lane's main competitor, having opened after she'd started her salon, and it tried to do what she did, only with a mediocre brunch included. Renée liked meeting here, something about keeping enemies close and annoying Lane. It wasn't great, but Renée didn't like many places in Pann, so Lane pretended to be more annoyed than she actually was.

No pretence now. She drained her cup and eyed Elleul as he sat at their table. The server approached with their food and set it down. She ordered more coffee, and Elleul piggybacked on her order.

It was all so fucking quaint and civil.

Lane dug into whatever she'd ordered. She couldn't remember the official name. It was all the same MangeX crud anyway. And she didn't have the stomach for it, even though she did need something solid in her stomach. Having that stupid stash in the office was a dumb idea, but she never seemed to remember that when she was restocking it or drinking it.

Wait, what *was* she eating? Shit—was that an actual egg? A real egg. Sweet heavens, how long had it been since she'd had a real egg? MangeX—the boring synthetic foodmeal that everyone used because it was cheap, nutritionally-complete *and* cookable in multiple ways, not that Lane would know—had to have numbed her taste buds if it had taken her this long to realise she was eating something fresh.

"And you, Madame Kovacs," Elleul was saying to her.

She looked at him. "Excuse me?"

"I'm glad to finally meet you."

"Mm." She scooped the entire egg into her mouth. Yolky bliss.

Renée was staring at her again. She'd been doing that a lot this morning. Not that Lane normally minded, but in front of this asshole, she did.

Elleul had an odd smile on his face. "You see, your reputation precedes you."

"As does yours, monsieur."

"Ah, but do you have a file on me?"

He lifted his tablet and showed Lane a screen full of information about her. Lane reached across and took the tablet for a closer look.

The Parliament *had* been tracking her. She'd assumed so— Intelligence seemed to have information on everyone—but it was nice to see the proof. She scanned down the screen. The displayed tab was about her work, though she also saw tabs devoted to general biography, family and friends. Her degrees, her notable projects, her research in quantum data, her work in the modification laboratory with human memory, the lab explosion, all of it was there. A tab titled *Informants* confirmed some long-held suspicions. Amazingly, Intelligence had almost everything until the time she'd fled the core planets with Helen.

However, they didn't have information *about* Helen. She thumbed over to the family tab. There were the names of her immediate and extended family. Parents were dead, which was correct, and everyone else alive. Helen's entry had a note that she'd left Lavele with Lane after the explosion—with an odd detail about said lab destruction being committed by one of the local resistance groups. Lane pressed on it and found herself back on her work tab.

Interesting.

And a damned relief.

"Your work is extraordinary," Elleul was saying. "You are quite brilliant, you know that? If it weren't for your unfortunate liaison with certain groups, the Parliament would have a permanent role for you in one of our own research institutes."

She shrugged. "I have a pretty nice gig here."

Elleul glanced her over. "Yes, a game parlour is certainly fitting for a mind of your calibre."

Renée looked surprised. "You're a scientist, Lane?"

Didn't she already know? Lane had assumed Renée had looked her up years ago. Apparently not. Huh. How sweet.

"Not only a scientist," Elleul said. "An engineer. A bioengineer. Modification programmes. You invented new technology, new ways for people to enhance their senses and strengths and bodies beyond natural capacity. These . . . *things*, these unnecessary mechanical instruments have no place in the human body. They have corrupted humankind beyond what's natural and good. You did that, Madame."

"I can't take all the credit." Lane tapped the biography tab in her file. There was her birthdate, physical characteristics, a rather terse *none* in the partners section, a timeline of her general movements in life, and all of her past core addresses. And some high school photos. Stars above. Not even Intelligence needed to see those.

"In fact," Elleul continued, "you helped run tech to groups specifically marked as needing Parliament protection from precisely such influence. So you weren't only an inventor, a researcher and a scientist. You were also an activist. Not a prominent one, of course, but you did enough to get our attention. You'll understand why I had to speak with you." He smiled at her. "We know everything about you, Lane Kovacs. We know how old you are, where you're from, how tall you are, what work you did, who your family is, where they are, why you left the core, and the name of the ship that brought you here. It seems only fair you understand the stakes involved, and, if you want to hear my opinion, I suggest it wise to cooperate with us."

Lane looked up at him. "I thought I was taller than 175 cm."

He took his tablet back. "We are investigating a murder and the loss of classified documents. We didn't find anything on the murderer or in your salon. Did Monsieur Fentiman approach you last night?"

At last, the point had arrived. "He did."

"Did he give you anything?"

"A headache."

Elleul's entire face seemed to tighten, and he started going red. It was a truly remarkable physical transformation. If Lane poked him, would he crack into pieces? Pop like a pimple? "Did he tell you anything?"

"Probably, but nothing I give a shit about, so I forgot it the minute he said it." Lane shovelled more food into her mouth.

"Madame Kovacs. You will tell me what he said to you."

She chewed thoroughly. Swallowed. "Let's see." Sipped some coffee. Swallowed. "He mentioned some sale he was going to make and that he was leaving Pann forever." Look at her, being all *cooperative*. She hoped Renée was taking notes.

"A sale? Of what, to whom?"

"Like I know? All he wanted to do was boast. I hear someone saying that every other day in my bar. They're usually back the next week, playing their woes away. Or drinking them away."

"I can confirm that," Renée said.

She could; when the sale never quite worked out, Renée's officers were normally involved.

"It's nothing new." Lane stirred her food around. Now that she was eating, she did feel better.

"Did he say anything about a ticket?"

Lane shrugged. "Sure."

"A ticket to Fides?"

He looked far too excited. Lane made sure to be casual. "Where else? People are always selling tickets to Fides. Some are legitimate, others are good fakes, but most are crap fakes." She glanced around and then leaned in to whisper loudly, "There's a black market here, Member."

He seemed to deflate right before her eyes. "I understand you don't participate in the black market yourself." He waited a beat. "Not anymore."

"No."

"Lane Kovacs operates above any markets. She is truly neutral." Renée grinned at her. "In fact, she supersedes any democratic form of government in favour of tyranny. A mere hint of tension and both parties are instantly thrown out."

Oh hey. She wouldn't put it *quite* like that. "I look out for myself."

Elleul frowned. "You weren't always so 'neutral.' This brings me to my next point: there are two persons of interest to our Parliament here on Salus. They are Tori and Ayumu Kusanagi. Perhaps you've heard of Tori Kusanagi."

"Perhaps I have."

"They will visit your salon and will no doubt try to solicit help in gaining tickets to Fides. That must not happen."

Lane polished off her plate. "And this concerns me because . . .?"

Elleul appeared to be grinding his teeth. "Because, Madame, you may have the prefect fooled with your supposed neutrality, but you don't have me fooled. You and I both know they will ask *you* for help. You will not help them."

For someone with so much information and power at his fingertips to get something so wrong was honestly hilarious. Lane leaned back and resisted the urge to cross her arms. "And what makes you think I'd help anyone?"

"Your record of sympathy with their cause."

"Well, I don't know about that. I'm just a business owner trying to make an honest living out here in the Neutral Zone."

Renée looked very much like she was trying not to laugh, the idiot. Luckily for her, Elleul's focus was fixed on Lane like a bloodhound. He was very ordinary looking, as far as Lane could judge, and the ordinariness abruptly irritated her. How typical for someone like him to jump to conclusions; how typical for her that he happened to be immensely powerful. The prick could have the decency to look evil and less like someone's overworked uncle. She stood. "If we're finished here, I have a salon to clean up before we open in the afternoon."

Renée stood too. "I'll be in touch, Lane."

"I'll wait with bated breath." She nodded at him. "Monsieur Elleul."

"Madame Kovacs."

And finally, Lane could leave. Pity Renée didn't have that luxury.

Outside was muggy and a touch on the warm side. She'd acclimated by now, but she could see other people still wearing scarves and gloves. Salus was on the outer edges of the habitable zone and therefore cooler than the core planets. The first year here, Lane had had several colds and constantly worn multiple layers, even during Salus's summer. Helen, of course, hadn't fallen sick at all.

And Helen needed to know the Parliament mutt was sniffing around. Pann being Pann, the presence of synths was higher than in the core—but that could be said about all the cyborgs or mods walking around. Synths were still rare, and while they'd been careful not to reveal what Helen was, it wasn't beyond crazy that others had noticed. They were safe here, but old habits died hard.

If that got back to Elleul, he'd . . . well. At the very least he'd add that information to their files and no doubt use it to make Lane look more suspicious in whatever conspiracy he was brewing in his head. If rumours about him and his past in Intelligence were true—and Lane was sure they were—then it wouldn't hurt to be careful while he was here.

Stars help them all if Renée's team had actually found the ticket and Elleul was trying some elaborate bluff.

She walked quickly to the salon. Inside, she found Helen and Serge picking up the mess left by Renée's team. Tables and chairs were overturned, the bar was in disarray, napkins were everywhere, and one of Helen's sculptures—the oversized guitar—lay in pieces near the toilets. Lane dreaded the state of the games room. Rakesh emerged from it to grab the vacuum bot and went back in, which actually boded well.

Helen waved, a broken chair in the other hand. "You're back. Any news?"

"Nothing we didn't already guess. Elleul knows about my background, but not about you. He—"

"Elleul?" Helen frowned a beat too late. "Was he there? I thought you were meeting Renée."

"I was. I did."

"So . . .?" Helen prompted.

She'd forgotten about that little moment they'd had. "So what?" Lane began righting the chairs nearest her.

"Did anything happen?"

"Like what?"

Helen tsked while Serge rolled his eyes. "Stop pretending to be obtuse, Lane. Renée asked you out for coffee. Early. You actually went."

"And?"

"*And* you were still in bed. You don't get out of bed for anything. It was a sign. I thought this meant the end of you two dancing around each other."

Serge waved a new stack of napkins. "Same here."

Lane snorted. "Neither of us dance. And no. She needed me out of here so her team could search in peace, and to give Elleul a chance to interrogate me. I knew it, she knew it, end of story."

That wasn't the end of it, or even the start of it.

She turned away from Helen's and Serge's smirking faces and spread her fingers over the surface of a table, feeling the grooves in the wood.

Lane wasn't stupid. Five years of watching their acquaintance turn into a tentative friendship and then into *something* didn't make her blind to what that something was, or what it potentially could be.

It just wasn't the kind of something Helen and Serge and everyone else liked to make cracks about. That's all. Nothing had been said, nothing had been done. Lane was all right leaving things there—after all, what was the point of pursuing anything with anyone?—but she knew eventually things would change and that Renée would be the one to change them. Today wasn't the timing she'd expected.

Renée was a lot of things Lane wasn't: Bright, open, welcoming. Mostly sober. Tech-free. Pretty strong on family, as was typical of Newportians and confirmed by a few absently mentioned details. Duplicitous and highly corrupt, obviously, and she'd dropped some hints over the years that indicated a past working for the current regime as a police officer. Somewhere in Lane was a horrified twenty-year-old, but her current thirty-five-year-old self didn't care. For one,

Renée was here like everyone else was, and for another, it was petty to care about something that happened over five or six years ago.

Lane didn't exactly lie about herself, but she didn't share either. She let other people assume things about her; that generally worked in her favour. In turn, she'd assumed Renée, given her access to various databases, had known her past and didn't care. Perhaps that was wrong. After Elleul's little display, Lane wondered if Renée would still want that date. The Parliament wasn't to be trifled with, even here in the Neutral Zone.

An ex-neolud police officer and an ex-bioengineer walked into a bar. A shit opening to a shit joke.

But if Renée was still interested, then maybe Lane could try some honesty and share the other reason she'd left Lavele and the core.

She glanced at Helen.

Or maybe not. It wasn't like she hadn't had the urge to talk to Renée before about what had happened. During some of their long evening conversations and drinks in Lane's office, and sometimes during the occasional afternoon with coffee and bribe negotiations in Renée's office, Lane had been tempted to lay it all out, about the research, Yui, and Helen. Strongly tempted. She couldn't tell if it was the normal weight of holding in a secret or if it was that quality of Renée's that drew people in and let them spill their stories—maybe both.

What was she thinking? No. *No.* Finally making a serious move didn't make Renée magically more trustworthy than last month or last year. If anything, given Elleul's presence, it called her already dubious judgement even more into question.

She took her hand off the table and inhaled deeply. "Helen?"

Helen turned to her. "Forget about me and Ren— Prefect Bellevue. Focus on Elleul. He showed me my file, and it doesn't have anything about you. Make sure you avoid his notice."

Helen scoffed. "Like he'll do anything."

"He could."

"Yeah, yeah, you don't need to tell me that."

Still her big sister, thinking she knew everything. Well, she literally did now, but that wasn't an excuse. Maybe five years was long enough to get used to relative safety in neutral territory, but they couldn't forget the danger that came with Parliament contact.

Lane finished straightening the tables and chairs in the section by the door, then went behind the bar to assess the damage there. A few bottles were missing, nothing too bad. The synthesising machine that made the espresso, tea, and other hot drinks had been moved. So had the music centre.

She straightened the synthesising machine first and reconnected the pipes back to the water and electricity supply that sustained it. Then Lane turned to the music centre. She edged it back into its nook, rewired it to the speakers around the bar, and opened the disc player.

The portal ticket stared back at her.

Oh stars.

She bit back a sigh of relief and closed the player. Time to change the atmosphere. Turning the centre on, she accessed the library and chose something upbeat from hers, Helen's, and Serge's collective adolescences. They needed something to lighten the mood while cleaning the mess.

CHAPTER
THREE

Renée went into the hotel first, because she was fairly sure the Kusanagis would refuse to see them if they knew Elleul was present. Like Lane might have, given a choice. Not that Lane hadn't received something out of it in the end; Renée had indeed paid for her brunch.

Elleul had been a little sulky on the ride over to the hotel, so Renée had avoided conversation by reluctantly reviewing Lane's file, and yes, she'd been a clear sympathiser and small-time black market supplier. She'd worked in tech development for most of her career, but her specialities had been in quantum data and human memory. Quite impressive. Shuttling modification tech to interested groups illegally was less impressive, but she'd hardly been the only one to do that. The restrictions imposed by Parliament had in effect created the black market; if someone of Lane's background *hadn't* participated, that would be more surprising.

In short: Lane's file didn't reveal anything too intense. What a relief. Renée honestly couldn't wait to talk to her about black marketeering; it had always seemed a very exciting industry. The one here mostly dealt with imported luxuries from the core, various weaponry, and portal tickets, as well as the usual niche taboos. Very occasionally something interesting would come up—information, usually—from the resistance cells; otherwise Renée largely ignored the darker trading in Pann. Lane would be sure to have some good stories.

She couldn't help noting how much more thorough this file was compared to what Intelligence normally sent to her officers. Not that she would bring it up, but it was an unexpected discrepancy. Career notes, links to other files, certain internal flags; all very thorough, especially the tab with all of Lane's living family and their last known locations.

She wondered if her own file was as detailed.

But first, the infamous Kusanagis.

By sheer luck, they'd decided to eat lunch in the hotel, and their table was where the staff led her. Renée studied them as she approached. They were dressed much like in the report photo, but their appearances were distinctively different. Ayumu wore slight stubble now, had dyed his hair a less-obvious dark brown and left it free around his face, which somehow, seemed longer, less tight, less youthful. Same with Tori: her face gave a different impression entirely, and her short spiky hair was waxed down and back. Quite elegant if Renée was allowed to give her opinion.

They fit in well with the other hotel clientele. Other guests ranged in age, but they all had the same air about them: middle-class to well-off refugees, waiting for the change in circumstances that would launch them away from this system.

The dining room was modern and comfortable, with light beaming through the large windows on one side. Salus's ring was framed beautifully in a skylight at the far end of the room. Chatter was muted but lively, with Renée catching snippets of Italian and Hindi on her way through the dining room. The smells emanating from the kitchen were sublime; Renée would have to come back here for a meal.

She stopped in front of their table. "Bonjour, Madame and Monsieur Kusanagi. I am Prefect Bellevue, head of Pann's police force."

They looked up, surprise clear on their faces, then Ayumu put down his cutlery and stood. "Hello, Prefect Bellevue. Is there anything we can help you with?"

Renée waved him back down. "Oh no. Please, don't trouble yourselves. I merely wished to welcome you to Pann, and to wish you a pleasant stay while you're here. We aren't used to such esteemed people visiting our little part of the system."

Ayumu and Tori exchanged glances. Ayumu gave a curtailed nod. "Thank you, Prefect. You'll forgive our . . . shyness. We're not used to government figures being welcoming." He indicated the spare chair. "Please, join us."

They sat. A server passed by, and Renée ordered a glass of wine. This meeting would require it.

"You knew where we were, Prefect." Tori's voice was firm and clipped the edges of each word. "I take it the person trailing us from the terminal was one of yours?"

Well, it wasn't the appointed shadow who'd clued her in to their precise whereabouts—the cameras did their bit too—but she would let Tori think so. Renée smiled. "Indeed, Madame Kusanagi! I'm surprised she was spotted. I must have words with her."

"Please don't. We've developed a sense for things like that." Tori sliced up the MangeX steak on her plate. "We were under the impression this is the Neutral Zone of the Janus system."

"And so it is. We're a separate entity from the core planets' Parliament, and from the Fides government. Our local procedures and politics are quite different. However, we have a stake in monitoring our visitors of interest, which you will be flattered to learn includes yourselves." Renée smiled encouragingly at them. "Don't take it to heart; we're not the Parliament and tend only to monitor for security purposes or for special requests. Alas, our neutrality also means anyone may travel here and make requests of us."

Tori frowned. "What do you mean— Oh." Her gaze fixed over Renée's shoulder and Renée turned. There was Elleul, smiling greasily.

Renée stood. "Allow me to introduce Member Elleul of the Parliament."

He bowed to them both. "Madame Kusanagi. Monsieur Kusanagi. A pleasure to finally put faces to the names."

Ayumu and Tori had frozen. Ayumu thawed first, clearing his throat as he did so. "Unfortunately, this is a pleasure we don't share, monsieur."

"Considering the circumstances, that's understandable." Elleul pulled out the final free chair, and Renée joined him in sitting at the table.

The server brought Renée's wine over. No one gave her a second glance as she gulped a third of it, then grimaced. Wretchedly sweet. Her mother would have cursed it, then poured the bottle away; alas, Renée was stuck until someone brought over a bucket or obliging plant.

"We won't interrupt your meal for long," Elleul said. "We merely wished to discuss the situation of your being here."

"This isn't really the time or the place," Tori said.

Elleul inclined his head. "I agree, but there are few better times or places than the present. I promise to be quick and direct. You're both citizens of core planet Arden and thus subjects of the Parliament. You, Madame Kusanagi, are a known radical who has organised opposition to Parliament policies and rule, and a criminal who has injured and killed civilians and government staff in pursuit of your subversive radical agenda. Fleeing to Salus is an offence on top of your many other crimes, and it is my duty to ensure you will not leave Pann— except under certain conditions."

Tori picked up her cutlery to attend to her food. "I expected no less from a member of this so-called Parliament. You must know we declare ourselves subjects of our better nature and of the democratic, representative government our system once had. You and your Parliament have no authority here. It's by no means certain we won't leave regardless of your 'duty.'"

"Ah, but you see, Prefect Bellevue must approve every portal ticket. The portal simply won't accept it otherwise. Prefect?"

Renée made what she hoped was a sympathetic face. "This is true. Unfortunately, there will be no tickets approved for you. I apologise deeply for this, madame, monsieur."

Ayumu shrugged. "Perhaps we'll like it in Pann."

"We heard the heat is quite bearable here," Tori said. "So far, that's proving true."

Heat? What heat? This was the edge of the habitable zone, the temperature was— Renée took in the situation and realised she wasn't talking about the weather. How droll.

"I wouldn't wish you two to be uncomfortable or inconvenienced. I can organise two tickets for you for tomorrow," Elleul said. "All you have to do is give me the names and locations of the major cell leaders in your little resistance. I understand you have them—every leader of every regional cell on the three core planets. Simple." This was an unexpected offer from Elleul; Renée supposed he thought himself merciful.

Ayumu muttered something under his breath that sounded Japanese yet distinctly impolite.

Tori finished chewing her steak, then swallowed it. "I *could* give you every name and location, but it wouldn't help you. Not at all, not one little bit. No matter what you do, whether you disappear us, assassinate us, imprison us, or torture us, our numbers are strong, and for each of us that falls, there are dozens to replace us."

Elleul smiled. "I see your reputation for eloquence and flair is deserved, but you're too humble by far, Madame Kusanagi. Your work has made too much of an impact, and much as I hate the description, you're an inspiration to the traitors and terrorists who follow your ideals. Your dedication to your cause is noteworthy but we both know you're here to retreat."

Renée forced down more of the wine, her stomach churning. Tori merely raised her eyebrows and forked in an overlarge mouthful of mashed potato.

"In short, you wish to live," he continued. "I offer you a chance to wash your hands of this pointless movement and start over elsewhere. If, as you say, your leaders are replaceable, then it can only benefit you to provide their names to me."

"We're not interested in your games," Ayumu snapped. Tori's arm moved under the table, and his mouth thinned.

Were they going to be much longer? Perhaps Renée could order dessert. Her glass was almost empty.

"I hope your situation is clear to you," Elleul said. "I will be around for some time, so there is no rush to make your decision."

Some time. Merde. That was worryingly vague. Renée wondered if quitting was a reasonable response to this. Dessert would be. But the atmosphere now felt as though they would be leaving shortly after all.

"Are you finished?" Tori asked them.

Elleul sat back. "Yes."

Renée emptied her wine glass. "I am now. Shall we, Member Elleul?"

They stood, gave small bows to the Kusanagis, and Renée followed Elleul out of the hotel restaurant. She glanced back to see Ayumu frowning at Renée's empty wine glass. Tori watched them go, eyes narrowed.

Oh yes, they'd be trying to get out of Pann. Legal routes wouldn't be available to them. It would take them a while to approach the hackers, if they decided to risk such a route. Much as the hackers loved organising illicit journeys, those slots didn't come cheap and weren't as secure as the standard procedure. Botched journeys were only reported when communication came from Fides a day or so later. For some the risk was worth it, but given how Tori in particular needed all her faculties intact, they'd probably attempt it as a last resort.

So what would their first resort be?

She pondered the possibilities during their taxi ride back to the station.

For sure they'd try Lane for the ticket. The evasiveness that morning was frustratingly typical of her, but Renée would bet another brunch she had it. The trickier question was if Lane would give it to them. Despite Elleul's belief that her past made her a likely candidate to help the Kusanagis, Renée wasn't so sure. He hadn't watched Lane kick mods and neoluds alike out of her salon nor seen Lane's expression whenever politics was mentioned.

Renée still found the focus on the diplomat's ticket difficult to swallow. Oh, she *understood* it, of course she did. Neither she nor Elleul could stop the bearer of that ticket from leaving.

However, the portal only did single journeys with a strict two-kilogram limit on inorganic material. One journey per charge. The machine's power cell stored twenty charges and required solar recharging, so the journeys were rationed out. If she were in the Kusanagis' shoes, she'd want two tickets, ideally two slots one after the other for some time in the next week or so, before Elleul became impatient and made another move.

It wasn't an impossible situation, but seeing them interact at lunch, Renée wasn't sure they'd settle for one ironclad ticket. Logically, it would be much better to seek a deal for two, rather than pursue one guaranteed journey and potentially wait months for a slot via someone else. Given who they were, waiting months in this small place was risky for them. They might end up separating after all. Hm.

If they couldn't persuade Lane to give them the ticket, they'd have to approach the black market. The local resistance groups would help them. That could prove difficult to monitor; the groups shifted as people came and went, and information was constantly updating. Renée hadn't bothered much. Maybe one of the more bored officers could do some inventory, update their records, follow a few people, buy some moles—the usual thing.

She made an order on her tablet.

It was also possible that Tori would pass whatever knowledge she had to Fides via the comms network. Individual tech transmissions had no chance of crossing the vast distance between Janus and Fides, even from this spot in the system. Only the official channel worked, and it was already tracked by Renée's comms unit.

There wasn't another way out of Janus from here, not unless the Kusanagis wanted to try another planet in the habitable zone. The only other planet doing outward journeys—to the Orion system, which really was a last resort—was all the way on the other side of Janus's star, a good two core years' journey via ship. It would have to be ship, as the portal could only connect to a planet in the same system when the star was out of the way.

No, they'd come here and here was where they'd try to jump out. Regardless of Lane's response, whether she'd help them or not, Renée was satisfied she could handle the situation. The Kusanagis' options were limited, and most of them were already monitored by her force. The pertinent thing was that there was very little extra work she had to do.

Which meant the most pressing matter was pinning Lane down somewhere private and making her finish whatever she'd been about to say before Elleul had interrupted them at brunch. The nerve and inconsideration of the man! Renée could still see the expression on Lane's face, the surprise and uncertainty, and she wanted to replace it with something happier. Hopefully she could.

She spent some time pretending to work that afternoon, then made her excuses and went to Lane's in the early evening.

The salon was open, as usual, and everything looked spotless. The heating was on and welcome, and the few patrons were quiet. Renée took in the interior, which looked slightly different somehow. Perhaps Helen had placed some new piece of work in a corner somewhere—but no, nothing new. In fact, the guitar piece that usually hung on the far wall was missing. Otherwise everything seemed in order and the place was relaxed.

Renée sat at the bar, and Helen nodded at her. "Prefect?"

"Wine, please. And it's Renée, Helen. You know that."

She poured a glass of MangeX pinot gris and placed it on the counter in front of Renée. "Add it to your tab?"

"If you don't mind."

Helen nodded and tapped at the screen behind her. Renée watched her for a moment, taking in her hair and the curve of her back. Lane had dark hair, but Helen's was lighter, almost blonde, and straighter. No matter how hot the place got, Renée had never seen her hair frizz or dampen the way Lane's did. Helen's skin was also more olive in tone than Lane's. She didn't match the photo in Lane's file.

She glanced around. No one was sitting close enough to overhear them—not with unenhanced ears anyway. "Helen, what made you come to Pann with Lane?"

Helen turned around, eyebrows high in surprise. "We have tech implants; we were scared of the neolud measures the Parliament was making; our friends were disappearing and our jobs were going the same way. You know, the usual."

Renée sipped the pinot gris and wondered if she'd ever taste the real thing again. She and Maman had made wine-tasting an annual tradition, which was when she'd fallen for the western wines, including the pinot gris this one was mimicking. Her mother had closed her eyes and hummed after her first swallow. This was a chemical imitation. Nothing here compared. "I know Lane was an engineer, specifically a tech engineer, and more generally a scientist of some kind."

Helen's face smoothed, and she leaned against the bar. "She was. That's not a secret."

"Well, not anymore. What were you?"

"Admin some of the time." She smiled, a hint of sorrow in her expression. "Musician the rest of it. I'd play at festivals and bars and parks. I didn't like school as much as Lane did."

"Oh! What instrument?"

Helen danced her fingers across the counter. "Piano. I could also play the drums a little."

"Superb. I'm impressed; I never learned an instrument. Hardly know the first thing about music. Do you still play?"

She shook her head. "No. I had an injury."

Renée swirled the wine in her glass, wishing she was home and wondering what Maman would think if she could see her now. "What happened? If you don't mind me asking."

"How could I mind the head of police asking me anything? I broke an arm and developed a neural problem. My hands don't obey me like they used to." Helen spread her fingers and gazed at her palms. "The muscle memory is gone."

"I'm sorry. That must be very disappointing." Did synths feel disappointment about something like that? Truly?

Helen smiled, then the smile saddened by a few degrees. Almost as though Helen had consciously done it. "It is."

"Could you relearn? Play us some tunes?"

She shook her head. "No. I've tried. I can do it, but it's not the same at all. It's . . . I prefer not to play. It's easier."

Interesting. "What a shame."

"What's a shame?"

Renée jumped a little in her seat, then swivelled to face Lane— who was wearing grease-stained overalls with a shirt and boots. Oh. *Oh.* There were smudges on her cheek and forehead. She looked so dirty.

"Your appearance," Helen said. "Go shower. You're a disgrace."

Lane rolled her eyes. "Big sisters. Am I right, Renée?"

Renée shook her head. "I'm an only child."

"That explains so much." Lane scratched at her cheek, then frowned at her blackened fingernail. "Hmph. This is your fault, you know. If your team hadn't shoved the machines around so much, I wouldn't have had to spend hours repairing them. One of Helen's pieces was wrecked, and the place was a mess. We barely cleaned up in time to open."

Renée spread her hands. "What can I say? You know how excessive destruction delights Parliamentarians."

Lane huffed. "I'm going to shower."

"Wonderful. I'll come with you." Renée stood, wine glass in hand. She'd never been upstairs, so this was going to be an occasion.

Lane facepalmed. "*Renée.* Watch the phrasing. And cut it out, Helen, don't *encourage* her."

Helen was grinning widely. "I'm just standing here."

"What on earth did I say?" Renée tilted out one hip and leaned forward. "My dear Lane. I only want to *talk* with you."

That seemed to necessitate a glower, but nonetheless Lane gestured at her and began walking. Renée sipped her wine as she followed her up the back stairs to the apartment over the salon. The door opened directly into a living area, and Lane locked it securely behind them, brushing against Renée as she did. She smelled like metal, oil, and dust. "Bienvenue chez Lane et Helen."

Renée looked around, happy to finally be in here. It was surprisingly cosy: soft rugs on the floor, pictures on the wall, a very worn sofa and coffee table ensemble, shelves filled with things, and several tall lamps. A number of open doorways led to other rooms—as Renée moved into the space, she could see parts of a kitchen through one and a bed in another. She turned instead to the sofa and sat down, resisting the urge to look at the walls and shelves. She wanted to study the pictures and Lane's belongings. There would be things here that couldn't be captured in an Intelligence file.

"C'est adorable," she said.

"Merci." Lane grabbed a rag hanging by the door and cleaned her hands. "You wanted to talk?"

"Indeed." Renée sipped her wine. "My dear, sweet Lane, we have unfinished business from this morning."

Lane wiped her face. "I'm not paying you back for brunch."

"My disappointment is boundless, but you can make it up to me by answering that question of mine."

Lane hung the rag back up and turned around. "Depends which question you mean. The one you asked or the one you avoided asking?"

"The one I asked."

Her expression closed off. "The answer is complicated."

A pang went through her chest, but Renée shrugged it off. "It's only coffee, darling, no need to—"

"Don't." Lane raised her arms to undo her ponytail. Her shirt shifted, exposing more of her collarbone and a stretch of skin at the side of the overalls.

Renée drank in the details—the lines of the shirt, the edges of hair peeking from the sleeves where they bunched in her armpits, how her muscles worked in her arms, the deftness of her hands, and the slow way her hair fell in damp strands on her shoulders—then looked away with effort. "What's complicated? If we need to discuss things, then we can. You didn't tell me you used to be an engineer."

"I assumed you already knew."

"Please. Background checks are more trouble than they're worth. I've flicked through your file *now*, but I admit most of it went completely over my head. What kind of tech work did you do?"

Lane walked behind her, moving things around. Renée wanted her to sit down, preferably on the supremely comfortable sofa and within touching distance.

Lane came back into sight, a bottle of something in her hand and a frown on her face. "I worked with hearing tech. Nothing too crazy." She paused. "The bulk of my research involved the connection between neurons and electric receptors, the intersection where biology fuses with hardware, and exchanges the signals which make the modification work as intended. I had been developing ways of capturing those signals as data and storing the data long-term." She unscrewed the top and took a swig. The smell of aniseed filled the air.

Renée was glad she had wine. "Fascinating, truly, but apart from the black marketeering issue—which you *have* to tell me more about—I can't see why Elleul would get so worked up about that. It's hardly unusual."

Lane's mouth quirked. "I was storing the data using qubyte chips."

"Right, the quantum work." Renée gestured at her. "So you were a quantum bioengineer. Interesting field indeed. That makes so much *more* sense."

Lane huffed. "The next logical leap is synths, Renée. The vast synaptic activity in the brain can be captured as data in qubyte chips. He suspects I worked with synth tech, not auditory tech."

And as long as he suspected that, he would have an eye on Lane. Much as Renée missed home, she did enjoy not having to care about things like this. "So what does this have to do with you and me?"

Lane went to the shelf on the opposite wall and put the bottle down. She didn't move away though. "If you're asking, maybe it doesn't."

"I think so." The problem was, Lane did seem to think it mattered. "We haven't shared our backgrounds before."

They'd discussed lots of things—including, but not limited to: Pann, the weather, the officers under Renée's employ, the staff under Lane's employ, the patrons of the salon, the mild terraforming happening on Salus, the portal mishaps, religion, things they missed about core life on Arden, mutual cultural references from their childhoods, drinks, games, old friends they'd lost contact with, information feeds and technology in general, the amazing capacity of humanity to expand across galaxies the way it had—but never their personal politics or family specifics. In Pann, there wasn't a tendency to do so, or a point.

Lane made a face. "We both know why."

"Seeing as yours as a filthy revolutionary has been exposed"—this made Lane smile, as Renée had hoped—"perhaps you would like to know about mine as a filthy cog in the machine."

"I'd gathered enough to know you were a police officer."

Renée nodded. "I worked in one of the major cities on Arden—not Lavele, where you were. I lived in Newport. Similar size."

"More conservative."

"By far, yes."

Her hemisphere had tended to be, compared to Lavele. But that was normal, at least growing up. Things had changed so dramatically over her twenties. Her time on the force had started promisingly. She'd been proud to serve her home as someone who kept the peace and helped others, and at first, that was exactly what she'd done.

Her family had been proud of her as well—her father especially, as he'd served in the army. She'd progressed a few ranks in a short amount of time, which had made her very proud and excited for the future. Then the new party had been elected, and things had slowly become more difficult.

"What brought you here?" Lane asked.

Renée couldn't quite look at Lane for this, so she eyed her glass. The wine wasn't real, but at least the colour was lovely. Hints of rose and amber in the soft evening light. "Our side of the planet held certain cultural values, if you remember. Newport was, I think you say, a guinea pig for many Parliament initiatives. Our service generally supported these initiatives, but as they became more and more restrictive, we became somewhat critical. Not that the critics were *open*, of course. Back then, there was already an understanding that questions weren't welcome." She sighed.

"You still asked," Lane said.

"You know me so well." Her parents had too. They'd advised her to keep her head down, to not make trouble. How right they'd been, and how easily she'd ignored them. "Of course. I raised a concern about one new rule in particular. I may even have refused to carry out a direct order from my superior."

Lane smiled. "And you called *me* a filthy revolutionary."

Her superiors and colleagues had certainly reacted as if she were one. Remembering it no longer hurt, but its place in her head was like a stain left from a badly healed bruise. "I was fired very publicly. They needed an example, you see. Afterwards, this was the only job offer that seemed remotely interesting."

Lane tapped her fingers against the bottle, then picked it up again. "How long ago was this?"

Hardly long enough. "Six years."

"I see."

"The time has simply sped by." The first year had been difficult, but Renée had eventually settled in. It'd helped when her family fell out of touch, hopefully because her disgrace had made it dangerous for them and not because they were actually disappointed in her. Not that she could check without raising a notification in a particular Intelligence Department that she wished to avoid.

She'd sent feelers out through less official channels, but nothing had come of them. At best they were safe and blocking contact to ensure that safety. At worst, they were somewhere exposed, and contacting them would endanger them. It seemed best to give up, but the powerlessness, the not-knowing, it was haunting.

Six years of no news, and stretching out under the relative benevolence of the Neutral Zone Committee. At least her work here was closer to what she'd originally imagined, not that it mattered.

And, of course, Lane had arrived in Pann just a year after Renée had. The last five years, upon reflection, could have been much worse.

Lane seemed amused. "You were fired for asking a question and refusing to do something you disagreed with. How *totally* unlike you."

The ghosts of her family were strong tonight—that was something her parents and cousins used to say. She ignored the pang. "Oh yes. I have my own file and everything." Renée leaned forward. "It's not quite running tech to protected groups or developing technology that's now outlawed by Parliament, and I'll never be at Tori Kusanagi's level, but I trust you won't think less of me for it."

Lane smirked. "I'll try my best."

"Now you know."

"Now I know."

Renée met her eyes, wishing she would come closer to the sofa. "And you? Why did you come to Pann?"

Lane bit her lip and looked aside. "All the usual reasons others do. Things were bad and getting worse. I had Helen to think about. Thankfully our parents were already dead, so it was easy for us to go. But, well, my work had been compromised too."

She fell silent, then swigged from the bottle again. "The thing is . . . Renée, I made a breakthrough in my research—a small thing, but it's potentially significant. I shared it with a few people I loved and one of those people . . ." She dragged her fingers through her hair. "Fuck. It ended badly, all of it—my work, the lab where I was, Helen's and my life in the core, and the relationship I was in at the time."

A badly ended relationship in Lane's past. How annoying. Renée tried not to interrupt, but it was difficult. "They were a fool."

A snort. "*She* was wonderful, actually. She was caring and reliable, and one of the most principled people I've ever met. So *intelligent*. The discussions we had about tech legislature, cyborg and synth rights, the nature of life and death—they were incredible."

"I despise her," Renée said.

Lane laughed, her eyes crinkling in a most attractive way. "She was wonderful, until she left without saying a damn thing and took my breakthrough with her. It happened the same day my life—our lives went to shit. There were riots in Lavele and the lab was destroyed. It's in my file. Wiped out my work and my reason for being in the core. Given the political situation, Helen and I decided to leave. We ended up here."

That seemed straightforward enough, but there was something missing from the story. Renée didn't know what, and certainly wasn't judging because she'd left out details too, but she couldn't help being curious. Lane had been working for a hearing modifications lab. Five years ago, that would have been acceptable to Parliament, as auditory tech was beneficial to people, and companies producing beneficial tech were generally left alone by both sides. So why had this one been targeted? And by whom?

It was unthinkable that mods or neoluds would do it, and it was simply odd if the Parliament had done so. Systemically targeting labs like that had come later, in the last three years, and the first one had been data feed injectors. It wasn't out of the realm of possibility that the Parliament had something to do with it, but *this* kind of lab, five years ago? Très bizarre.

Perhaps it was related to this "small" breakthrough of Lane's. There had been nothing in the file about any breakthrough, just some hasty notes about the known implications of quantum bioengineering.

Of course, it might have been the riots. Rabbles weren't known for good decision-making.

Another strange detail stood out. Unlike Renée, Lane had a tradeable and in-demand skillset. Why come *here*? With her skills, Lane could have gone anywhere and been safe.

Ah, Helen, of course.

Regardless of the vague details, the memory was clearly painful. "I'm sorry, Lane." But Renée had noticed that *she* in Lane's past relationship, and she couldn't help feeling hopeful at that.

"Don't be. I'm not." Lane placed the bottle firmly on the shelf, then walked around the coffee table and sat on it, right in front of Renée. One denim-clad knee was mere millimetres from Renée's. "I came here to escape the people who'd wrecked my life and to forget Yui. I'm not sure I succeeded."

Perhaps they had more in common than Renée had originally thought. "I don't think anyone ever forgets someone who broke their heart."

Lane gave her a sad smile. "You're right."

"And did you escape those people?"

She shrugged. "Did you?"

Silence fell between them, punctuated by a gentle murmur of music and voices from the salon downstairs. Renée set her wine on the table, then reached out and pressed a thumb against Lane's index knuckle, enjoying the hard curve of it. "You're still in love with her?"

Lane met Renée's gaze, and the conflict on her face said everything. Renée tried not to feel too disappointed, but something in her expression must have given it away because Lane's hand turned and gripped hers.

"No. Stop. I am but I'm also not." Lane's hand was slightly oily, but warm and firm. "A lot happened, but there wasn't closure. She left. So did Helen and I, and everything changed. It's a long story." Her face was turning pink. Even that was lovely to see. "Look, I'm a wreck of a person, Renée. I don't give a crap about anything anymore. I never fell for people easily, or felt any kind of strong attraction, ever, so this isn't straightforward. Okay? That's what you really need to know, if you're serious about this. Whatever you're looking for, I don't think you'll find it here."

Ah. And this was so terrible?

Renée scooted forward so that her knees brushed up against Lane's thighs. She couldn't take her eyes off the blush on Lane's face. Were they really, finally here? They were so close she could see individual streaks of dirt on Lane's cheeks. "I'm not looking for any particular thing. I'm looking for you, and there is just one place where I'll find that."

Lane exhaled. "Oh, damn. Renée, you're too smooth for your own good. Your gamble, then."

From where she sat, this wasn't a gamble at all. Renée reached for Lane's other hand so she could hold them both, running her thumb along the ridges of Lane's knuckles. Lane's hands were wiry and strong, and there was a small but deep joy in finally feeling them. She had to take a second to clear her mind and remember what she wanted to say. "Lane. It's very simple. Do you want me?"

Lane's gaze flickered over her. Heat rose slowly, deliciously, in its wake. It was a little dizzying to be under this much focus, to finally touch Lane like this and be close to her. To understand each other better than they had before. Honesty was more intense than Renée remembered.

"Well, shit," Lane said finally. "I actually do. In the way I can want someone, yes." She gave a short, low laugh. "Maybe we could take our time and figure this out."

That was the best thing Renée had heard Lane say all evening. "I will follow your lead, ma chère." She pulled Lane's hands towards her as she leaned in. Lane wryly smiled, then closed her eyes and met Renée halfway.

Kissing her was more than she'd hoped it would be. A firm press of soft skin with the barest edge of wetness, the delightful huff of a shocked inhale. Lane kissed her back, letting their hands go so she could run one up to Renée's shoulder. Renée gripped Lane's thigh, wanting something solid under her, wanting to touch more of Lane. Nothing seemed real except Lane—her body, her breath, her taste. Not even Renée was in a kiss like this. Everything was her and them and this.

She kissed the aniseed off Lane's lips and tried to pull her nearer. Lane smelled different up close—under the dust and oil was sweat and hair, spice and metal. So many layers. Renée wanted to press her mouth and nose into Lane's skin for days, seek out every nuance of taste and scent. She hoped she would get a chance to do that. The need to roll them both onto the sofa and get started rose fierce and hot.

Instead, she sat back and waited for Lane's eyes to open.

In Lane's old lab there had been a creaky old fossil of a machine that she'd used to make the outer skeleton of her qubicon. It had bitched and groaned while processing the models Lane had fed in, occasionally needing two whacks to the engine before purring into motion and spitting prototype skeletons out like shiny treasures.

Kissing Renée felt like that. Something in Lane was being prodded to life, processed and reformed. When Renée leaned back, Lane wanted to chase after her mouth again, so she did. That was new, the want to stay connected with her. Precious. Rare. Good.

Beyond the aniseed lingering in her own mouth, Renée tasted like wine, crisp and full. Lane nudged gently with her tongue, pressed one knee further in, and broke the kiss when Renée made a small noise.

Somehow Lane had ended up kneeling on the sofa, with her hands on Renée's shoulders and her knee pressed between her thighs. Renée gripped handfuls of Lane's overalls, keeping them together. Lane had forgotten the intensity of being so physically close, how to touch and explore. She'd never quite had the compulsion to keep looking at her loved one; now she couldn't pull her eyes from Renée.

Each part of her face seemed simple in isolation—the line of her cheek, the curve of her nose, the fan of her eyelashes, the crinkles around her eyes—but the combination of everything formed something more, something wholly lovelier than each individual part.

Renée beamed happiness, her expression bright as the sun. As Lane took her in, her face softened to something sweeter. All the times they'd talked in the bar or drank over a game or argued in the police station, and not once had Lane ever seen *this* expression on her face.

Just from kissing. Imagine if . . . and what about . . . but Lane couldn't—no. Now wasn't the time to think about the things they could do, because now wasn't the time they would do those things. The past, Renée's position, their future in Pann, none of that seemed to matter, and they could deal with it later. Now was for being present and looking her fill of this woman. This infuriating, surprising woman. Shit, this was insane.

She was grinning. So was Renée.

"I adore these overalls," Renée said, giving them a tug.

"I can't say the same about this." Lane stroked her sleeve.

Renée raised an eyebrow. "I can take it off if you want."

Still smiling, Lane shook her head and let Renée go. "No. I should— I have to shower."

Those fists balled her overalls tighter. "Not yet."

Lane hesitated, then ran her fingers gently down Renée's cheek. The skin was soft, so soft. Renée's fists released and Lane straightened, Renée's hands falling to her lap like loose feathers. "Stay if you want, but I can't. I need to be downstairs, and unlike some, I take my job seriously."

Renée picked up her wine and reclined against the sofa, eyes dancing. "I'm so happy from that kiss that I'm going to pretend I didn't hear that. I believe I'll recover in the exact time you need to clean all that grease off, but I make *no* promises."

Lane shook her head and left the living room. She tried to stay focused as she entered the bathroom, acutely aware Renée was a few walls away. Not that Lane was afraid Renée would come in here—

she wouldn't—but her presence was palpable despite physical barriers between them.

She took off her overalls and shirt, then bra and underwear, dumping the lot into the washing machine. Turned on the shower and waited for the water to warm, then stepped in and let the heat and pressure rinse off the grease in her hair and on her skin.

The echoes of Renée's hands and the press of her knees remained under the flowing warmth of the water, as though Lane's body was still being touched. Funny how welcome that was, after all this time. Funny how Lane could feel this way again about someone. Especially about Renée Bellevue, of all people.

Yui never kissed her like that. Yui had been gentle, building up closeness slowly, easing Lane into the physicality between them. Renée kissed her like Lane had always been hers, as though there was a magnetism equal to the planets and moons and sun between them.

Lane pressed a fingertip to her lips. She needed to get back to earth. Somewhere between kisses, things had fallen into a before and after, and there wasn't time to reflect. She *should* reflect.

When she was clean, she dried off and dressed in her bedroom, deliberating a little too long over her choice of shirt and trousers. Then she returned to the living room, combing out the tangles in her hair.

Renée remained where she'd left her, glass depleted in one hand and head back against the sofa. If she hadn't explored, Lane would be amazed, but there wasn't much to discover in their living room. Only pictures and mementos she and Helen had brought from Lavele, and stuff they'd accumulated since moving into the building. None of the other people in their pictures would matter to Renée. Hopefully not to Elleul either, though Lane suspected—hoped—Renée didn't tell him anything she didn't have to.

Lane moved forward and Renée sat up, eyeing her hair. Lane didn't want a comment on her appearance, so she said quickly, "Are you working tonight?"

Renée stood. "No. However, there should be certain people coming here, and I did want to confirm something with them, so I'll be around."

Lane paused in her combing. "You're not going to arrest someone again, are you?"

"My *dear* Lane. No. I don't arrest people *every* night."

"Is one of these people you're meeting Elleul?"

Something darkened in Renée's face. "No. We're not friends, Lane. You understand that, yes?"

"Yeah. Not friends, but colleagues."

Renée's mouth set. "He's a government representative investigating the murder of a government official. I'm duty-bound to help him. You know that."

Lane rolled her eyes. "If that's what the committee has on paper, whatever. You know better."

"You distrust him."

"Me and the rest of the planet. And you're not telling me you think he's here for just that, because I know you don't."

Lane finished combing and pulled her hair to one side to put it up. Renée came over and gently reached out to her hair. Lane dropped her hands.

Renée separated out three strands from the rest and then began intricately braiding down the side of Lane's head, gathering strands of hair as she went.

"You're right. I do not." Renée's voice was very low. "Be careful around him, Lane."

Lane exhaled. Renée was warning *her*? "Somehow, I don't think I'm the one who needs to watch her back around him."

"Mm."

"I mean it. You're useful to him now, but that only goes so far. He's dangerous, Renée, and you're standing right next to him." She dropped her voice. "Didn't he rise up through Intelligence?"

"For someone who doesn't give a crap about anything, you seem awfully worried."

Lane didn't know what to say to that.

"I'm flattered, naturally."

"Fuck's sake. Don't be."

Renée laughed. She was unexpectedly gentle and firm as she worked. It felt nice to have fingers running through her hair, to feel the odd warm breath on the skin of her neck. Lane resisted the urge to close her eyes, preferring to watch Renée focus instead.

When Renée was done, she took a band from Lane and tied the braid, resting it against Lane's left shoulder. Her hand grazed that shoulder, then slipped off.

Now what? They rarely made plans to see each other again, as they seemed to meet every day or other day. Lane didn't want to change that. She ran her palm over her braid and said, "Merci."

"De rien." Renée was close again, and smiling that incomparable smile of hers.

"I need to go."

"Me too."

As though walking through mud, Lane took a step past her, then another. Pulled on shoes and picked up her key. Renée stood behind her as she opened the door and the noise from the salon increased. She locked the door behind them and led the way downstairs, glaring at Helen when Helen caught her eye and smirked. *No, it's not what you think*, even though it definitely was, for once.

Renée touched Lane's side. "Until later."

"Yeah, yeah."

Lane waved her away, then slyly watched Renée walk to a few prominent leeches at a table on the other side of the bar.

Lane checked in with Helen and Serge first. The bar was stocked, though they were running low on rum. She put in an order for more via her internal channel. Helen complimented her braid. Then she checked on the bouncers at the front door, and after that, the games room. The atmosphere there could get rowdy.

The dim lighting was meant to allow people to find and queue for games and nothing more. Depending on the game, people could connect using their tech or could use the equipment provided. Around the room, people played in their designated game areas, the machinery transforming around them in response to their movements. It was loud, but only because Lane didn't have equipment to block the noise.

The employee on duty, Rakesh, nodded at her. "No problems so far."

"Good. Everything okay with you?"

"Yeah. Liz's sister is coming on the next ship from Lavele, so we're going to be more crowded at home."

"That sucks."

"True, but it'll be nice having more family here." He smiled. "It won't be for forever anyway. We'll get out of here one day."

"Sure."

Rakesh leaned in. "If you could put in a word with the prefect, we'd appreciate it."

Lane snorted. "Even if she listened to me—which she doesn't—you know I don't do that."

He shrugged, a half smile on his lips. "Worth a try anyway."

"Make sure no one spills their drink in here." She turned away but still heard him chuckling at her.

Honestly, her employees had to be the worst in all Pann, after Renée's search team.

But she wanted to laugh with him. That was new. Everything felt, well, not exactly *good* but okay. In balance. She could have honest moments with Renée. Her employees could have uneventful evenings. Her patrons could behave. There wasn't an atmosphere of trouble, only entertainment and chatter and relaxation.

Either she'd been here so long she'd forgotten what trouble-free life could be like or something about kissing Renée had tripped some wires in her head, but for the first time in a long time, Lane felt something like content. Serotonin didn't mess around.

She emerged into the brighter bar and did a quick scan. A few new faces. Helen was standing by someone's table, waving her arms around—and the light closest to her was flickering. Shit. She was emitting.

Lane walked quickly over to her and grabbed Helen's arm. "Remember what we talked about, H."

Helen turned to her and pressed her lips together, then jerked her chin at the people sitting at the table. Lane followed her gaze and her blood froze.

The man she didn't recognise.

The woman she definitely fucking did.

Yui stared back at her, eyes wide. "Lane."

CHAPTER FOUR

She looked the same. A little worn around the eyes and mouth, but otherwise the familiar round face, smooth skin and expressive features were all there. Her hair was shorter though; slightly over the length of a pixie cut, slicked back.

Lane's heart drummed in her ears.

Her voice sounded *exactly* the same.

How was her being here and virtually unchanged fair?

The man with her glanced between them, frowning. Helen tugged her arm out of Lane's grasp.

"Ah! Lane. I see you've found them." Renée had appeared, smiling cheerfully, on Helen's other side. "These are the people I hoped to meet tonight. Please, allow me to make introductions. Madame and monsieur, this is Lane Kovacs and her sister, Helen Kovacs. Lane, Helen, this is Tori and Ayumu Kusanagi, special guests to our little city."

Tori Kusanagi? *The* Tori Kusanagi?

But she was Yui . . . Oh.

Oh.

Oh.

"*Helen?*" Tori gasped.

Lane noticed Helen's face was blank and nudged her. Helen changed her expression to polite interest and stepped back. The light stayed steady. Lane sucked in a breath and tried to process the fact Yui was here. Yui— No, Tori. And her husband.

Husband.

"We've met before," she managed.

Renée's eyebrows flew up. "Really? You never mentioned this, Lane."

"It was a long time ago. In Lavele." Tori's voice was oddly scratchy. "I gave you a different name."

"You really did," Helen said.

There was a heartbeat of tension.

"Well! I think this calls for a celebration." Renée turned to Helen. "Could I trouble you for some champagne and glasses? Verve Claquet. My tab, please."

"On it." Helen left with a speed Lane envied.

"I'll help her." Lane followed Helen to the bar.

Helen busied herself with a bottle and glasses while Lane pulled out a tray and ice bucket. Helen made sure Serge was down the other end before hissing, "What the *actual fuck*?"

"I know."

"That's Yui!"

"I know."

"And she's actually Tori fucking Kusanagi! And she's *here*!"

"Helen, I was there too. I *know*."

Helen dumped ice into the bucket, then leaned in. "Don't join them."

Lane wanted to look over her shoulder at them. Made herself count the glasses on her tray instead. "I can't believe she's here."

"Lane." Helen's voice was hard. "I will make you the strongest Sazerac in the galaxy if you stay here and let me take this stuff to them."

What was she doing here? How was she Tori Kusanagi? Her Yui, *the* Tori.

Wait, did she still have—

Lane gripped the counter. "She might have the qubicon, Helen." The idea made her force in a deep breath. Her qubicon. The only remaining evidence of it, here.

"I meant it about the Sazerac."

Lane stared at her. "We deserve to know what happened."

"I agree, but not in the middle of the fucking bar in front of fucking Renée." Helen popped the cork and stuck the gently steaming bottle into the ice, then picked up the bucket. "Wait here."

"No." Lane took the tray of glasses and followed Helen back to the table.

Now that she wasn't reeling, she could take a closer look. Tori looked well. Better than Lane remembered. Back on Lavele, when

Tori had been Yui, she'd been thinner and sadder. Lane didn't have an opinion on Ayumu beyond a numb incomprehension that he'd *married* her.

She set the glasses down, and Helen poured a round. This happened in silence, as did the pointed glare she shot Lane before placing the bottle back in the ice bucket and walking away.

Lane sat down, feeling faintly detached from everything around her.

Renée beamed. "Lane, I met these two earlier today. I hoped to see them again soon, and how wonderful, here we all are."

"This is unexpected." Ayumu's voice was deep, almost gravelly.

"Well, this *is* one of the best nightspots in the entire city." Renée grinned. "And we're honoured tonight! Lane never drinks with her customers. I attribute that to your presence, madame."

Tori looked as though she'd swallowed all of the bar's lemon slices. "I'm sure that's not the case."

Something seemed to click in Lane's head. "As though I wouldn't share a drink with the famous *Tori* Kusanagi." She raised her glass to Tori, then drained it. Tori flinched.

"You'll find plenty of fans in Pann." Renée picked up the bottle and filled Lane's glass. "Many people are in your shoes too. Wanting to get to Fides, it's a popular pastime."

Lane couldn't seem to stop staring at Tori. "You're heading to Fides?"

Tori nodded. "Of course."

The Kusanagis were leaving the movement? No, impossible. Heading out of Parliament's reach, that had to be it. Lane couldn't believe otherwise, not if these two were everything the web said they were.

Ayumu gave a tight smile. "Both of us." He turned to Renée. "This champagne is excellent. Dances on the tongue."

"But of course, that's why it's called—"

"Lane."

She turned to face Tori, who seemed to have gathered herself. "Tori."

She spoke hesitantly, voice softened so it wouldn't be heard over Renée and Ayumu. "We were wondering. Do you know someone called Fentiman? We were supposed to meet him here last night but were delayed."

The Kusanagis had been his sale? Idiot. *Idiot*. She was never doing favours for anyone again. Look at this mess.

Lane thumbed her glass, enough to feel the chill of the wine. "He was arrested last night."

Tori's face fell but she smoothed it over quickly. "I see."

"If you want to find him, go to the police station before . . ." Lane wasn't sure what would happen to Fentiman. Leeches were held until charged (or until Renée liked the amount of bribe they offered), then they went free. Depending on the charge, they were sometimes sent to another city for further legal action.

But with a murder on his tab? And Elleul watching the case? Fentiman was likely headed for a one-way trip back to the core or into the earth.

"I see," Tori said.

Tori *would* see. She'd had that talent back in Lavele. The two of them, avoiding their pasts and work, talking about them without having to say a word. How easy it had been back then.

Lane sipped her champagne, tasting it for the first time. Ugh. Renée's ridiculous preferred brand. The excessive carbonation almost hurt her tongue. She glanced over at Renée, who was laughing at something Ayumu had said. The braid lay heavy over Lane's shoulder.

"It's good to see you again," Tori said.

"Is it?" Lane said without thinking.

"When was the last time we saw each other?"

Also without thinking: "Park Aurora, in Lavele."

Tori smiled. "You remember."

"It's an easy day to remember. The Parliament implemented that law about everyone registering the technical modifications they had. There were riots in the streets. The laboratory blew up. We had a picnic in the sunshine at lunch, and you told me you'd meet me for dinner."

Tori winced, her smile fading.

"The hearing tech lab?" Ayumu asked.

Lane looked at him. "Yes. You knew about that?"

He nodded. "It was the first modifications company to be, ah, targeted by the Parliament. Since then, many companies, factories, and laboratories have been shut down."

Renée leaned forward. "I thought it was instigated by the same people who stoked the riots."

"A *hearing* tech lab? No way."

"You sound very sure of that," Renée said.

He shrugged. "No mod movement would target an organisation like that. Neoluds, definitely."

"Rioters are capable of anything," Renée said. "Even counterintuitive acts of violence. And my understanding was that Parliament didn't target beneficial tech."

"Not at the time. They do now. But who else could it have been? Your 'understanding' doesn't match ours, Prefect."

Renée chuckled. "I wouldn't expect it to."

Ayumu turned to Lane. "So you met Tori while she was in Lavele?"

"I did." Lane eyed Tori. "We were . . . friends."

Renée threw back her champagne, then topped everyone up. "What a small system it is."

"Absolutely." Ayumu didn't smile as he drank.

"So you and Helen came here," Tori said. "I often wondered about you. I hoped you were both all right after that day in Lavele."

Lane couldn't do this anymore. She sank the rest of her drink. "I have some business to attend to. Excuse me." She stood and walked from the table.

Fuck her. Just . . . *fuck her.*

She didn't know where she was going, but she found herself holding the stash of vodka in her office. She looked up, and there was Helen in the doorway, a worried look on her face. "Give me that."

Lane held the bottle out to her, and Helen took it. Lane turned and sank into the seat opposite her desk. "Helen."

"I know."

"She's *married.*"

"I know."

"And she was looking for Fentiman."

"I know—I listened in."

Right, her enhanced hearing. She could adjust her range to extraordinary levels, as well as turn off her auditory input entirely if she wanted to. She rarely did. Still as nosy as ever; *that* hadn't changed. Lane sighed and sat back. "They'll be sniffing around for tickets."

"We don't have to let them in here."

"You know the door policy."

"How about you take a break, then? Go on holiday? You're due."

Lane scowled. "So are you."

"Yes, but unlike you, I didn't have my heart broken by one of the leaders of the fucking mod resistance, so I can handle myself."

"I'm handling myself!"

Helen held up the bottle with a raised eyebrow.

Lane groaned. "Fine. *Fine.* But she knows about you now. I'm not leaving you by yourself in this salon."

Helen exhaled sharply, then went over and sat in the other chair. She took Lane's hands in hers. "Lane. She didn't recognise me when I first went up to her. Obviously she knows now, but it's clear she didn't keep track of us. Remember where we are. What's she going to do anyway? Out of anyone, she can definitely be trusted to keep quiet."

"We don't know for sure. And another thing: What if she still has my qubicon?"

A strained pause. "So what if she does? She's probably broken it by now. I know what it means to you, but it's been so long. I thought you were done with all that." She put one arm around Lane's shoulders. "Lane, we'll get through this."

Helen's skin was cool. Her nails were sleek and round, not a ragged edge or calcium spot to be seen. She'd been through so much to get here. They'd managed several months on a tightly packed passenger ship without anyone spotting Helen was synth; they'd managed years here without any trouble. This was momentary. The Kusanagis would move on, one way or another, and Lane and Helen would still be here.

Lane bent her head to rest against Helen's shoulder. "Yeah, we will."

Helen turned her head, then kissed Lane's hair. "I have to go. Serge is grumbling."

"Okay."

"Don't stay in here too long."

Lane waved her away. She managed the place; she knew the drill.

When she was sure Helen was gone, she stood up and closed the door for some privacy. Then she dug through her desk and found a spare hip flask she vaguely remembered taping to the underside of a drawer. The whisky in it had a metallic aftertaste, but still took the edge off.

She sat at her desk and stared at the books on her shelves.

Yui had been, was Tori Kusanagi.

Back then, Lane had heard of Tori Kusanagi, though her fame was limited. She'd been an underground celebrity and something of a daredevil, taunting the Parliament with bulletins to major newspapers and local zines, interrupting factory shutdowns, and hijacking Parliament propaganda with resistance ads.

She'd spammed chat servers and public regional boards with updates on the Parliament's more distasteful activities. There had been rumours of rescues from a "detention centre" and an encrypted server to run a dark web market for brain modification tech organised by her.

Around the time that Lane had met Yui, Tori had been inactive, to the point of mass speculation on the net, but Lane had barely noticed. She'd been too wrapped up in discovering love.

Well.

Certain things made more sense now.

And Yui was *married*. That is, Tori was. Strange to realise that the woman Lane loved years ago had fallen for someone else enough to marry him. It didn't really fit with what she remembered of her. They hadn't discussed their pasts, which made discussing the future also off-limits. That had been all right—something about the social climate made it feel appropriate, almost necessary.

The Yui Lane remembered had been loving and affectionate, but incredibly independent. She hadn't been interested in marriage at all. Lane definitely remembered that conversation—what was the phrase Yui/Tori had used? *Legal hegemonic shackles*. Something overblown. It had made Lane laugh at the time.

So when did Tori meet and marry him? Ayumu's name had become widely known a few years ago—Lane couldn't remember how many. It was the kind of thing someone at Tori's level would keep under wraps for as long as possible. Who knew how long they'd actually been together.

Maybe even when Tori was in Lavele with Lane.

She fidgeted with the end of her braid.

Honestly, she'd never expected to see her again—much less with a different name, a spouse, and a system-wide resistance movement behind her.

And not with a diplomat's portal ticket intended for Tori stashed in Lane's music player. All of this spelled out trouble. What in Salus's grey earth was she going to do?

By the time she emerged from her office, she wasn't any closer to an answer, and both the Kusanagis and Renée had left.

CHAPTER
FIVE

Renée woke up groggy and sleep-deprived. Nothing like a certain amount of champagne to ensure bad sleep. It might have helped if she'd left the bottle at the bar, but Renée Bellevue had never been one to leave important things unfinished.

Soft orange light crept under her blind and inched across her floor. This was as vibrant as it got, usually at dawn or sunset, so the rest of the day didn't bode well. She gingerly sat up to rub her eyes and curse at her headache. *Merde*—what time was it exactly? When she checked her tablet and confirmed it was still early, she fell back on her bed with a groan.

It would be a three-coffee morning. She could tell already.

She covered her eyes with one arm and listened to the building around her wake up with the rising sun. Her apartment was on the top floor of this building, allowing for ample opportunity to hear the rafters expanding in what passed for morning heat. It was an old Haitian settler building, wooden and traditional, one of the originals from the first wave of people to terraform Salus to a planet humans and other carbon-based creatures could live on.

The facilities were basic but functional and beautifully vintage. Her wraparound balcony offered views over the river on one side and the small hills to the west on the other. The floor had an intricate wooden overlay, and tall wooden shutters framed the large expensive windows.

It was a vast step up from the blocky shoebox she'd lived in near her station in Newport, and, yes, now that she was thinking about it, one of the nicest things about life here. Her father would like this place. He enjoyed historical architecture. Though the morning creaking was interminable. She should really move to something newer and more stable, less prone to reacting to the seasons.

Or leave Salus entirely. She might have chosen to come here, but it hadn't been a true choice, all things considered. By now, her time was done, her dues paid. She wouldn't land a similar position as before, and starting over would be immensely, horribly hard, but she'd find *something* where she could keep her head down. Political schisms back on the core were the roughest they'd ever been, yet it wouldn't be impossible to live there again.

Elleul might deliver on that little "promotion" of his. Maybe she'd find her family and friends. Hug her parents. Joke with her cousins. Throw night-long parties. Drink good wine. Soak up proper sunshine.

Or be carted off to a reassimilation centre.

What was she thinking? It was for sure easier here. The apartment, lifestyle and weather left much to be desired, but the job wasn't bad, when she was interested in it, and Lane was divine. After last night, though, things felt different. The tension at that table had been palpable—and the expressions on Tori and Lane's faces!

Renée didn't have to be a master in body language to put two and two together: Tori was Lane's heartbreaker ex, and neither of them were past it. Irritating. Much as she had a sudden urge to kick the Kusanagis onto a ship to the other side of the system, that wasn't possible, not with Elleul throwing his weight around and the NZC watching her closely.

Lane's discomfort while explaining about Yui—Tori—came to mind. So did her various disgruntled expressions while she spoke with Tori. Then there was her smile after the kiss they'd shared, lovely and gentle as moonlight. Renée wanted to see that again. She wanted to taste her and feel her skin and run her hands through her hair, make her brighten again.

Perhaps Tori wasn't the concern she seemed to be. But she was *something*.

Bah. Too complicated for this time of the morning. Lying here fretting did nothing. Renée had better things to do. Like sleep.

When that didn't work, she rose and put on some exercise clothes. She could at least jog out the frustration and hangover. As she started through the streets near her apartment, her thoughts went back to details of the previous evening's conversation.

After Lane had departed so abruptly, Tori and Ayumu had looked tense and uncertain, which was only to be expected. Tori had turned to her and said, "We can be open together, yes?"

"I'd prefer it, madame."

Tori had paused, then asked, "What has Fentiman said about us?"

"Absolutely nothing. While we're being open, it's very kind of you to confirm the connection we've been speculating about."

Both Kusanagis winced, and Ayumu muttered something about having no damn luck lately.

Tori straightened her shoulders. "We noted in the news channels that he didn't have the documents he supposedly stole."

Renée spread her hands. "Alas, madame, that is true."

"Do you know where they are?"

She picked up her champagne. "Alas, not at all. We expect he sold the missive already, but kept the portal ticket for someone willing to pay the right sum for it." Sipped. Ah, so good. "He was arrested in this very salon. We've searched the place but didn't find it." She shrugged. "Who knows where he may have left it. Or whom he may have left it with."

"I see." Tori glanced at Ayumu.

"If you happen to stumble across it, I'd be very appreciative if you told me."

Ayumu coughed. "If that happens, Prefect, we'll do our best."

"Excellent."

Tori stood. "We must be going."

Renée had said her goodbyes, watched them speak to some random person trying to sell them jewellery on their way out—it was never just jewellery—then she commandeered the bottle and headed home.

As she jogged her usual route, she wondered if Tori had approached Lane by now about the ticket, and what Lane would do in response. Before last night, Renée hadn't known what Lane would do with it. But now? With their past relationship? Tori would likely tap into Lane's repressed conscience to get it from her, maybe even lean on their shared past.

Was that true though? Lane had said she wanted Renée. Had kissed her. Had been happy. She'd moved on enough to consider other options and wouldn't fall for anything so trite. Yes, she might give it to the Kusanagis. She might *sell* it to the Kusanagis. Or use it herself, offload to someone else, rip it up, ignore the entire situation . . .

To be honest, it seemed just as possible to Renée that Lane would deliberately lose it and let the universe decide its fate.

Ah, and perhaps this was why Fentiman had gone to Lane with the ticket in the first place. Anyone else would've taken the ticket and gone straight to the terminal—anyone but Lane. *If*, indeed, he had given it to her, but it was rare that Renée's gut was wrong about something like this. It was exactly like him to cover his bases and for it to pay off.

What a pity Elleul was sniffing around the whole affair. It made things infinitely more difficult than they had to be.

She came to a stop.

Wait. Where *was* Elleul? She had no idea where he'd been and what he'd done yesterday afternoon and evening. The best-case scenario was lounging around her headquarters and berating her officers—but how likely was that?

Hm.

She turned back to her apartment building. Morning ablutions went quickly and she arrived at work early once more. One coffee in the staff kitchen, then she began looking for Elleul.

She didn't get very far: Atkins stopped her outside the bullpen, his face scrunched up and his hands fidgety. Now that she was standing still, the other officers on morning duty seemed more reserved than usual. Hm. She braced herself as Atkins skipped his usual cheery *Salut*. "Prefect, there's a, uh, problem. Fentiman is . . . ah . . . He's . . ."

A minute later, in the station jail, she found herself staring at Fentiman's corpse hanging from the ceiling of his cell. It wasn't a particularly clever set up: a belt connected his neck to the light, there were electricity scars at his temple and under his jaw, dried blood on his nose, nothing in the cell accounted for what he'd jumped from, and when she looked closer, she noted the absence of tension abrasions on his neck.

"He hanged himself?" she said.

Atkins sounded very nervous. "Um. Yes."

"With an item of clothing we take off prisoners for precisely this reason."

"A-apparently."

Plenty of people carried electric weapons—cheap ones were widespread in Pann, as they were easily printed and charged. None of her officers carried ones with lethal charges on normal duty. None of her officers would have done this. She turned and looked at the camera in the corner that monitored the cell block.

"Our cameras captured the whole thing," Atkins said. "His . . . hanging."

"I see."

"But the recording was, uh, damaged."

Typical, to be expected. She turned back to Fentiman. He'd been alive and due for trial, and now he wasn't. Bastard. What was the phrase? This was a pickle.

"Also, Member Elleul is waiting for you in your office."

Of course he was. Renée eyed Atkins. "How long has he been there?"

"I'm not sure. A few hours?"

She gestured at the cell. "And how long has this one been dead?"

He swallowed. "Also a few hours."

Putain de bordel de merde. It was just as well that she wasn't enhanced; if anyone picked up the kind of language she thought, she'd never be hired for anything.

All this stress was going to give her wrinkles. More wrinkles. Bah. Why did this connard have to *be* here? And what had he said to her officers? How had he done all this? Seemed like Lane was right: Elleul had a background in Intelligence, because this stank of the Intelligence handbook.

Honestly, she felt vindicated. Janus government visitors brought nothing but headaches and bad procedures, so she'd refused them since arriving in Pann. She'd disliked the way things had been going in the Newport service before her fall from grace, and this was why. Bureaucrats were blowhards and Intelligence agents were pests, and this was the worst of both worlds. The next time the mayor yelled at her for ignoring visit requests, she was going to point to this. Years of deleting emails from Parliament wasted.

"Well. It won't do to leave our illustrious guest waiting. Do the usual forensics on Fentiman, fill out the basics of the report, and send it to me. I'll handle everything else."

Atkins practically swayed in relief. "Yes, Prefect."

First: more coffee. She picked up another cup on the way to her office and had finished it by the time she walked through the door.

Elleul was sitting in the visitor chair, a pastry on a plate in front of him. She didn't have the impression of a person so much as a squat thing sucking energy from the room. Her room. This was her space, and she didn't like him in it. Black holes surely contributed more to the universe.

He waved at her. "Good morning, Prefect! Have you tried these?" He held up the pastry.

Renée watched a thick gob of MangeX raspberry jam plop out the end of it to land in a bright red splatter on his plate. "Yes. They're delicious." She sat at her desk and put her cup on the side before taking out her tablet. Time to play the game. "I understand there's been a grave incident in my station. Member Elleul, were you—"

"My dear Prefect." Elleul smiled at her. "I know about Fentiman, and let me be absolutely clear: I do not hold you or your officers responsible in any way."

She eyed him. "No? He was awaiting trial in our care."

He gestured with his free hand. "These things happen. Criminals often can't face up to justice or to the weight of their crimes. It's quite sad, really. We see a lot of this kind of thing back in the core. I certainly did during my stint in Intelligence." He bit into the pastry.

The shiver running down her spine could just be due to the sight of him eating. "You don't say."

He swallowed. "Yes. A lot."

"Which division?"

"Criminal investigation. I saw some truly despicable acts, Prefect. Constant vigilance and immediate accountability are what's needed to maintain safety and order." He tilted his head. "I'm sure you agree. Of course, it's so unfortunate when things like this happen, but I usually find it's for the best for *everyone* involved."

"I see."

"I'm glad you do."

She mindlessly tapped at her tablet. "Once the report comes to me, I'll file it as suicide by hanging."

"That would be wise."

"I do hate these kinds of things."

A cold tone came into his voice. "What do you mean?"

She realised she'd opened the messaging app. The last message from Lane was on her screen. *You buying?*

She looked up at Elleul. "Extra paperwork. This will generate a lot, and I have a backlog of ticket requests to process too."

Elleul actually chuckled. "You have my sympathies, Prefect, and my apologies. I have taken up a great deal of your time over the last two days."

"On the contrary, I neglected you yesterday."

He put the pastry on the plate, scattering crumbs. "Not at all, I assure you! I took a small walk around town in the evening. Saw the local sights, tried a restaurant, did some shopping. I feel so refreshed. I was even up early today." His raised hand shifted the lapel of his jacket, and Renée spotted a glimpse of a holster there. He hadn't been carrying a weapon yesterday or the day he'd arrived. The shape of it was familiar too—a particularly prolific electric handgun in Pann's black market.

"If you don't mind," Elleul said, "I would like to work in here with you today. It would be interesting to see your approvals process."

It involved her tapping at her tablet screen for hours. Surely he'd handled requests before—in fact, he was *known* for approving multiple kinds of requests. She didn't like this at all. "Of course, monsieur."

"I, in turn, can share the extra information Intelligence provided to me—with their full and supportive permission."

So there *was* extra information. Core Intelligence always answered her team's requests for information promptly; she'd assumed what came back was complete. Damn.

He waved his tablet at her. "I don't only have files on the Kusanagis, Fentiman, and Kovacs, I have files on most criminals present in Pann or en route here. Oh, and nearly everyone working at this station. Including you."

Renée raised her eyebrows. "I'm sure my file is excellent bedtime reading, monsieur."

He smiled at her and picked up the pastry again. "Please, don't be worried, Prefect. Everyone reassured me you would be helpful, and, so far, I can tell them you have behaved within the bounds of the law and your duty."

More jam fell out of his pastry as he took a bite, sticky clumps that threatened to miss the plate. Renée leaned back in her chair and waited for him to finish. There was no need to respond to this.

Once he was done chewing, he smiled again. "I confess, I was curious about you. I know you were on the core for most of your career, but then moved here, to this little outpost of a planet barely in the habitable zone of this system. I thought that was a strange career move. Turns out it was the only one you were offered."

That was entirely false. She'd been offered a number of other positions, but this was the only one she'd been able to stomach. The others had been demotions or isolated posts off in wilderness territories or retail.

The Neutral Zone Committee had described the role as a promotion, which it *technically* was. Then the representative had admitted they very much required a Janus-born officer to balance the Fides-born mayor and could she please consider it because they kept being shut down by other candidates who were scared of Parliament intervention, and no one else had even remotely relevant credentials, and they were desperate.

She'd already been disgraced, so what was a little more? And, thinking back on it, this was the position that had made her least angry at the time. Orion's arm, it was like looking back at another person. Where had that anger come from? And where had it gone?

"I chose what seemed to be the most challenging out of a number of alternative positions," she said.

"Interesting choice for someone who lost her position due to gross insubordination."

She clicked her tongue in annoyance. "They promised me it would go into my file as a management reshuffle."

"Ah, I'm sorry to disappoint, Prefect." He tapped at his screen. "Let me see. You protested the arrest of a group of young delinquents, despite clear evidence they were wearing tech in a designated tech-free space."

"To be correct, that was the example I used. I was questioning the no-tolerance policy being implemented at the time."

He raised his eyebrows. "They weren't where they were supposed to be, and you knew it."

"Of course they weren't. But they were *also* barely teenagers and weren't harming anyone. It felt pernicious to be arresting children for crossing a street." A gentle warning would have been more appropriate. There had been many situations like that—Newport had been divided into zones overnight and people had needed time to learn the new places they could or couldn't go.

Even the phlegmatic people of Newport had rebelled against the change. Monitoring the zones alone became full-time work for some of her colleagues, yet they'd been expected to continue their other duties as though nothing had happened. The no-tolerance policy had been unnecessary pressure on top of an already difficult situation.

Plus, the paperwork that went with arresting children was especially irritating.

"If they've succumbed that young to foul alterations, they need the discipline and safety a service or detention sentence would provide. You should've realised you were helping them." He waved his pastry, and more crumbs fell on the floor. "However, I do understand the reluctance. It says here the youngest was ten, which is depressing. Nonetheless, I see that you requested the *removal* of the no-tolerance policy. That seems disproportionate, all things considered. What are your thoughts now?"

She shrugged. "It was a long time ago. I hardly think at all these days."

His eyes narrowed, and he took another mouthful. Swallowed. "The committee which reviewed your request acknowledged the problems the force had experienced, but, well, a no-tolerance policy is expected to encounter those sorts of issues."

"I can't deny that."

"Your request was badly worded. I can see why it raised alarm bells." He ate the final piece of his pastry. "But your performance prior to this was stellar. In all honesty, I was a little surprised at the committee's decision. The judgement of you as 'subversive' and 'great potential for radicalisation' was over-the-top. Sometimes even those in positions of responsibility get things wrong, Prefect, and I feel I must apologise for this miscarriage of justice."

She inclined her head. "That's very kind of you, but unnecessary, Member."

"I imagine it's all forgotten about by now," he said. "You've been here, oh, six years?"

"Or so."

"Your behaviour since has been exemplary, and you must be overdue a change. I imagine the Janus police service would welcome you back." He began droning on about loyalty and promotions and career changes.

Renée took in his expressions, the relaxed pose of his body. This was an interesting line of questions, and one he'd asked before. Typical Intelligence spiel. Would he bring up her family situation? Those old friends she didn't let herself think about anymore? Past achievements? Perhaps that extra-informative file of his contained notes about her parents.

Yes, this felt familiar. No doubt Elleul had subjected a few other officers in her station to similar conversation. Not everyone would receive a promise of promotion or return to the core; some would have their remaining families or friends threatened. Her Fides employees would receive a file of their own in the database and some empty words, but the Janus ones would be easy to sway one way or another. Was it too early to drink? She glanced at her tablet. Damn, it was.

Oh well. The hangover still lingered.

He wrapped up with, "What keeps you here?"

"The weather," she replied.

He laughed. "No, seriously. I'd like to remind you that good service is much appreciated. Keep helping me, and I'll ensure this"— pointing at his tablet—"is forgotten. You could return to your home. Your family. Life as normal, as it should be."

Her family—they *were* still around. A hint. An offer. It was more than she'd had in years. And a clean file. A ticket out of here. A chance to find and see her parents, her cousins, her aunts and uncles once more—if they were still around. An opportunity to work without the past hanging over her head. A chance to go *home*.

Her breath caught, and his smile widened. "I would *ensure* it."

She smiled at him. "What a kind offer. I'll be sure to consider it."

"Yes, do that."

He returned to his tablet, apparently finished.

She swiped at her own tablet with a finger that trembled. How silly. She put her hands under her desk and shook them, trying to release the tremors. Up came the overnight reports—and one from Kusanagi's shadow was top of the list. She'd trailed Tori to a dance studio in the middle of the night, then back again to her hotel an hour later.

Resistance meeting. Had to be. However, no cause for concern. Not illegal.

And obviously not something Elleul needed to know about just yet.

She irritably ordered her expected third coffee via the online system, filed and archived the overnight reports, then brought up the ticket approvals queue and began working through them. Her hands were steady by the time Elleul asked to oversee her methodology for approvals.

Lane woke up to unimaginable noise. She cast blearily around, then almost fell over her own feet as she got out of bed. Stars, she felt awful. Shitty fucking hip flask whisky and a long fucking night and *what* in *all known worlds* was making that *racket*?

She stumbled out of her room into the living room, then followed the noise to the kitchen. Helen stood in front of their industrial blender, apron around her front, mask over her nose and mouth, and finger on the pulse button. Something grey crunched inside the blender, while toxic-looking dust wafted from under the lid.

"What the actual shit, Helen?" Lane yelled into the noise.

It stopped and Helen faced her. "You're up."

"Me and half the damn block! What time do you call this?"

Helen arched an eyebrow. "Midday."

Lane groaned. "And you couldn't do—" she squinted at the blender "—whatever you're doing downstairs?"

"Well, no. We serve drinks down there." Helen pointed at the dust on the counter. "People shouldn't inhale this."

"Then *why* is it in our *kitchen*?"

Helen scoffed. "Because I don't eat, and you never cook." She tilted her head. "You look terrible. Maybe you should go outside. Get some fresh air, some sun. See Prefect Bellevue."

Lane scowled. There was definitely something she needed, and it wasn't fucking sunlight *or* Renée. "I regret saying you could live with me."

Helen gave her a wide smile and pushed the button.

Lane fled back to her room, wishing hell on older sisters with the ability to turn off their auditory inputs. She rooted in her shirt drawer for the breakfast port and took a healthy gulp, then pulled some clothes on and lurched out of the apartment. The noise was less in the street, but it wasn't until she was a block away that she stopped hearing it. By then she felt better—still tired and aggravated, but tension was draining away rather than building.

She dragged her hands through her hair, then twisted it into a bun on top of her head. Now that she could think, the stuff in the blender looked like another attempt at making sculpture clay. Heavens knew why Helen was so determined to make her own, especially at midday while other people were *sleeping*. Helen's attention to detail had always extended into unfathomable depths; *that* trait had managed to stay through the change.

Well. Lane was outside, with time to kill. Perhaps taking in some sunshine and *peaceful* solitude wasn't a bad idea.

She bought some meat wraps from a street vendor and began walking towards Parc Rouge. It was a standard weekday, which meant she only had to keep half an eye out for the normal amount of thieves and opportunists. Eating the wraps on the way was pleasant and unhurried.

However, she didn't realise she was being followed until she was close to the park. Her senses had grown rusty with disuse—and that was a nice thing, she mused as she entered the park. It was good to live in a place where being followed wasn't something that happened as a matter of course.

Parc Rouge's name derived from the perennial red leaves on the majority of trees. Terraforming wasn't always a precise science, and certain tree seeds from the original Earth system had mutated with something in the soil on Salus, turning what should've been green and brown into red and black. The grass and various flower beds were all the expected colours, and once the problem had been realised and adjusted for, later trees had grown in decidedly normal ways, so the park was a riot of colour all year. The person following her didn't blend in at all—their grey hoodie stood out.

It *was* lovely. She really should come here with Renée.

Renée.

That confounding, irritating, magnetic woman.

That *kiss*. It had been a long time since Lane had last kissed someone, and never quite in that way. Now, in the light of day, feeling something for Renée and acting on it seemed somewhat dangerous. At the very least, misguided. Especially with Elleul on the scene.

But was it really so bad? So odd? She walked through a park with red trees, on a planet at the edge of the habitable zone, far from home and with nowhere farther to go. Given everything, how was kissing Renée so strange? Compared to Yui turning up again?

Or, rather, Tori turning up again. And revealing herself not as some unemployed service worker, but in fact Parliament's most wanted, the leader of the mod resistance and proponent of synth rights. Hell and earth, how was liking Renée any stranger than *that*? What was one more ridiculous thing in a world of ridiculousness?

There was zero point in thinking too much about this. Thinking had never served Lane well in romantic situations.

Her stalker seemed to have narrowed the distance between them. Lane made for a nearby bench and sat down. The person following her sat on the other end, and now Lane recognised her.

"Tori," she acknowledged.

Tori pulled her hood down and tucked her hands into the front pocket. "This place is colder than I expected."

"We're on the outer edges of the habitable zone."

"I know."

They fell quiet. Why was she here? Couldn't she get to the point? Abruptly annoyed, Lane leaned back and waited. Tori would speak eventually; she hated awkward silences. Well, she'd used to. Maybe that had been a lie too. Either way, Lane wasn't about to ease her into any conversation between them.

This bench faced a field circled by trees, beyond which was a skyline of Pann, edges and corners cutting up the clear air. Almost familiar, except for the non-core colours and shapes. Above them, Salus's ring bisected the wide sky. Some people hated the ring. It permanently divided the stretch of blue; a visceral reminder of where they weren't. That was exactly why Lane liked it. This view was lovely. No wonder Renée kept asking Lane to come here.

"It's good to see you again," Tori said.

"Is it?"

"I have to say: a gaming salon?" Tori glanced at her. "I never pegged you for customer service."

There was nothing to say to that. Lane did it because she and Helen needed to do something while they were here.

When she didn't reply, Tori said, "I suppose I shouldn't comment."

"Where's the hubs?" Lane asked.

Tori flashed her a knowing look. "Out. We hoped to lose the tail, but I was still followed." She turned to face the view, mouth thin. "I thought that would stop here."

Lane shrugged. "It'll be one of Ren— the prefect's people. They won't bother you."

"That's not the point, Lane."

Oh, that phrase. Tori had said it a lot back in Lavele, with exactly the same hint of frustration and stress on the word *point*. Hearing it again brought back a rush of nostalgia and confusion. Lane also shoved her hands into her pockets in an effort to avoid clenching them.

Tori made a face. "I'm sorry. I don't mean to snap at you. It's just . . . Oh, Lane. I didn't expect to see you ever again."

"The feeling is mutual."

"You or . . . *Helen*. Oh my goodness. Is that . . . From the bar, is she *really* . . . ?"

Lane scowled. "Nah, she grew six inches, blonde hair, and two cup sizes for kicks."

Tori shook her head. "I can't believe it."

"Try."

There was a tense silence. "What happened to her?"

"Take a wild guess." Lane had to forcibly relax her jaw. "Actually, don't. You don't deserve to know. You weren't there."

Tori flinched. "You're right. I wasn't. But you were, and you *saved* her."

Eh. Lane wouldn't put it that way.

"This means your qubicon worked," Tori breathed. "Right? Of course it did, how else would Helen be here? I know you didn't have a synth body on standby. I . . . Wow." She paused, clearly thinking things through. "Your projections were correct. The qubicon kept her safe. And she's alive, walking, living. Holy crap, Lane, I *knew* it."

This was also familiar: Tori's intelligence, the way she figured out the right conclusion on minimal information, and the light in her eyes as she did it. "You haven't changed a bit."

Tori hadn't understood the finer details of Lane's research, but she'd known the overall principle, and she'd been very excited at the implications. She obviously still was.

"Do you realise what this means? What this could do? How many people this could save? This could revolutionise life and mortality as we know it!"

Lane rolled her eyes. She'd heard it all before. Mods loved to wax lyrical about *the next phase of human existence* and that *synths are no different to humans* and *it's all data in the end*. Cringeworthy.

Tori's face shone with excitement. "Lane, this kind of breakthrough, you have to share it. You *have* to. I'm shocked you haven't already, frankly. You could be the mother of the next evolution in humanity. You'd go down in history."

Somehow, her quick mind had been more charming four years ago. "I suppose so."

"You *suppose* so? Lane, why run here? Why hide this?"

Lane scowled. "Oh, I don't know. You're not totally wrong. I attempted the grand scientific breakthrough in quantum entanglement that I'd dreamed of. It worked under real life conditions and Helen's still around. Sort of."

"What do you mean, 'sort of'?"

Where was that quick mind now? "You're jumping to conclusions. Helen isn't complete."

"Seems that way to me."

"You don't live with her." And see a daily reminder of what had happened. "You're also forgetting a few minor details. Helen was killed. She *died*. I had to find a synth body before the entanglement collapsed *and* deal with you leaving with the last prototype of my work, while my city was shut down due to riots and my lab burned down with all my notes in it." Lane should've brought some wine with her. She could use something to lessen the edge of this conversation. "You're honestly surprised that we're here? On Salus? Out of anywhere in the system? No, of course, the *science* is what's important."

Tori turned away. "I'm sorry, Lane." There was a long, heavy pause. "I won't say anything to anyone about her."

Lane did believe that. Tori was good at secrets.

The silence stretched out, uncomfortable and thick. Lane didn't remember such long periods of quiet between them before.

Tori brought her legs up so she could sit cross-legged on the bench. "But really, though—why the gaming salon? When you're sitting on this kind of knowledge? It's such a waste of your talents."

Tori had dodged the allusion to her prototype. Perhaps that meant she still had it.

"I have many talents," Lane said.

"Yes, but—"

"I was tired. I still am."

"I'm serious, Lane." Tori's hands fidgeted, though she didn't stop looking at the skyline. "Please. This is the first time we've seen each other since . . . well. Since. I hoped so many things. This first meeting, I thought our conversation would go better, that we would still have that wonderful honesty we used to have."

What was one of Lane's bitterest memories from before Helen's death? Lane and Tori in bed, lazily exploring each other's skin while dawn broke through the curtains. Lane tracing circles across Tori's cheek before saying *So you're aware, I'm definitely in love with you, Yui.* Tori's eyes had lit up, her smile had widened, and she'd pushed in closer under the blankets, wrapping legs and arms fully around Lane, and replied, *I love you too.*

Lane couldn't look at her.

"Your work used to be everything to you," Tori said. "I remember how it drove you. I just struggle to understand how that changed so dramatically. How *you* changed."

Lane felt like swinging at something. Or diving into a vat of beer. Maybe both. Her fists had clenched in her pockets, and she forcibly unclenched them. "Life does that."

Yet another gap of tense quiet.

"Is that it?" Tori asked. "All your passion, gone, because of *life*? What happened to Helen is terrible, but we've all lost people. The person I knew wouldn't give up on her work because of that."

Fuck this. "You took my last prototype. My *best* prototype. I had nothing left, so I moved on. Like you did. Too bad I didn't get a spouse out of it." She stood and faced Tori. "We done with the pointless reminiscing? I'd appreciate you getting to the real reason you followed me."

Tori stood too, scowling. "I didn't lie to you back then—not about my feelings for you. And I'm not lying to you now. I loved you then and I love you now and I'm *worried* about you."

"Get in line. And don't stall. I meant it: ask."

Tori held her gaze, her own unflinching but sorrowful. "No. Besides, don't you have your own question to ask me?"

Seriously? She had to ask about the ticket sometime. She must have figured out by now where it was. And if reviving the past was more important than getting off of Salus, then she really wasn't the Yui Lane had once loved.

Lane shrugged. "I was wrong. You *have* changed."

Tori pressed her hands to her face. "Orion wept. You never used to be this infuriating to talk to. Let me *explain*." She flung her hands wide, as though in supplication.

"Don't bother." Tori wasn't the only person who could put pieces of information together. "Knowing your real name explains a lot— why you never told us your history, and why you took the qubicon with you. Why you left so suddenly. Something happened, a crisis you and only you had to deal with. Right? I can understand that. What I can't fit in is Ayumu. Did you leave me for him? Did he sweep you off your feet?"

Tori's mouth twisted, and she slumped back onto the bench. "No, I didn't, and yes, he did." She ran her hands down her thighs. Lane remembered that habit. "I married him about a year before I met you."

Hell. Lane closed her eyes, then opened them and looked away from Tori. She'd thought the surprises were over. A whole year, huh. *Already married.* The reminder not to assume everything was probably necessary; it would be *welcome* in about two hours when this conversation was over and the effects of visiting the bar had kicked in.

"We were carrying out an operation in Lavele, and it went bad," Tori continued. "I managed to get away, but I was injured and had to lie low. Recover. I thought he was dead." She scrubbed at her eyes. "Those were dark days. You pulled me out."

Lane drew in a deep breath, clear and scented with leaf and grass. She did remember Yu— Tori recovering from injuries. At the time, Tori had said she'd been in a fight. It had been plausible—Tori was decked with tech and brawls happened often with aggressive neoluds.

Tori's voice kept going, thickening with each word. "And you're right. I left because of a crisis in the resistance. I was needed. I found out he wasn't dead at all. And Parliament agents had found me. Don't you see? I left because I had to. For me, for him, for you. They were tracking me and I wanted them to ignore you. It all happened too quickly to tell you, and *I'm sorry* for that, but I'm not sorry for protecting you. Or for loving you."

She was hunched over now, her eyes brimming and mouth twisted. Lane watched her, trying to figure out if she meant it or not. Her upset seemed real and the story wasn't outlandish. When Tori wiped her eyes again and looked up, Lane turned away.

"Lane. Please. I never expected to find you here, but I can't help seeing it as a sign."

Lane struggled to keep it together. "And here's me thinking it was just bad luck."

"We loved each other once," Tori said.

Oh please. "You lied to me."

"I was real with you."

"Not about your name. Your story. Your *husband*."

Tori stood up. "They didn't mean anything, not with you. They don't change a thing about me. I was more myself with you than I've been before or since."

"They matter to me."

"I don't believe you."

"Fine. They matter to you, and you didn't share them with me." The sky stretched wide above her, and this park felt vast around her. The distance between them could have filled the universe. It was shocking to realise that was possible for them; back then, Lane would've said there was nothing between them. They'd been together in a space of their own. "I was a stopgap."

"You were *everything*."

"No, *you* were."

Tori reached for her. "Lane. I have enough money for three tickets."

And like that, everything retracted back to its normal size and place. Lane straightened her shoulders, stepped back. "No."

Tori's arms dropped. "I'm not leaving you behind again. I won't. I can't."

"It's not up to you."

"*Lane.*"

She'd had enough. "Thanks for the explanation." She turned and strode away, sending dead leaves fluttering around her ankles. Her stomach twisted, and she flexed her hands deep in her pockets.

Shit.

Why couldn't anything be easy? For Tori to come back, to look at Lane like that again, to say those things, it was incomprehensible. To suggest Lane could *leave* Pann like that. Leave her business, her employees, Helen, Re— Absurd. Nonsensical. Things had changed. Things were different. *They* were different. Fuck it all. Fuck everything.

Renée's face kept coming to mind, but Lane kept shoving it back. Her salon waited. Business never stopped.

CHAPTER
SIX

Renée made sure she sat at an angle that was becoming when viewed from the door. Feet up on Lane's desk, chair tilted back, legs crossed winsomely, a glass of substandard red in one hand, and her tablet in the other, her face illuminated. She'd let her hair down tonight, and was deliberating whether to sweep it behind one ear or let it hang freely like a curtain behind her. It was a little short for the first option, but she could manage it for the vital first few seconds.

Decisions, decisions.

After all, Lane had spent almost half an hour with her ex-girlfriend in the park that Renée had been inviting her to for months. Said ex-girlfriend had barely been here two days. Renée wasn't sure where she stood with Lane now, and of course what was between Lane and Tori was their business, but she couldn't sit back. So creating the right impression was vital. When she'd arrived tonight, Lane had been busy breaking up an altercation in the games room, so Renée had sneaked in here and had time to plan her ambush.

Steps approached the door. She shook her head to make sure her hair fell the way she wanted it to. The door opened and Lane stepped in, then stumbled back. "Fuck! *Renée*? What the hell?"

Renée lowered her tablet. "Oh! Lane. What a surprise to see you here."

"In *my* office. Yeah, sure. What are you doing here?"

Renée smiled at her. "Isn't it obvious? Waiting for you." She sipped her wine.

Lane rolled her eyes and shut the door behind her. "Funny. Get out of my chair."

Get out of my chair wasn't *get out of my office*. "But it's so comfortable."

She scoffed as she went to her shelves of books. "Stars forbid you ever be uncomfortable."

"Lane, you don't understand the total pain of a day I've had." Renée turned off her tablet screen and set it down. "Elleul had the gall to sit with me and monitor my work *all day*."

"Yes, that sounds terrible."

Renée spread her arms, taking care not to spill her drink. "It's *unconscionable*! If I wanted to be micromanaged, I'd go back to the core. If I wanted my work to be interfered with, I'd simply let my lieutenant do things for me."

Lane pulled out one book after another, opening them, then placing them back on the shelf. "I thought he did do most of your work for you."

"Lane."

"But you're right, someone breathing down your neck makes work very tense."

"Exactly. Hence, I'm here, relaxing in your office, avec une verre." She raised her glass to demonstrate.

"Which you *no doubt* paid for." Lane glanced her over. "Where's Elleul?"

Ugh. "Why on earth would you make me consider his precise location?" Renée shrugged. "I suppose he's sitting in his hotel plotting how to make tomorrow worse for me. Maybe more paperwork. Maybe he'll rid the city of all its newborns overnight and set my station on fire while drowning kittens." When Lane shot her a pointed look, Renée smiled. "*Or*, perhaps, he's considering how to ship the Kusanagis to the core."

Lane turned back to the shelf. "Sounds like him."

"Mmm. I don't see a way they'll possibly escape him. Unless you help them, of course."

"I thought I wasn't allowed to help them."

"You're not, but this is Pann. Not even I abide by what I'm *allowed* to do."

"I couldn't comment." Lane pulled out a book that turned out to house cherry liqueur.

"That stuff is vile."

"Helen's blocked the top shelf." Lane unscrewed the bottle and took a gulp. Winced. "Ugh. Not worth it." She put it back. "You're not here just for my company."

"I am, actually." Renée checked her glass and swirled the drink around it. Red lapped at the sides of the glass. "I'm fond of our chats."

Lane raised her eyebrows. "Huh."

"What?"

"I didn't realise you were that lacking in friends."

It was easy to fall back into the old pattern, but this wasn't why she'd come here. Renée scoffed. "I am and you know it. Lane, darling, please. I thought we were past this."

Lane eyed her for a long moment, then left the shelf and rounded the table. She settled on the desk next to Renée's shoes. "I'm happy to see you, as always, but I'd appreciate it if you didn't break into my office."

This was better. "But how can I have my way with you if I don't corner you in here? And it can't be breaking in if Helen opened the door for me." Lane groaned and covered her eyes. "Ma chère, I must check something with you. Last night. She's the Yui who broke your heart, oui?"

Lane nodded. "You noticed." Her hands clenched the desk edge while her legs swung free. Her thigh flattened distractingly with each downward fall. It was a lovely thigh, encased in black denim. No dirt today. Renée had a vivid image of sitting up and reaching for Lane's thighs, running her hands up the fabric to rest on her hips, leaning between the V of her legs—

"I had no idea she was Kusanagi," Lane said. "None. She met me today to explain why she left."

So that was what they'd discussed in the park. "And?"

Lane met her gaze. "And what? I was right. She left because she had to." Her eyes narrowed. "One of your people was watching her. You must know all this already."

Renée shook her head. "I have a report of you two meeting, not what was said. We haven't got close enough to plant any bugs."

Lane shook her head. "Tell me again why I like you. Why do you bother asking when you already know the gist?"

Renée poked her foot into Lane's thigh. "I most certainly do not. I completely expected her to ask about the ticket you have. And you do have it, don't you?"

"What ticket?"

Renée laughed. She should've known. "All right. The report said you were both emotional, clearly close, but that could mean any kind of relationship. You told me you still loved her. Does she feel the same?"

The swinging stopped. Renée found herself examining her glass. Somehow, that was easier than seeing Lane's expression right now.

"She says she does."

Merde.

Renée closed her eyes, then took a large mouthful of her drink. When she opened them, she forced herself to meet Lane's gaze. "I suppose that's to be expected. There are a few exes of my own that I would consider welcoming back."

"She's not *welcome*, believe me."

That was a relief to hear, but Renée wasn't stupid. She'd seen the level of emotion in their faces, both last night and in the video snippets her spy had filed with the report. Lane was deliberating and so was Tori. Had to be.

Lane muttered something she didn't catch.

"Quoi?"

"I said, 'Now isn't the time.' Look at what's happening around us. She'll be leaving again soon. What does something like this matter?"

Renée shrugged and drained her wine. "That's a very logical way of looking at it." She pulled her feet off the desk, set her glass down, and stood. "But allow me to respectfully disagree."

She stepped in front of Lane, her thighs pressing against Lane's knees, and placed her hands on the desk on either side of Lane's hips. Lane angled back slightly, eyes a little wide.

"You're forgetting something very important, which is that people are the most illogical beings in the universe." Renée could smell a faint hint of cherry, as well as the metal and dust that apparently never left Lane. "Even her, *principled* though she is. So is this world we find ourselves in. Timing is overrated. And you, ma chère, underestimate the effect you have on people."

A breath shuddered out of Lane. "I could say the same about you."

Renée noticed how Lane's pupils had dilated and how her pulse jumped in her throat below her razor-sharp jaw. Good. Glorious. "I underestimate nothing about myself."

Lane tilted her head, her mouth curving slightly. "Least of all your modesty."

"Life is too short for modesty." Renée gently pushed one leg forward, along Lane's knee and up against her inner thigh.

There was the start of a very pretty flush on Lane's cheeks. "You worried about her, Renée?"

"Of course not." Lane smirked and Renée cleared her throat. "My *point*, my darling, is that these things do matter. They matter a great deal. Maybe more than anything. Stop being logical."

Lane took Renée's face in her palms and kissed her. Renée closed her eyes, wanting to sink into the feeling of Lane's soft lips and the berry-vodka taste of her mouth. Callused fingertips brushed down Renée's face, leaving goosebumps on her arms and neck in their wake.

She tasted divine, like a cry of joy, a revelation, a star-filled autumn sky.

Renée pushed one hand against the small of Lane's back, bringing her forward and prompting a soft noise from her as their bodies met. Renée deepened the kiss, wanting them as close as possible.

Lane broke away. One hand twisted in Renée's hair, sending a delicious shock down her spine, and Lane used the grip to keep their faces close. "Don't worry about her."

How could she not? A lump rose in Renée's throat; she forced it down. Before she could respond, Lane let her hair go and rubbed the back of her neck. "Your argument has merit, but I'm still not convinced."

Renée grinned. "I can argue as much as you want."

Lane smiled back. "Things don't matter just because you say they do."

"Alors. They don't matter, therefore we might as well do them, because we can. What do we have to lose?" Renée pecked the corner of Lane's mouth, nosed her way to Lane's ear. "We're alive. We're here. We feel good. It is enough." She stroked down Lane's side, following the curve of torso and waist down to her thigh, prompting Lane to wriggle slightly.

"Much more compelling." Lane ran her fingers along Renée's throat, perching on her collarbone like a diver on a springboard.

"Oh good. I can argue all night." Renée nuzzled along that wonderful jaw and down to her neck, kissing and nipping as she went. Lane's breath hitched—

Someone knocked on the door. "Lane?"

Lane tensed against Renée. "That's Rakesh."

One of the staff members here. The bartender? The enhanced being who lumbered around the games room? One of the servers? Who knew or cared. He was in the way. Renée moved both hands to Lane's thighs and gripped tightly.

"One second!" Lane called.

"It's urgent, madame."

She muttered, "Yes, yes, it always is." She leaned back with a sigh, letting go of Renée. "I'm working. Sorry."

Renée stepped back reluctantly, keeping her fingertips resting lightly on Lane's knees. "I know a park where we wouldn't be interrupted."

Lane pulled a wry smile and jumped to her feet. "I had no idea you were this fond of the outdoors."

"I'll have you know that I like the outdoors very much." Lane's shirt was slightly dishevelled. Renée reached out and adjusted it for her. "Especially when it means neither of us are at work."

"Madame!"

Lane gave her a knowing half smile. "Hold that thought." She walked to the door and opened it. "Yes?"

"Someone has won fifty thousand francs at poker," said a lanky man that Renée vaguely recognised from the games room. He had ports studded in a pattern over one eyebrow, plus a clear wire implant running from one ear down his neck into his shirt. His gaze flickered to Renée, then back to Lane. "Not the prefect this time. I'm so sorry, but we need your approval to let the transaction go through."

"Yeah, yeah, got it." Lane glanced back. "This may take a while, Renée. You're free to wait here if you want, but if you have other things to do . . ."

Renée had multiple things to do, most of them on Lane's body. How else could she show Lane what she meant to her? Lane might not be concerned about Tori's presence here, but Renée knew she'd be persistent in chasing her. Tori would be back, and Lane would be drawn in thanks to the sentimentalism she refused to acknowledge, and Renée would be left with sweet memories of what could have been. Merde, why couldn't things be simple for once?

"I noticed Monsieur Elleul is here tonight," Rakesh said.

Of course he was. That was exactly how this evening seemed to be operating. No doubt his presence would eventually require her attention. Damn.

Renée picked up her empty glass. "I suppose he's due for more flattery." She strode over to the door and slid past Lane. "I'll see you later, Lane." That was a promise, as she wasn't anywhere near done with her yet.

Lane didn't do a good job of scanning the poker logs. The irritation at being interrupted, plus the implication of more to come, was somewhat distracting. Relative sobriety sat under her skin like an itch. The win looked legitimate enough and her contact confirmed the event logs were correct. She approved the money transfer and informed Rakesh.

After that, she retrieved gin from bar storage while Helen was clearing empties from the tables.

Then an argument broke out between a mod and a neolud, which she directed outside using her stun wand and Serge's muscle.

By *that* time, Helen had gone on a break, freeing Lane to reach for the good vodka and pour herself a reasonable three fingers over ice. As she went to take a sip, someone cleared their throat behind her.

She turned and fumbled her glass.

Ayumu Kusanagi frowned at her. "Can we talk in private?"

Oh good, now she had an actual excuse to drink. Lane took him in as she sipped. This was good stuff—clear with a slightly sweet edge. Distilled with neat consumption in mind. If the night wasn't done annoying her, she might as well push a layer between it and her.

He seemed stressed. It was difficult to tell, as his face had all the expressiveness of granite, but there was a telling tension in the angle of his shoulders. She inclined her head towards her office.

Once they were seated—he in the visitor chair and she in the chair Renée had been sprawled across not three hours ago—she waited for him to begin.

He took a breath, gaze direct and unfaltering. "I know my wife spoke to you today. She was a little vague on the details, but I can imagine what the conversation focused on. She told me everything last night."

Tonight had just turned from annoying to fucking *excruciating*.

"You should know I don't usually fall in love with married women," Lane said.

He raised his eyebrows. "I'm not angry. Tori needed to hide in Lavele for some time, and she thought I was dead; you weren't given her real name, let alone the details of her life with me. No one is to blame."

"How unexpectedly understanding."

Ayumu's hands clasped each other tightly. "If anything, I'm glad she found happiness during that time. I really am. We have a difficult life, and the good parts are always gifts."

"Nice sentiment."

He settled better into his chair. "To be honest, after hearing Tori's description of you, I find myself surprised. She said you were . . ." was that a tic in his cheek? ". . . someone who wasn't a salon owner or who wouldn't date the prefect of police."

Lane could well imagine how Tori had portrayed her. "What's wrong with owning a bar? And I'm dating the prefect? News to me."

"And to my wife. Our informants had some interesting things to say when we asked. You're relatively famous, you know that?"

She did not. "I'm a small-time salon owner, that's it."

He made an irritated noise. "Don't play that game with me. It's unnecessary. Your connection with the prefect is obvious to everyone; *less* obvious is your connection to the local hacker group, and that's probably for a reason, correct?"

Someone somewhere had spilled some beans. Lane was going to have their hide, whoever they were. She hid her anger behind another sip.

His dark eyes flicked to her drink, then back to her. "Enough. I came here for one reason."

"Superb."

"You have the ticket, the one Fentiman was going to sell to us."

She raised her eyebrows. "You sure about that? Prefect Bellevue had this place searched."

"You're too smart to leave it somewhere easily found. There's nowhere else it could be." Ayumu's jaw clenched. "So yes, I am sure you have it."

Lane glanced him over. His face was steely and flat, betraying little emotion, but his hands gripped each other tightly, and the tension in his back and shoulders was obvious. He didn't want to be here anymore than she wanted him here.

What was it about him that drew Tori? That made her keep him?

It was useless to figure something like that out. Like anyone, he had depths Lane couldn't see. Probably. If he ever relaxed enough to take that stick out his ass.

She took a big gulp of vodka, instantly regretting it as it burned going down. "Say that's the case—" she coughed "—why would I give it to you and Tori?"

He blinked. "Why *wouldn't* you?"

"Did Tori tell you the full story of us in Lavele?"

He straightened. "No. I didn't want to know . . . certain things. I trust she told me the details I need."

"Maybe you should rethink that."

"What do you mean? What happened?" He glanced at the vodka again. "Does this have something to do with why you and your sister came here?"

"Something, yeah."

He frowned. "I know there's a painful history. Tori didn't elaborate, but having seen what I've seen, I can imagine what happened. Even so, the things I've heard about you don't describe a person who'd keep a grudge, let alone be petty about it."

And that right there was the problem with trusting other information sources. "You heard wrong."

He let out a deep sigh. "I know my wife hurt you, but this goes beyond you and her and me. You know who she is and what she represents. You know that she's saved countless lives. You know what it would mean to get her out of this system and somewhere safe."

"True, I do know all of that. But the thing is, why would I care?"

His mouth set. "Madame Kovacs. Lane. It's not too late. We still have a chance to push back the Parliament. There are forces in Fides and other nearby systems waiting for the right opportunity to act. We can really make a difference."

"I'm sure you think you can."

Anger rippled over his face. "Has this place sucked all the hope out of you?"

"Not at all." She put her glass down. "It was gone long before I got here."

He leaned forward now, elbows on the desk, expression so guilelessly intense that Lane had the abrupt urge to laugh.

"Lane Kovacs, you were a brilliant scientist dedicated to furthering modification technology. You helped get parts to those who needed them. You gave my wife a technological miracle. You abstain from political action now, you pretend not to care about anything or anyone, but we all know that's a lie. Your sister—"

She slammed her hand on the desk. "No."

He scowled. "Our cause was once your cause. It still can be. It still is."

"My cause disappeared years ago."

"It didn't, Lane. It's alive and well. You can help. You can get Tori to Fides."

She crossed her arms. "The ticket is a one-use, one-way ride. Did Fentiman tell you that?"

"Yes." Ayumu straightened. "We were going to arrange another ticket with him, but apparently Bellevue and Elleul anticipated us. It's proving difficult to source another one as ironclad, quick, and safe as this one." He paused. "Did you hear about Fentiman?"

"No."

"He's dead, and I doubt it's as innocent as the police are making it seem. That will be us if we don't leave. That will be *Tori* if she doesn't leave."

Fentiman, dead? How? He'd been in the local station, which was an incredibly secure place. Back in the core, people disappeared or had strange ends in many places, but here? No. Though, clearly Ayumu thought his death was suspicious. And with Elleul on-planet perhaps Ayumu's suspicions weren't unfounded.

And how telling that Renée hadn't mentioned it. Presumably it contributed to her very hard day. Hopefully it would contribute to her kicking Elleul back to the core.

Still, what did any of that have to do with her? "You must be used to that kind of threat by now—and it's one everyone on Salus lives with, by the way. This may be neutral territory, but—" she shrugged "—people bring the politics with them."

He made a frustrated grunt. "That's not the point."

Lane wondered if he was where Tori had picked up the phrase. Or did he get it from her? Either way, hearing the same inflection from a different person necessitated another gulp.

"No one should have to live with a threat like that. Look, we can pay you. We have the funds. Twenty thousand francs."

"No."

"Fifty. One hundred."

"You could make it a million and change and I wouldn't sell it to you."

Ayumu proved himself capable of expressing emotion by finally glaring at her. "You're not the person my wife said you were."

When his eyes moved to her glass *again*, she deliberately picked it up and cradled it. "If you mean sober and overflowing with the milk of human kindness, then alas. I haven't been that person in years."

"I'm not above begging, but if you won't be swayed with reason, I don't see the point."

Swayed with reason? *Reason*? That was rich. What a cheap shot. "You're as good with words as Tori is. I can see why you two are together."

He stood, entire body stiff. "I should leave."

"At last, something we agree on."

"But first, I want to know *why* you won't help us."

Lane stood too. "Ask your wife." She nodded at the door. "Elleul is out there. Be sure to avoid him."

"How can you allow him through your doors?" He kept his voice low, but anger dripped from every word. "How can you allow *anyone* on their side to drink here?"

"Their money is as good as anyone else's. And believe me, if they're *here*, it's not because 'their' side is helping them." For someone who'd seen the things he had, Ayumu Kusanagi seemed to be suffering from a massive blind spot.

Another tic in his cheek twitched and he walked out.

Lane sat back down with a sigh.

This was why she didn't allow politics in the salon. At least he didn't throw a fist along with the sentimental bullshit.

That reference to the hackers infuriated her. She pulled up the messaging on internal view and voice recorded a swift message to the usual encrypted number: *Leaking me to the Kusanagis is still leaking. That wasn't the agreement.* Sent with a command.

Then she slumped in her chair.

Today was officially terrible.

Her gaze fell to her desk.

Well. Not so terrible. Renée had her pinned right where Lane's vodka currently rested. It was easy to resurrect the scene: Renée's eyes darkening right before she dove in, the urgent press of her hands against Lane's body, the noises she'd made whenever they'd brushed against each other.

Something about Renée had been irresistible tonight. The endless charm, the surprising hint of insecurity, the smooth way she'd moved into Lane's space. She made it easy to be affectionate, to take that leap into a new level of their relationship.

Lane had liked kissing Renée. The way they'd connected felt natural and almost a relief. Remembering the kiss sent a slow warmth through her. Between her legs felt pleasantly heavy and full, and she sank forward to let her forehead rest on the desk. It had been years since she'd responded like this to someone. She wanted a moment to sit and *feel* before the reaction subsided or someone interrupted her with another task.

She could guess what Renée had in mind for later. Lane didn't regret that they'd been stopped; there were things she and Renée should say to each other, things Lane wanted to convey that she couldn't via sex. It seemed this part didn't get easier, despite time and experience. While she was long past judging herself for what she did or didn't feel sexually, she hoped Renée would be one of those people who would understand. She seemed to be. Exploring each other could take a different path and Lane wanted to show her that.

She was doing this. She was considering this kind of connection once again, and with *Renée*. Lane must be going crazy in her apathy. Yet it was so easy with Renée, and in a way Lane hadn't expected.

A new message notification popped up. A response from her hacker contact. Without moving her head, she opened it, closing her eyes to help her focus on the text: *We were vouching for you. They're safe to tell. But we understand and apologise. It won't happen again.*

It was too late now though. She groaned into the wood of the desk and dismissed the message app.

"Anything I can help with?" came Helen's voice from the door.

"Can you make people go away?" Lane's voice was deeper this close to the desk.

"With the right weapon, yes."

"You're your own weapon."

"I could say the same about you. Are you all right?"

Lane opened her eyes and rolled onto the other cheek so she could face the door. "I'm fine."

"Uh-huh. Is that water next to you?"

"Of course."

"Liar." Helen came over and stood beside her. "I'm hearing talk tonight."

"Oh?"

"Fentiman committed suicide in jail, only no one thinks it was actually suicide. He apparently left a very valuable portal ticket here, despite Prefect Bellevue's search turning up nothing."

Shit. Seemed Ayumu was onto something. Poor Fentiman. Lane closed her eyes. "People have nothing better to do than talk."

"To me, the conclusions are logical and the probability of them being true is high." Helen's voice went quiet. "Lane. If you have that ticket, you need to move it on. People aren't going to burgle us yet, but they will if the rumours persist. Sell it or give it away or, crazy idea, use it yourself."

"Noted."

"I mean it." Cool fingers ran through Lane's hair, rubbing gently at her scalp. "You got us here, which was huge. But you shouldn't stay, not when you have a real chance at leaving. I'm safe. If you have that ticket, you need to use it."

Lane scowled. "I'm not leaving you."

"Do you honestly think I like seeing you like this? You're not happy, Lane. You're not using your amazing brain to the best of its abilities. Frankly"—Helen's voice turned sour—"you seem determined to destroy it. You need to stop. Get out of this place. Find brilliant people and live a better life."

Lane opened her eyes. "I can't imagine a good life without you in it."

"I'll be fine. I'll be here, waiting for Parliament to be annulled."

"You really think that could still happen?"

Helen nodded. "I do. Or a coup, or for the masses to rise up and reintroduce the guillotine. The laser kind, for extra show."

It had been a few months since she'd cracked that particular joke. Lane gazed up at her. After this many years, she was used to this face, but at certain points, she would've given multiple ironclad portal tickets away to anyone in order to have the real Helen gazing down at her. She knew her sister was in there—most of her, a version of her—but this deep pang of longing for *her* didn't seem to care.

"I know you can look after yourself, but I would miss you too much," Lane said.

Helen smiled. "I love you too."

Lane slung one arm around Helen's waist and hugged her close. "It might make me happier if you stopped making clay smoothies while I'm sleeping."

"Stop moping until the early hours of the morning and you won't be woken up by my smoothies."

Lane huffed against Helen's thigh. "How dare you use logic against me at a time like this." Helen hummed and kept combing through her hair.

They stayed like that for a while. When Helen moved, it was to sit on the desk. "If you won't use the ticket for yourself, what are you going to do with it?"

Lane shrugged. "I don't know."

"The Kusanagis have asked for it, right?"

"He has. She hasn't."

There was an expectant silence.

"I said no to him, Helen, and I'd say no to her too."

"Really? Even though she's Yui?"

Lane scowled. "*Especially* because she's Yui. If I give it to them, Elleul will have me arrested and before you know it, I'll be following Fentiman."

"The prefect won't let that happen."

"She will. She won't like it, but going against a Parliament member would be suicide for her, for all of us. And, you know, I do have it. Pretty sure that counts as holding stolen goods or something. The NZC is watching her movements with Elleul, so she's got to be careful." Lane sat up and gazed at Helen. "I don't want to put her into a position like that. I don't want to give her a reason to arrest me. I don't want their attention at all."

"Bit late for that."

Understatement. She should've told Fentiman to fuck himself with the damned ticket.

Helen kept running her fingers through Lane's hair. Eventually she said, "You haven't told me what happened the night I died."

"And I'm not going to."

Some of Lane's hair was gently tugged. "You'll have to someday. You haven't told me, but I can guess some of the details. There's a definite difference in the before and after of my memories. Not just of me, but of you too. You changed that night. I know you had to in order for us to get out without problems, and you didn't change so much that I don't recognise you, but whatever happened, you're different."

Lane opened her mouth to answer, but Helen shook her head. "Let me finish. I know you're going to say you did what you had to do, like everyone else. But it wasn't nothing. It cost you something. And maybe this is an opportunity to recover what you lost."

Helen was talking about her research and the relative innocence of their life together in Lavele. Did she really think it could be that simple? Lane wasn't sure how to tell her that it wasn't. Yes, she'd left a lot of things behind, and some of it had hurt, but it had been necessary. On balance, she had few regrets.

This situation demanded something new from her. And unlike in Lavele, Lane had no idea what she wanted to do. There was no clear purpose, no obvious methodology to follow, no nice rules to get from here to a place where life would be simpler and safer. No right answers.

Lane didn't know what she would do or what would happen, but she had to consider the facts she did know. Threats were at hand. Maybe it was time for the old precautionary measures.

"I'll think about it," she said. "And while I'm thinking about it, I'll get some air. Do you need anything from the store?"

Helen frowned. "No, but Serge was complaining about running out of mints earlier."

"Okay." Lane checked her account balance on internal view. "I'll be back in an hour."

"It doesn't take an hour to get mints."

"I'm going the long way."

Helen stood up. "Fine. Be cryptic. Come back soon. I don't think Elleul's presence here means a calm night."

Lane nodded and they left her office. She surveyed the salon as she walked through: no one seemed to be causing issues, everyone seemed to be having a good time. Even Elleul was laughing at something Renée was saying. Her waving arms promised that whatever it was, it probably *was* funny. The colour in her cheeks hinted at the colour of the wine in her glass, and how much she'd had of it.

Outside, the air was cool and smelt of its usual whisky-pollution heaviness. Clouds drifted across the night sky, scattering the ring's light into bright shards. Lane went to the nearest dispenser and drew out the francs she needed in cash. Then she visited the corner store and bought Serge his mints.

After that, she walked a few blocks closer to the terminal and down one of the side alleys where people sold unlicensed goods. Doorways stood open into dimly lit stores, dark gaps between the brighter-lit stalls full of clothes, shoes, food, and gimmicky semi-permanent tech. Unlike in Lavele, the illicit goods here specialised mostly in luxuries and nostalgia items smuggled from the core past the tariffs and Parliament restrictions.

Salus didn't have the planet-wide network platform that would have automatically broadcast their wares into her tech; instead the sellers transmitted locally and people with the appropriate tech had to tune in. She turned her receiver on and flagged the wares she wanted, then walked, letting her tech search for the right channel.

Though vanilla wares predominated, Pann's black market had the same five things as every black market across the inhabited galaxy: drugs, extreme pornography, dubious tech surgeries, body parts, and weapons. Lane tuned out the stuff she didn't want—though neurastim upgrades and spinal jacks were bargains—and carefully avoided glancing at the alley that led towards the body parts sellers.

The darkness loomed overhead, and despite this black market being infamous on the ground in Pann, the tight maze of alleys and stalls thronged with people. Proxy on, input channels locked down. No digital signatures identifying her were going to be left here. She kept her hands in her pockets and face angled down, only stopping to browse when her flag alarmed at lethal and surveillance hardware.

She skipped the firearms for the accessories and optional extras. She bought some signal jammers, new scanners, a supplementary booster—the kind with lethal voltage—for her wand, and some extension wires for the games. The tech went into a specific bag under her shirt and the wires into her pocket alongside the mints. Then it was time to block off her tech and make a very quick beeline back to the salon.

CHAPTER
SEVEN

What a lovely evening. Pann could be outright beautiful at the oddest moments. The ring shone burnished gold against the velvet dark of the night sky, drowning out all but the strongest stars. On the ground, little lights dotted the inky masses of buildings and snaked through the streets. The river gleamed silver in places, and it was all a bit wonderful. Lane was very lucky to have this kind of view from the salon's front door, and Renée was lucky in turn to see it now. She leaned back to appreciate it.

It seemed like she blinked and there were thick clouds intruding in her night sky. This made enjoying the ring a little difficult because she could only see the whole thing well when the clouds weren't there, but when they weren't there, the ring was *exceptionally* beautiful. And anyway the visible sections were also very pretty. But clouds tended to bring an awful mugginess to the air, and Renée decided she didn't like that they were there.

As well as that, it appeared the wall behind her was shaky. Thinking about it, that was probably because Renée was mildly drunk. Well, moderately drunk. Mildly moderately drunk. She was one of those lucky people who barely showed how drunk she was when she was drunk, which was a shame because there was a curfew, and no one was in the street to see how not drunk she appeared.

Oh dear. She was breaching the curfew, which was naughty of her, but it didn't matter because what was she going to do, fine *herself*?

By all the stars in all the galaxies in all the universe was she *drunk*. Why was she here at the salon again?

Something about Lane, as per usual. Renée should be a little embarrassed at her strength of feeling for Lane, but the thought disappeared as she acknowledged it. Probably for the best.

She squinted up at the sign on the side of the building: *LE SALON DE LANE* with *et jeux de vidéo* underneath in smaller curlicue. A stamp for digital scanners to play a preview and browse the drinks menu was printed underneath.

Member Elleul. Yes, that was it. He had wanted to talk, which meant Renée had needed the booze to stay sane. The couillon tended to drone on and on about enhanced beings and the sanctity of organic flesh and adhering to nature's laws, blah, blah, blah. Idiotic. And so dull. Just remembering it demanded another glass of wine. If she didn't have new grey hairs by the end of the week, it would be a miracle.

But she'd received a break from the tedium when they'd seen Ayumu Kusanagi stroll into Lane's office and stalk out looking rather peeved. Elleul had left a short while after. Intriguing and odd. Naturally Renée was dying of curiosity about what Ayumu and Lane had talked about, and what Elleul was now doing—and hopefully not doing—but she had to wait to talk to Lane and Helen. Because Lane had also gone somewhere. But she'd come back, right? Which was now. Wasn't it?

Wait, when had Renée even left the salon?

She blinked. Pulled out her tablet. It was much later than she'd thought.

Ah, now she remembered. She'd been put into a taxi, had told the driver to head to her place, remembered that she'd wanted to see Lane again, had told him to turn around, and he had and now she was back.

Merde, she was drunk.

Possibly too drunk.

And outside after curfew. Oops.

Wait wait wait.

She carefully looked up and turned around. The salon door was shut tight and the lights were off. Above the salon, the apartment windows were dark. It was closed and Lane and Helen were sleeping.

What a fool she was. Now who was the couillon?

Time for her to do the same thing and go to bed.

She took a deep breath, then let go of the wall. One step. Good. A second. Yes, she could do this. Ah, wait, this reminded her of that trip with her cousins to the coast, where they drank far too much and missed all the night trains home and had to stagger together back to their hotel. They'd been too loud, and one of them had sprained her ankle, and Jacques had almost fought a bicycle, but they'd made it with a constant chant of *one step at a time.*

Above her, someone opened a window.

She turned around and staggered. Damn ground slipping under her feet. When she managed to look up, she saw Helen smiling at her and waving. Renée waved back.

Helen climbed out of the window, hung by her fingertips, then dropped to the ground feet-first and rolled onto her back next to Renée.

"Good evening," Renée said down to her. "I mean morning."

Helen smiled. "Hi, Prefect Bellevue. Why are you outside our salon at this time of night?"

Renée extended a hand to help her up. "Taking in the very pleasant view while doing my duty by keeping order and peace in the city."

"Now that you've said it, it's so obvious." Helen gripped her hand, and Renée pulled her up, then held on to her when the ground did the weird uneven thing again. "Are you all right, Prefect?"

"Fine, fine, fine. I'm perfeck—perfectly well, thank you." Renée blinked. "And you?"

Helen laughed and dusted herself off. "How about I walk you home?"

"That would be very welcome."

Helen extended an arm, which Renée took gratefully, and they began walking. One step then another and another. Granted, this was much easier with someone as steady as Helen helping her. Once they were a few buildings down the street from the salon, Helen remarked, "I thought we put you into a taxi."

"I think you did too."

"I suppose you wanted to see my sister. I'm sorry, she's already asleep."

Renée waved this away. "No. Maybe, but no. Not at all. Just a bit. I only . . . I'm a little tipsy and not thinking straight."

"You mean, you don't want to see my sister?"

Quoi? Where had that come from? "What has she said to you? Whatever it was, it was wrong. I want to see all of your sister."

Helen snorted. "Got it. I suppose that's good."

It should be. After five years, it was *supposed* to be good. Lane seemed to be cautious, but that was all right. Renée simply wanted to *be* with Lane. Goodness, wine had the ability to bring out the sap in her. "I hope so." Renée squinted at the street ahead of them. "Is that a person or a rubbish bag?"

"It's a garbage bag. Why aren't you sure if things with my sister are good?"

"Timing's a little—" she waved "—unfortunate."

"Oh. You mean Tori?"

"Yes. Her wonderful heart-breaking ex who happens to be an illustrious resistance leader and who *happens* to show up at *her* bar." Renée turned to Helen. "It's a little strange, no? Unlikely things aren't supposed to happen in real life."

"Real life is full of unlikely things." Helen seemed to hesitate. "Perhaps I shouldn't say this, but I don't like that she's here. I'm not sure what Lane said to you about her."

Renée made a vague gesture.

Helen's eyes narrowed. "She took Tori leaving badly, and I mean *badly*. I don't want to see Lane like that again. I don't want Tori drawing her in again."

Images of a sad Lane came thick and fast, followed by a seductive scene featuring Tori, Lane, and a certain office desk. Renée gripped her arm. "Do you think she'd do that? No. Surely not. Tori is married, after all."

Helen shrugged. "So what? That means different things to different people."

Now that Renée had started, she couldn't stop picturing them together. "What were they like? Her and Lane?"

There was a long pause. "Disgustingly sweet together. They complemented each other well. My sister never made relationships a priority, you know? Yu— Tori was good for her in that way. Made her happy."

Renée regretted asking. "And the same the other way around?"

Helen frowned. "If you mean did Lane make Tori happy, then yes. At the time I thought Lane helped Tori through a hard time, but knowing who she is now, I think I understand the attraction better."

"You didn't before?"

"I did, but her being Tori Kusanagi makes it more meaningful." Helen glanced at her. "Don't be jealous. It won't happen. We've all changed, Lane included. Perhaps too much." Her voice was soft and bitter.

Renée stared ahead. The street was a little busier and less dark, lit by intermittent streetlights placed according to a formula that calculated the most efficient coverage of light for the least usage of solar battery. A sole person occasionally scurried past in the shadows, avoiding eye contact or averting their face. Breaking curfew, like her and Helen. Disappointing. At least the ground was steadier. Or she was less drunk. She relaxed her grip on Helen's arm.

In the office that evening, Lane had been happy, or something close to it. She had smiled. Whatever made Lane want to kiss Renée had to be a good thing. Renée wouldn't go so far to call it trust or desire, but it was something that Tori didn't have. And Lane had said not to worry. Even if Tori was persistent, maybe things had changed enough that it didn't matter. Renée felt a little better. Helen was right. She didn't have to worry about this. Well, perhaps not so much.

To be frank, it was quite bizarre that she was even having such thoughts. Her? Worry this much over someone else's ex-lover? Had to be the alcohol. "Whatever happens between me and Lane is up to her."

"And if nothing does? What will you do?"

Terrible question. Renée wasn't going to entertain that for an instant. "What everyone else does, of course. Remove all pictures of her from my tablet, drink too much, cut my hair, sleep with someone to affirm my desirability, then take up a new hobby for a few months until it all happens again with someone else."

Helen was watching her closely. "I see."

Renée turned her attention from the street to Helen's smooth, poreless face. From here she could tell. "Helen. You're being very nice to me."

"Despite my better judgement, I do actually like you."

Renée beamed. "Moi aussi! Wait, why 'better judgement'?"

Helen didn't say anything.

"Is it me being prefect of police?" Renée rolled her eyes. "Please, don't let a little thing like that come between us. Forget this being prefect. I'm a servant of the Neutral Zone Committee, not the Parliament."

"Yes, but the NZC has a cooperative agreement with the Parliament and you have Elleul breathing down your neck. Also, weren't you previously a core officer?"

"The agreement only extends so far. As does the agreement with Fides. Elleul can go to hell. And indeed, I was. Does that matter?"

Helen shook her head. "I want to get the lay of your convictions."

"Oh that's easy—j'ai rien. I fly with the prevailing wind."

Helen laughed. "Understood. I wondered if it was a good idea, taking a walk in the dark with the prefect of police."

"Why wouldn't it be a good idea? Am I boring you?"

Helen laughed again. "No, no. It's, well . . . I doubt Elleul would approve."

"Ah, mais non, you miss my point. The joy of having no convictions is that I can do what I like." Renée winked at her. "I am the master of my own fate! I act according to my own rules, not other people's rules."

Helen nodded. "Sure."

She didn't seem convinced for some reason, but Renée hoped she'd made her point. "We've known each other for several years, Helen. I consider us friends. You can trust me on this, I'm very unreliable."

Helen glanced at her, was quiet for a beat, then said, "I'm glad to hear that. I have a question for you, as a friend. How much do you know already about us? About why we left Lavele and came here?"

Renée blinked. "My darling Helen, you know I don't read anyone's files unless I have to. Now that I've had to, I know Lane's place of employment was destroyed and her job went with it. I assumed there were the usual political reasons too."

"That's definitely some of it. You might have noticed she and I don't look related."

Renée nodded, then stopped because it still made things spin in odd ways.

"I died. She brought me back. And that meant it wasn't safe for me at all in Lavele."

Aha, vindication. "I knew it!"

Helen winced. "I thought we'd been careful."

Renée tapped her chest. "I am a police officer. I notice things like this. Don't feel bad."

"I'll try my best." Helen's affect was incroyable, really amazing mechanics. Truly, she was very humanlike.

Renée told her so. "You are very well made. It took even me a while to notice. Your internal programming must be superb."

"But you see, that's part of the problem. My memories are incomplete."

Incomplete? Renée frowned at her. Why would her memories be incomplete? Organic-to-synth transfers were total and took seconds. Maybe a minute. Oh, she was too drunk to worry about this.

Helen continued, "I don't have the last day I was alive in my organic body. Lane told me that I died in an accident, but I don't think that's true."

Curious. "Why?"

They had walked a fair distance by now, but Renée's place was still far. The ground was more stable now, especially if she kept her head still. Bien.

Helen's expression was smooth and calm, but her voice modulated with caution and thoughtfulness. Truly, technology could do marvellous things. "It happened on a day where so much *else* happened. Tori left. Protests and riots shut down our city. Lane's lab was destroyed. I died. I mean, really? It doesn't feel right. I wouldn't have been out in the streets, I would have been at home avoiding the trouble." Accidents were entirely plausible, but Renée couldn't imagine Helen's gut or intuition or whatever had been programmed for her was wrong. "Most important of all, there should have been an official record of me receiving medical treatment or undergoing mind capture and having this body assigned to me. But there isn't."

"Ah." Put like that, yes, it was certainly strange.

Helen sighed, her hand lowering. "Lane is insistent there was an accident, and so far I haven't pushed her. But I think if it was entirely innocent, she would have shared all the details."

Renée agreed. She tried to think this through more, but the pieces of this particular puzzle didn't fit together very well in her head. "How inconsiderate of her. You're entitled to know the details of your own death."

"I am, but I think the truth is painful for her, and possibly for me too." Helen spread out the fingers on her hand, then twisted it to gaze at her palm. "Not that it hasn't been painful considering the idea that someone killed me. Adapting to this body wasn't easy either."

"I can literally only imagine," Renée agreed.

"It's not all bad. I'm glad my sister did whatever she did, and it was a good thing we left. Maybe it doesn't matter that the details why are fuzzy to me. I'm grateful to be alive in any definition of the word. But it's not the same."

Renée privately assumed that would be the case, but here was an opportunity to confirm. "Not the same? In what way?"

Helen's expression turned hard. "Look, I know what the mods say, and believe me, I'm no neolud. We need tech and it's not going to hurt us. But they don't *know*. No one does, only those of us who've gone through this. I have the memories of being in a biological body and they don't match with how I process reality now. Though I've gained some things, I've lost others." Her mouth twisted in a wry expression. "Some of those things were important to me. But losing them doesn't feel important. There's this vast—" she gestured angrily "—disconnect between what I was and what I am. I see myself as two separate entities. I'm not the same. I would say I don't like it, but 'like' is a concept to me now, not a feeling. I'm certain the previous me wouldn't like this, but she's gone."

She fell silent for a while. This didn't seem a good time to interrupt, so Renée focused on moving forward. They entered a quieter quarter, which was nice. Fewer curfew-breakers to ignore, fewer to overhear.

Helen sighed, perhaps for Renée's benefit. "While I'm not happy to find out my sister's ex-lover is in fact one of the leaders of the mod resistance, it's given me a new idea about what happened to me: someone from the government came looking for Tori and found me instead."

Renée wasn't convinced. If that had been the case, why kill Helen? She'd been human and a citizen, and certainly *not* Tori Kusanagi. A few basic questions and a DNA scan or file check would have verified that. Sympathy with the enhanced being resistance wasn't reason enough to kill someone. "Were you enhanced at the time?" she asked.

"Ahem. I was a person with some tech, like most people my age. I never protested."

"Was your city targeting citizens like you?"

Helen shook her head. "No, actually. Not then. I see what you're getting at, but I *would* have been an unwitting associate of Tori." Helen shrugged. "Perhaps that was enough."

"Enough to pull you in for questioning, not to kill you right away."

"It's just a guess."

It was a good one, given who Kusanagi was, but there were missing pieces. Renée was in no state to collect them together, but she seized at one particular detail. She carefully stopped and pulled out her tablet. "What was the name of Lane's laboratory?"

"Why?"

Renée waited, and when Helen didn't give the name, she decided to find it herself. Lane's file was still in the case portfolio and the name was in her work tab: the Lavele Hearing Research Institute. Excellent. Out went a request for information on the lab and on events in Lavele on that date. This would be more interesting than ticket requests in the morning, assuming Elleul had kept his hands off the people in her jail cell overnight.

When she looked up, Helen was giving her a wary look. "What did you do?"

"Made a request for information about the lab."

Helen made a noise of surprise. "You're not as drunk as you seem. Why do that? What could it possibly have to do with me?"

Renée glanced down at her tablet before putting it into her pocket. "Call it a hunch."

Helen toned her expression down to serene. "Renée, are you really attempting to solve my death five years later and from another planet?"

Renée grinned. "I'm a police officer. Why else did you bring it up?"

Helen smiled. "You got me." She faced forward. "I like us being safe. If you find anything . . . *sensitive*—"

"There's nothing which could shock me, Helen." Renée placed her hand over her heart. "I promise, I'll guard your and her secrets as well as I guard my own."

"I regret this already," Helen said.

"But regret is better to live with than not knowing. Yes?" Helen didn't say anything. Renée glanced at her briefly. "I completely understand."

They walked in silence for a while.

A beam of violet streamed into the sky, and they looked upwards. The beam shot straight up through one cloud, just missing Salus's ring, and penetrated the star-studded black. It held for a few minutes, powerful and vibrant, a cord connecting Pann to the cosmos. As abruptly as it started, it disappeared.

The hackers were staging their illegal journeys again. Had Renée received a bribe recently from them? It didn't feel like she had. She should check that.

Helen turned to her. "You know now why Lane and I haven't moved on. But I'm wondering why *you* haven't. What brought you to Pann, and why haven't you left?" She nodded at where the beam had been. "You could sign yourself a ticket anytime."

"Well, it wouldn't be *that* easy." Renée tucked her hands into her pockets. "I was reshuffled here. And how could I go when there's such fun to be had in this town of mine?"

"Right, right. Why were you reshuffled?"

"The usual reason anyone is. I disagreed with my boss on a minor point of policy."

"Aha. That must have been difficult."

Difficult. Her career, her life, up in smoke; her colleagues and friends branding her a subversive rebel and kicking her away; her family, supportive, but also advising she apologise and keep her head down to earn her way back into good graces. Perhaps she should've done that. One disagreement. She wasn't even enhanced. The bitterness remained strong, and who could blame her? She'd lost her family, her life, because of *one question*. "Oui, it was."

A second burst went up into the sky. Renée really should follow up on how they did these trips. It involved a spare power cell that was temporarily swapped in, and keying in a different port location in the corresponding terminal in Fides, as well as a few other things involving satellites and relays and matter transmissions. Something like that. Highly illegal but ingenious. She thought her force had raided the spare power cell recently though. Yes, that was it, they had it in the station and was waiting for the bribe for its return. Hm. It seemed they'd found other sources of energy.

"Shouldn't you be calling this in?" Helen asked.

"What? Those?" Renée waved it away. "Too much effort."

"I suppose it *would* be suspicious if you reported this while tipsy and outside during curfew."

"Exactement."

They counted thirty bursts of light by the time they reached Renée's building. Renée almost felt sober, and it exacerbated her discomfort with the hacker trips. There were too many. They should have exhausted their battery. Something was wrong.

She yawned. Something was wrong, and it was a concern for her future self.

Helen stopped outside her front door. "Thank you for the walk, Renée."

"You're most welcome, Helen. Will you tell Lane about this?"

Helen shrugged. "She's my sister. I make no promises."

Renée watched Helen turn and start running. In seconds she was at the other end of the street. Their walk across the city had taken them over half an hour; she would do it in a few minutes. Upon her return to the salon, she'd also jump back to her window. Synths really were enhanced compared to organic beings. Renée would never be tempted—she didn't want to be placed in a different body, nor did she like the implication of living longer than humans usually did—but she couldn't deny there were benefits to having a synthetic body.

Not that Renée needed to climb through windows regularly. That was what tablet trackers and bugs and cookies were for.

Her tablet vibrated and she checked it. Several news articles and investigative reports about the lab had come through. Oh good. She needed something useful to do when she woke up hungover and grumpy in the morning.

Despite seeing the headlines a few minutes after waking up, it was midafternoon by the time Lane dragged herself out of bed. Stars, waking up had to be the worst part of the day, regardless of the time.

And when that was accompanied by headlines like these and the resulting need to visit Renée, no one with any sense would fault Lane for staying in bed.

On her way out, Helen waved at her from the room they'd turned into her studio, where she sat in front of a hunk of clay, hands and arms coated in thick grey. Lane waved back, locked the front door, bought food and coffee, then headed to the police station as she ate. She turned what she wanted to say over and over in her head and kept checking the headlines.

KUSANAGI JOINS FORCES WITH HACKERS, FREES TRAPPED REFUGEES

QUEUE JUMPER BLITZ

KUSANAGI AND HACKERS: BUT WHO'S FUNDING THEM?

PANN EXODUS: NEW RECORD REACHED

Not much of a new record when the old one was twenty a day; forty if you counted the hacker trips. Still, the local press never let something like the truth get in the way of a scoop.

Thick round clouds hung low, trapping heat and moisture to the earth. In the streets, the air lay heavy and stank of frying oil and electricity. Lane looked forward to the rain; she preferred the smell of petrichor to pollution-laden dust. Precipitation on Salus was less acidic than on the core planets, given terraforming was ongoing and the planet's population was crowded into relatively small city areas. The rain here was the most refreshing Lane had ever known.

When she reached the police station, she paused before going in. She knew the public parts of this place so well by now, almost as well as her salon. Bribes, complaints, dropping off drunks, and occasional coffees with Renée meant she could step inside and the officer at the front desk would wave her in without a second glance.

Back home, if she'd willingly gone into a police station in the middle of the day and been so familiar with police officers, she'd have been under suspicion from the cyborg activists she'd known. It was a relief no one gave a shit here.

Inside, the officers were restless and curt, the atmosphere tense and heavy. Instead of waving her in, an officer physically led her to Renée's office, glancing around the entire way.

When Lane entered the office, Renée was at her desk, tablets displaying text and images scattered around her. The place was in more disarray than usual—someone had left a crumb-strewn plate on the coffee table at the far side of the room, multiple mugs dotted the furniture, and there was a blanket on the small loveseat.

Renée looked awful: sallow skin, dark circles under her eyes, a firmly entrenched frown. Typical hungover Renée. She'd been wasted when Lane and Helen had shoved her into a taxi last night. Now she didn't seem able to summon a smile when she looked up. "My darling Lane. Not that it's not wonderful to see you, but today was a mistake."

Lane paused in the doorway. "How's that?"

"My head has the worst pain I have ever experienced in my life, the Kusanagis are running riot across my city, and I am in the middle of so much *paperwork*."

"The hackers last night?"

"C'est ça," Renée agreed, glowering at one tablet. "And also you."

"Me?"

"Analytics have told me there's a connection to you. I don't know if it's your name in an account or data link or what, but it's something."

Lane had been right to come. She closed the door behind her and went to the desk. "Ayumu Kusanagi told me yesterday I'm relatively famous. It would be weirder if I *wasn't* mentioned."

Renée raised her eyebrows. "You're not that famous." She gestured at the chair in front of her desk. "Sit down and tell me why you're here."

Lane sat. "I'm here to report a crime."

That earned her a deliberate long blink. "Quoi?"

"And I wanted to see you too, of course."

That seemed to help; Renée relaxed in her chair and rested her face on one fist to listen. Lane explained about the recently discovered security gap in the salon's network, which had "allowed" a "trojan" into the financial protocols. She left out how her and a hacker contact had set up that gap and "trojan" a few months after the salon had opened, in return for the hackers adjusting Helen's Intelligence file with updated information and wiping records of their travel to Salus. "I found it this morning. It's been skimming money off the game transactions for months."

Renée's expression was priceless. "Maybe even years?"

"Maybe! Who knows how long they've been robbing me?"

Renée pressed one hand to her forehead. "Allow me to use my substantial intellect to guess that this leads back to the hackers?"

Lane spread her hands. "How could I possibly know? I don't have anything to do with them."

"Mm. And in terms of 'skimming money,' this actually means . . . ?"

"About 0.00005%. A tiny fraction of a centime per transaction."

Renée raised an eyebrow. "How many transactions per night?"

". . . Many."

"Naturally."

Lane batted her eyelashes. "Please. You have to track down the vile hooligans who did this."

Renée's fingers flew over her tablet. "How coincidental that you discover this on the exact day we're focusing our efforts on the hackers and the endless leads which have turned up in their wake."

"Life works in strange ways."

"Life is currently attempting to drive me insane." Renée glanced up at her. "You could have reported this to any of my officers."

"True."

That won her a knowing smile. "What else?"

"I heard Fentiman hanged himself. Is that true?"

Something about the ensuing pause and immediate disappearance of the smile gave Lane a sick feeling in the pit of her stomach.

Renée's lip curled. "*Someone* certainly hanged him."

Lane could imagine who. She glanced at the door. "Was it—"

"Don't. You know better than that."

Was her office bugged? If so, things were bad. Lane leaned forward over the desk. "Renée. Seriously. It was him, right?"

Renée covered her eyes. "I have *no possible idea* who you're referring to."

This worried Lane. She hoped Renée knew what she was doing. "Don't fuck around. And don't let him fuck you around." She lowered her voice. "I like you in one piece."

That finally earned her a small smile. "Bien sûr." Renée cleared her throat and moved a few of the tablets around. "Anything else that needs my attention?"

Lane dragged the chair closer and rested her elbows on the desktop. "Did you get home safely last night?"

Renée blinked, then groaned. "*You* put me in the taxi?"

"Yes."

"Merde. Helen sai— Ah, but it would have been you *and* Helen. I think I remember now." She glared at Lane. "Your drinks are bad. What do you cut them with, antifreeze?"

"My liquor is fine, you just had too much." Lane took her in, liking the glint in her eyes and the way her collar framed the pulse at the base of her throat. She reached over and clumsily straightened her collar. "I did miss the follow up you promised me last night." The heated gaze she received back seemed to indicate Renée appreciated the gesture. "What happened?"

"Elleul happened." Renée jabbed at a tablet and closed whatever document she was working on. "Orion's eye, he's a difficult person to entertain. How anyone can talk to him without alcohol is beyond me. All the usual blah blah about purity and naturalism and bodily integrity, *so* boring. Doesn't anyone have anything better to talk about?" Her hands went up in the air. "He's certain you're going to help the Kusanagis and has all sorts of bright ideas about how to prevent that. Today he insists we find and arrest all the hackers who sent those people last night. There's just the small matter of *evidence*." Renée glanced at the door, then began whispering. "I cannot tell you the damage this is doing to my carefully-obtained exchange agreement with the main hacker group."

"The bribes you mean?"

Renée lay one hand over her heart. "Lane, I'm shocked at that insinuation."

Lane snorted. "So he's got you churning out paperwork?"

"Oui." Renée looked ready to throw the tablets off her desk. "He doesn't seem to understand that he cannot snap his fingers and we will all follow, regardless of the rules."

"Since when do you care about rules?"

Renée waved her hand dismissively. "Sometimes they're useful. His end goal is the Kusanagis behind bars. Despite what the headlines say, it's not clear yet what their role was last night beyond their usual pep talks, and those were streamed from an as-yet unknown location.

I can arrest the hackers for illegal operation of the terminal portal, but I cannot arrest the Kusanagis unless there's clear evidence they were there too."

"And of course there isn't."

"Analytics is working on it." Renée's voice went hard. "Elleul is overseeing them. He has everyone's Intelligence files, so of course my team are doing what he says. Perhaps I should learn something from him."

"I wouldn't use him as an example of good leadership, personally."

Renée rolled her eyes. "Of course not. My point, if you would let me get to it, is that he's proving troublesome, and I find myself at a loss to stop him."

Lane slid one hand over, nudging the tablets out of the way, and interspersed her fingers with Renée's. "What is going on here?" Lane had never whispered so much in her life, but they couldn't take chances. "You're working for the Neutral Zone now. He's a guest, and he has no control here. You know that, right? *You're* the prefect. You have that power. Don't forget where you are and who you are."

Renée's hand tightened around hers.

Lane searched her expression. "What does he have over you?"

Renée turned Lane's hand over with both of hers and kissed the palm. "My darling, you know the answer to that question. Everyone seems to know."

Lane hadn't expected that. Her face went hot, but she pushed on. "I'm charmed, but somehow I don't think it's me. Look. You don't care about Intelligence files. From what you told me, yours is a joke. So what is it really?"

Renée looked away. "What is it always? Information. Influence. Power. Promises. He says he could get me a pardon. I could go home. Find my family."

Go home? *Home*?

Lane straightened, her hand jerking out of Renée's. They stared at each other for a moment, then Lane reached for her again. Renée's hand was soft and warm in hers, but the desk under Lane's knuckles was hard and cool. Their combined grip sat amid glossy black plastic and varnished wood, a living knot interrupting the smooth lines. She kept her eyes there as she spoke. "Getting out of here. Welcomed back with open arms. That's a hell of an opportunity."

"I want to know they're okay." Renée's voice was rough. "I want to see them again."

"Yeah, I bet." She managed to look back up. "Difficult to turn that down."

Renée shrugged, her mouth a tired line. "Oh please. You know what politicians are like. Liars, all of them. Nothing will happen."

Possible. Or not. Lane could see the hope in her face. If she had the opportunity to go home without bad consequences, to find her family, the way Renée did, Lane was certain she'd hope too. Renée had mentioned her family a few times, always with smiles. Her father had cracked terrible jokes, her mother had loved wine and puzzles, and there had been half a million cousins with varying eccentricities.

Times like this, Lane was glad her parents were gone. No one could hold them as a promise over her head. But this wasn't only about family, it was restoring Renée's reputation. A full pardon was almost unheard of. "You're betting on him being the one who follows through." There was a slight buzzing in Lane's ears, and she was aware for the first time this day that she was stone sober. "He's done that with other promises."

Renée gave a small, deliberate shake of her head. "We shall see."

"Would home be safe?" There was a tense pause. "I suppose for you, with his recommendation and a pardon, it would be."

She didn't say anything.

Lane found the thought of Renée not being in Pann an odd one. Her predecessor had retired out of the position, apparently typical for Pann's prefect. Renée might have assumed the same would happen to her.

But it was true that she saw being here as a kind of punishment, and that unlike most of the refugees, she wasn't desperate to go to Fides. The idea of home was heady. Lane's home was long gone. Perhaps Renée's was too—or perhaps it wasn't. Could Renée just slide back into her old life, her old job, after all this time and all the things she'd gone through?

"Would you miss me?" Renée asked abruptly.

Lane realised she'd been staring into space above Renée's shoulder. She met Renée's dark eyes, somehow darker with the circles under them. Lane had the urge to reach over and brush her thumb under them, as though that might wipe away the effects of the bad night. "I can't imagine being here without you."

Renée smiled then, big and delighted. An answering giddiness rushed through Lane. It wasn't a promise to stay, but it was a hope Lane could hold for herself. She squeezed Renée's hand and moved forward to show her, to kiss her.

The door slammed open behind them as someone barged in midrant. "—never, *in my life*, seen such utter incompe— Prefect?"

Lane twisted back to see Elleul, his face a worrying shade of purple. She realised her hand was still twined with Renée's.

"Excuse me, Member Elleul," Renée said. Lane faced her again as she patted Lane's hand. "As I was saying, Madame Kovacs, we will find the criminals and serve justice. I promise. You were correct to come to me. Everything will be all right." She continued patting Lane's hand as she looked up at Elleul. "It's very bad, Member. Lane has discovered a skimmer in her game systems. She's out thousands of francs. So unfortunate."

Aha. Lane gave a big sniff. "I thought I had everything covered. I'm so good about installing updates and patches, you know?"

The expression on Renée's face could've gone in a stock image directory under *concerned sympathy*. "Of course. No one could do more! Once Analytics is done with last night's illegal departures, they'll begin looking into your systems."

Elleul was making a strange noise behind Lane, something between a wheeze and a choke.

Lane stood up. "Thank you so much, Prefect."

"You know you can come to me anytime. We're here to serve."

Something flashed on one of the tablets, and, distracted, Lane looked down. A news article with a photo of a familiar building displayed behind a message notification before the screen went dark again. That had been her old lab, the LHRI.

She glanced at Renée, then nodded at Elleul and left the office. As she walked through the station towards reception, she wondered if she'd seen that correctly. She'd never mistake the building though. Was Renée looking into her? If so, why?

She exited the building, not liking this development one bit.

CHAPTER EIGHT

As Member Elleul ranted about the audacity of her team needing time to investigate the events of last night, Renée thought through the implications of Lane helping the hackers. Lane was no hacker herself, but everyone knew enough about firewalls to prevent basic nonsense like skimmers infiltrating a system.

Renée saw right through her. And if Lane was letting the hackers skim money off her, others were too. The question was, how many other business owners were doing it? It was an ingenious way of making the money needed to keep their operations going, and an inspiring one too. She made a mental note to check with Atkins about getting a skimmer setup of their own.

"And furthermore," Elleul continued, "*why* haven't these hackers been shut down earlier? Your team seemed to think they weren't a concern at all."

She shrugged. "We only have so many resources here, monsieur, and the Neutral Zone Committee has made it very clear to us that we should prioritise higher-degree crimes."

"But these degenerates are allowing people to circumvent the system! *How* is that not important?"

Renée made sure she looked inoffensively confused. "You mean you want enhanced beings to stay in Janus?"

Elleul went red and began blustering.

"Simply put: homicides, rapes, arson, and so on have been deemed more important." She picked up the tablet that was tracking Analytics' reports. "Even if we somehow caught every hacker in Pann, more arrive every month. It would be an ongoing struggle."

"I find that inadequate as an explanation."

Analytics had indeed discovered multiple sources of money flows in the hackers' finances. "Then consider this an insignificant portion of local industry that isn't worth the resources to disrupt," she replied absently.

"For someone who is meant to be reducing crime, you seem very close to criminals," Elleul snapped.

Renée set the tablet down. "Excuse me?"

"Your force doesn't attempt to stop these absurd midnight portal transports, you *still* haven't arrested either Kusanagi, and you were practically comforting Lane Kovacs. What *are* your priorities, Prefect?"

Crétin. "Following procedure, Member, like any head of a police service. I require airtight leads and evidence, and the NZC so far has had no complaints about my leadership." Minimal complaints counted as *none* at this level.

He leaned towards her. "And what does that mean in terms I understand?"

"It means that my officers and I follow procedure, and if you have concerns about our methodologies, you may raise those concerns via the official channels. I remind you that this is the Neutral Zone."

The ensuing silence raised the hairs on her arms. His mouth pulled down, his eyes bored into hers, and he seemed unable to speak. It wouldn't do at all to leave him in such distress; time to soften her words. She wakened the tablet with the LHRI article and pulled her case notes onto the screen. "Look at this."

He took it and scanned the screen. "This is old news from Lavele."

"In a way. One thing I've wondered about Lane is why, with her background, she's remained here in Pann instead of moving on to Fides. I've been digging, and I suspect she wasn't just running tech to the black market." She paused for effect. "In reality, I think she was leading a concerted mod ring at the engineering and technician level that infiltrated multiple laboratories to distribute enhanced being propaganda while also enabling systematic theft."

She wondered if this ability to spout nonsense was a talent or not. "This is related to Lane Kovacs's departure from the core planets. According to this article, the resistance movement labelled this laboratory destruction an act of provocation from the Parliament, but the Intelligence file states the resistance movement did this."

He frowned. "That's . . . inconsistent."

Exactly. Renée was surprised too. Intelligence reports tended to place a rather *particular* frame on their information, but they never outright fabricated data or contradicted reality. There was always enough truth in the information to be useful; the real difficulty was sifting it out. Had this lab been targeted as part of the tech shutdowns, the Intelligence report would have been gleeful about it. It was most puzzling.

Renée nodded at him. "Exactement. Where there is inconsistency, there is a problem. And given this concerns Kovacs, I believe it may have implications for the current situation."

"You think *she* did this?"

Renée paused. "I'm not sure. It doesn't fit her profile. But something about this is relevant. My gut says so."

"I see." He said it in a tone that implied the opposite.

"I think something happened at this laboratory. Someone discovered her, most likely, and in her anger and betrayal, she and her fellow thieving engineers committed this gross act of arson. Or they decided to make an example as part of the riots, add chaos and a blaming game into the arena. Perhaps they were even under orders from the top of resistance."

In Lane's Intelligence file was a very detailed entry for work: "bioengineering, synapse exchange, data storage, quantum engineering." Something about that was pushing at Renée. On the face of it, working at the Lavele lab would have been ideal for someone in Lane's position, but she'd never expressed any kind of sadness at its demise.

Renée had requested the lab data from one of its exterior data centres. Apparently everything was corrupted when the lab burnt down, but they'd sent it anyway. She had people trying to recover the data. If she could find what Lane was working on, it might offer some insight into what happened.

"Or perhaps it's sheer coincidence. She might have had one too many and dropped her beer into the wrong chemical." He put the tablet back down on the desk with a sneer. "I'll be impressed if any of this proves she's involved with the hackers somehow. When you're done investigating a five-year-old incident on the basis of your gut, do let me know how you plan to arrest Kusanagi on the basis of her aiding known criminals in your jurisdiction."

There was a tense silence.

"Or I will take the matter out of your hands entirely."

She stared at his putrid face, relieved when he turned and walked out. Then his words sank in.

Merde.

Renée did not like Elleul and she did not like Tori, but most of all, she did not like the nonsensical assumption that because he was a Parliamentarian, he had authority here and she must obey it. Lane was right. This jurisdiction was hers. It might be perverse and petty, but regardless of what Tori Kusanagi had or had not done in this situation, Renée decided she would not be arresting her on Elleul's say-so.

And no doubt Elleul would take matters into his own hands regardless. Hopefully Renée had delayed him a little now. If he acted against Kusanagi, then she was on her own, but Renée suspected the methods Kusanagi used to evade Parliament spies and assassins in the core would also work here. Kusanagi knew how to keep herself alive.

Satisfied, she bent to the article about the lab. There was something important here. She could feel it.

When the article revealed nothing of any interest, she tried to recollect what Lane had told her before that first kiss. It was difficult, as the kiss had obliterated most events around it. Renée had to get Lane's hands and lips on her again, soon.

Something tugged about data storage and a small breakthrough of some kind. Lane had also said Tori Kusanagi had run off with her breakthrough, and that the notes had been lost in the explosion. Perhaps Kusanagi still had this thing, perhaps she didn't, but if it was related to the lab destruction and Helen's death, it might be relevant to the situation now.

She pulled over the tablet featuring Lane's Intelligence file. The sentence on her work and research specialities hyperlinked to other parts of the database. *Bioengineering, synapse exchange, data storage, quantum engineering.* Putain, even the keywords were tedious. She tapped at *quantum engineering*, which pulled up an extra note.

Quantum mechanics form integral parts of our physical world and the basis of many useful medical and military technologies; however, the application and development of quantum technology in the field of human modification technology and cybertronics is considered unnecessary and unethical. The implications of recent developments in quantum engineering, particularly around stabilising qubyte storage, seamless communication, cryptography, and synapse integration, cannot be overstated and are under active monitoring by Intelligence. Any work that facilitates human or organic encoding/incorporation/fusion with technology is abhorrent, unnatural, anti-life, and is to be stopped and destroyed.

Well then.

The thing was, this stuff was all terribly complicated and most of it went over Renée's head. What did work like this *look* like? All she knew about quantum things could be counted on three fingers: computing, the mind-to-synth transfer process, and transportation portals.

Mind-to-synth.

Oh. *Oh.*

Everyone knew that in order for the process to work, a person's mind had to be read and converted into digital files stored in qubytes—the only units capable of holding the vast human mind— then those qubytes transferred that data into the memory storage of the synth body. The transformation process was called entanglement, for a reason Renée didn't care enough to understand. It was one of Parliament's most hated analogue-to-digital conversions, but lucky for them it was a very unstable process.

The qubytes had less than a minute to do the transfer before they collapsed and the data dissipated with them. A successful procedure was quick and the person lost perhaps a few seconds in the process. Due to the instability and timeframes involved, synth creation was a rare and expensive exercise, done only in the last few days of expected life and only in cases of terminal illness.

Renée had never heard of it being done after a lethal accident.

Helen hadn't told her quite everything, but she'd shared enough. She'd lost *a day.* How was that possible? How was Helen walking around at all? How had Renée *missed* that?

She pulled her personal tablet over to her and stared at her notes. *Lane, breakthrough—tech some kind. Lab destroyed. Lab data corrupted. Responsible: Parliament/neoluds? Mods?*

Under that she added, *Helen mord. One day synth transfer—impossible?*

Then she sent a message to Helen: *Did you and Lane have a spare synth body ready for any accidents to either of you?*

A few seconds later, Helen wrote back: *No.*

Has Lane ever said anything about finding your body?

She mentioned once that looking for a spare synth body had been the worst thing she'd ever gone through. It took a day and nearly all our savings.

Day? A *full* day? How would a day after her death result in a functional Helen? The qubytes would have collapsed long before the data of her mind could be transferred. Très bizarre.

Renée deliberated, then wrote: *Helen, what had Lane been doing with qubyte data storage? And did she experiment on you?*

The answer took far longer to come this time. *She had been working on a way to hold data in qubytes for long periods of time without decay.*

A second message followed: *Yes, I was one of her guinea pigs.*

No, Helen hadn't shared everything. Renée felt like she'd passed some kind of test. She was on the right track.

Renée: *She succeeded.*

Helen: *Yes.*

If Renée understood all this correctly—and she made no such guarantees—this would be an incredible breakthrough. A way to keep a person's data active, complete in qubyte storage, for almost a day. It was unheard of. That would be the basis for developing that timeframe further—days, months, perhaps even years. The flexibility extra time would give people, the options it would provide, were immense.

More people would be able to use the process. It would make synth creation easier, cheaper, mainstream, more accessible, more widespread. The enhanced being movement would be galvanised like dogs running after a rabbit. Quantum technology could expand exponentially as data storage and exchange was stabilised.

It would also bring the wrath of the Parliament and the current neolud ideology down on Lane with the weight of a supergiant star.

A "small" breakthrough. How oddly modest of her.

And Lane said she'd shared her breakthrough with Tori—who had then run away with it.

The question then was: Why hadn't Tori shared it with the wider world? She of all people would recognise its impact. Renée had little interest in the contradictions of Tori's inner motivations and actions, but it was notable nonetheless.

She pulled up the feed from the Kusanagi shadow. Scanning it in its entirety, there was nothing mentioned of any strange technology on either of them. If Tori still had whatever Lane had made, she and her husband didn't flaunt it.

The notes from the previous evening stated the shadow had followed them into the industrial district near the terminal but had lost them somewhere in the warehouses. She'd spotted them a few hours later as they'd left—right before the large number of hacker-organised departures. They'd returned to the hotel and hadn't left again.

Until now. A few minutes ago, the shadow had sent an update that Tori was on the move.

Renée still remembered the pained and bitter expression on Lane's face when she'd discussed her research. Lane wouldn't be exactly forgiving of its theft. There was every possibility that whatever Lane had made and given to Tori was broken; experimental technology wasn't known for stability or durability.

However, if Lane wanted it enough, she'd take it broken. If Tori gave it back, that might be enough to convince Lane to hand over Tori's ticket out of Janus. If she did that, Renée would have to arrest her and keep her in the station jail.

Renée sent a message to the shadow: *Ascertain if she's carrying anything and where she's going.*

A few minutes later, she received a response: *Scans indicate nothing unusual on her. She is headed in the direction of Lane's Salon, but actual destination is not certain yet.*

Damn. If only Renée knew something about what this tech looked like. It could be tiny, huge, standalone, integrated . . . Merde.

Another notification: *Confirming successful bug placement.*

Her people still had the ability to astonish her. A bug was perfect. Tori would encounter a bug scan eventually, but maybe they'd pick up something implicating before she did.

She made a note about a bonus for the shadow, then tapped on the streaming icon sent via the feed and began listening in.

After visiting the station, Lane spent the afternoon uninstalling the skimmer and negotiating a new one with her hacker contact. It was wearying to correct code and read documentation via internal view—she'd had her optic nerve bolstered as part of tech integration, but the mental drag was insane—so she dug out the salon's one and only tablet and knuckled down to work. Using the tablet felt odd and quaint, but the lack of headache thanked her.

It hadn't stopped bouts of distraction. Damn Renée and her inflated self-confidence. Like hell Elleul had bought their little performance. If Renée thought he'd be keeping that promise now, she had to be mad. No way he'd keep it. If he forced the issue though, if she danced to his tune, that would spell so much potential trouble—

Worrying was stupid. So what if Renée was looking into the LHRI incident? So what if Elleul was throwing his weight around? It wasn't Lane's problem. There was zip she could do about it.

Intense knocking at the bar's front door interrupted that fun little thought, and she stepped out of her office. At the bar, Helen paused in slicing MangeX lemon slices out of the usual moulded block. They exchanged a long glance. Knocking at the door during closed hours wasn't good. No one ever came by just for a visit.

The person knocked again. Helen stayed behind the bar while Lane answered the door. When she found Tori standing in front of it, she almost closed it in her face.

Tori held the door open with her hand. "We need to talk."

"I think you and I define 'need' very differently."

"Please, Lane." Those big brown eyes pleaded with her. "We have unfinished business and we need to resolve it."

Shit.

Lane let her in and locked the door behind her. Tori still aimed to blend in: she wore a zipped hoodie, unbranded sneakers, and nondescript trousers. Her hair wasn't slicked down today; instead it waved in soft strands around her ears and jaw. Lane had an abrupt memory of when Tori's hair had been longer and her face sharper with grief and healing. She'd liked brushing Tori's hair back from her face.

Lane avoided her gaze as she led Tori toward her office. Helen eyed them, cutting in silence.

"Hi, Helen," Tori said.

Helen nodded at her, face expressionless. "Tori." She coughed suddenly, deep and hacking.

Lane paused, then opened the office door for Tori. "Go in. I'll be a minute."

Tori entered the room, and Lane went back to the bar. She leaned in close to Helen. "What is it?"

"She's bugged."

Lane frowned. "You scanned her?"

"Yeah."

"You do that a lot?"

Helen gave her the textbook expression of outraged disbelief. "Of course I do. Don't you read the statistics on illicitly planted tech?"

"Nope. Sure it's not normal tech?"

"Positive. It's in her hood."

Lane had to think it through. The hood was so obvious. Who here would— Oh, of course. Renée. Or Elleul.

"Thanks." She turned and went into her office.

Tori stood by the shelves, head angled so she could read the books on them. "You brought books with you?"

"Only a few."

"I remember these." Tori faced her, taking in the room. "This is a nice office. Can Helen hear us in here?"

"No." She'd had the office soundproofed for privacy—with the door closed not even Helen could hear anything said inside. Unfortunately, that only worked for analogue soundwaves; she couldn't block wireless signals.

Tori heaved a deep breath. "I know I shouldn't be here, but I had to come. I have so much to say to you, and our last conversation went so badly."

Lane crossed her arms. "Just get to the point."

"I wanted to say I'm sorry. I made some assumptions and didn't consider everything you might have been through."

She looked so earnest. Lane tried to remember that Tori was very good at being earnest. She also tried to remember that being argumentative wasn't a great way to have a conversation like this. "I did too. And I'm sorry too."

"What's happening in the core has changed all of us. It's unrealistic to expect you to want to see me again, or for you to be the same person I loved back then. I know things happened to you and Helen." Tori took a few steps forward. "It's, well . . . Lane, I had to . . . I *understand* your anger."

"Marvellous."

Her face fell. "Don't. You used to be so open with me."

Lane glanced at Tori's hooded sweater. The hood looked so innocuous. "Maybe I don't like double standards. Me being open, you turning out to be considerably less so. Feels kinda uneven."

"What do you want to know? I'll tell you anything."

There was an edge of desperation in Tori's voice that Lane recognised. She'd heard that edge in the voices of her patrons and people bargaining at the station about their portal ticket denials. She'd heard it in her own when she'd met with the skeevy sonofabitch who'd eventually handed over Helen's synth body. Hearing it in Tori's was a little strange—but helpful.

She went over to Tori, ignoring her expression of hope. "I've got plenty of questions for you. First things first." She reached past her for the book with the cherry liqueur and pulled out the bottle.

Tori's mouth twisted. "Oh, Lane. Really? You need a drink to get through a conversation with me?"

Lane twisted it open. "Booze has never disappointed me. Can't say the same about you." She took a sip, grimaced at the sweetness, then upended the bottle over Tori's hood. Liquid soaked through the fabric.

"The hell?" Tori unzipped the hoodie frantically and shoved it off. "What are you *doing*?"

"Oops."

Tori held it at a distance, head swivelling between her and the dripping hood. "Lane, have you gone crazy?"

Sure felt like it these days. Lane yanked the sweater from Tori, dumped it on the ground, and stomped on the hood for good measure. Something crunched under her sole. Good. The somewhat emptier bottle went back in the book on the shelf and she rounded the sofa to stand closer to Tori, who watched every movement, eyes wide.

"What's weird to me," Lane began, "is that you helped the hackers transport a bunch of people last night, extra people, yet you and Ayumu are still here. Why? They'd have put you both through."

Tori glanced at her ruined hoodie, then looked up at Lane as though seeing her for the first time. "I could ask you the same question. You've been funding their operations for years."

"Answer the damn question."

"It didn't feel right jumping the queue. Did you know there are thousands of people lined up for the hackers to send over?"

Lane did—everyone in Pann did—but Tori looked a little wary now. Hm. "Sure. Thing is: you've got better reason than most to jump queues." She plucked at a loose fibre in the sofa back. "You know what I think? I think you didn't want to end up a mangled meatsack."

Tori gave a small shrug. "It's true that there's a heightened risk with their transports, but that didn't factor into our decision."

Bullcrap. "It's okay for the rest of us, eh?"

"No. *None* of this is okay. If we can't go legally and safely, we'll use them. We're not there yet though, so why make anyone else wait longer?" She looked hurt. "Lane, you know me better than that."

Lane perched on the arm of the sofa, crossing her arms again. "Ren— The police force confiscated the power cell this morning. How did a power cell like that even happen? Where did the group find a spare power cell in Pann?"

Tori shrugged. "We have engineering contacts who printed a new one."

Cold trickled down Lane's spine. "*Printed*? You *printed* a portal gate power cell? Are you insane?"

"It'll work for a while. Isn't that what matters?"

"It could die mid-transport! There's a reason those cells are built the way they are! Fuck's sake, Tori, there are safety standards around those things for a reason."

A huge smile crossed Tori's face. "I knew it. You *do* care."

Lane tried her best to contain herself, but it was a real struggle.

Tori continued, "You're not the only one with questions. I've heard things about you here, things which have made me question if you're the person I used to know. But," and there was an awful hope in her voice, "you are, I can tell you are. You've been through so much but you still help people. I don't get it, why you insist on performing this strange, bitter act. I know you. You cared so much about the cause back then, and you still do. Listen to yourself, to your anger. Why limit yourself? Why pretend otherwise?"

This damned sincerity. Fuck it was hard to resist. "It's not an act. I look out for myself."

There was a small pause. Tori's mouth pursed. "You might have convinced Ayu, but you haven't convinced me."

"He told you what we discussed yesterday?"

"Yes." She sounded a little reluctant. "He said you have the ticket and you're not going to sell it to us because of me." Her hands clenched, unclenched, then began fidgeting together.

Lane didn't remember her having a habit like that. "And?"

"I'm not going to pretend I'm not disappointed. Of course I am. It's just that . . ." She dragged in a deep breath and set her shoulders. "Lane, you know who we are, what we're running from. It's the same thing you and Helen ran from, that everyone here is running from. You see the headlines, but the reality on the core planets is worse. Things are getting so bad there. In our *home*. I know I hurt you, but the situation goes beyond our personal feelings. You must see that, you have to if you're helping people all the time, and Lane, I—"

"Stop." The cherry turned tacky in Lane's mouth. "I get how bad it is. We all fucking do. And I'm aware that you and your work are important. I stopped caring. Your darling partner tried the same tactic and no dice. Like I said, I look out for myself and my own."

Tori closed her eyes briefly. When she opened them, they were hard. "Fine. *Fine.* You hate me and don't want to help me. At least give the ticket to *him*."

Give the ticket to Ayumu, not Tori; *that* was a novel suggestion. Selfless too. "How romantic."

"Don't mock me." Tori was calm, hands still.

Lane resisted the urge to laugh. "Why would I *ever* help your husband?"

"He's done nothing to you."

She was right, which irritated Lane.

Tori stepped closer. "You could. I know you could. I'll be all right here. I can protect myself if I have to, and we have friends who would help me. I'd risk the hacker transport as the last resort." Tori's eyes began looking shiny. "Oh Lane. You don't see what a good person he is. How kind and strong he is. He's one of the funniest, sweetest people in the world."

Lane blinked. ". . . Really?"

"You don't understand him the way I do."

"Yeah, no shit."

Tori wiped at her eyes, then headed for the other end of the sofa and sank into it. "I wanted to tell you everything at the time—and I still want to. Will you listen? You of all people deserve to hear it."

And damn it all, despite everything, Lane *did* want to know. She steeled herself.

Tori must have taken her silence as encouragement. "We fell in love at university. We were in the same groups, marching for progress and technology, the rights of cyborgs and mods. So young, so idealistic." She shook her head, hair drifting around her. "A better, more naïve time. The talks we had, the things we taught each other, the growing up we did together . . . He's not only my husband, he's my best friend. My rock, my anchor. We didn't intend on marrying, but it happened anyway. I wish you knew him better, I really do. In another lifetime, I think you'd have been friends."

In another lifetime wasn't worth thinking about, not when it wouldn't make a difference. Lane made a noise expressing as much.

Tori gave her a sad smile. "I wish we had met in another time and another place. Perhaps I could have shared a life with you *and* him. Maybe I would have married you instead of him."

Lane couldn't picture it. A hard-eyed, steely husband didn't fit in the space Lane knew as hers and Tori's. Or maybe she could and she just didn't want to.

Tori wiped her eyes again. "I love him and I want him safe. I don't want to lose anyone else. Can't you give me the ticket for him? If I promise he'll use it to leave?"

She thought Tori would follow through with that, but— "No."

Tori exhaled shakily. "Even though you help others, you won't help us?"

Lane stood, tiring of the conversation. "I don't help anyone."

Tori surged to her feet too, tears slipping down her cheeks. "You do. You *know* you do. You help the hackers. You let people make money in your salon. You give people information and you influence the prefect, but for whatever stupid reason you pretend not to do any of that. Stop lying, Lane. He called you a coward and a liar, and he was right. He missed petty and spiteful too." She reached into a pocket.

"Sorry to disappoint—"

Tori pulled out a gun and aimed it at her.

Lane stared at it. Cheap, plastic, the printed basic model sold everywhere on the streets here. Easy to obtain and carry around, didn't show up on tech scanners. She'd ignored numerous models exactly like it in town the other night. She touched her pocket, confirming her electric wand was to hand, booster attachment making it bulkier than normal. "Tori, what are you doing?"

Tori sniffed. "I'm sorry, Lane." She stepped forward, her other hand held out. "Give me the ticket."

"A gun? *You*? On me? Wow."

"I use what I have to. You're not being reasonable. You're not." Tori's voice thickened, matching the way her hand shook the gun. "I insist you give me the ticket."

Lane stared at the gun. Stars. It could be that simple? Just like that? One second and everything would be over. For her it would be permanent.

Had Helen thought like this when she'd been confronted with a gun? Lane wouldn't ever know, and neither would Helen.

Maybe this was her time to find out. Lane stepped forward until the gun pressed against her sternum, right below her breasts. "Do it." At this proximity, it would sear Lane's heart and lungs like steaks on a grill.

She kept her gaze on Tori. Tears continued falling from those big brown eyes, one after the other, and her teeth worried her lip. The gun trembled. Lane leaned in, the press of the barrel turning into a bite through her shirt. "You'd be doing me a favour," she murmured.

Tori made a wounded noise. Her mouth twisted, and she dropped the gun with a *thump*. "I can't do it. I *can't*."

"Tori."

"Not you. I can't." She shook her head. "No. Ayu, he needs to be safe, but so do you, oh *hell*." She covered her face and sobbed, broken Japanese emerging between cries.

Lane glanced down at the gun.

Orion wept.

They'd really gone there tonight. And she had thought— There was no point now. The moment was over.

Tori cried as though she'd lost something precious. Lane moved forward and hugged her, tucking Tori against her chest and neck. She fit the same against Lane; shorter, small-boned, slight, as though if squeezed too hard she'd break. Lane took in a deep breath of Tori's scent: soapy citrus with an underlying chemical tang. It wasn't unpleasant or familiar.

Tori clutched her tight and let her tears flow into Lane's shoulder.

Had Tori cried like this when leaving her? Lane would never know. After a while, she said, "You really love him."

Tori shuddered in her arms. "I do."

"And the other day, in the park, that was—"

"True. All of it. I love you too."

Fuck. It was good to hold her again. Lane closed her eyes and resisted the urge to once more run her hands through Tori's hair and kiss her forehead. It was care, the need to soothe someone upset, that was all. She honestly thought she'd never have this again, with Tori or anyone else, and Neptune's eye this brought back how charged their time together had been. All the intense feelings and discussions and connections; all of that returned as if it had happened yesterday. But it wasn't painful, not as much as she'd thought it would be. Like peeling a callus.

"You . . ." Tori sniffed loudly, fists digging into Lane's back. "You have to believe me. Those months in Lavele with you were everything to me. I was lost, grieving Ayu, and then I met you and I was lost again but in a different way." One fist dropped from Lane's back and Tori wiped her face. "The whole thing was so unexpected, wasn't it?

I found new parts of myself with you, parts I'd forgotten I had, parts I didn't realise were even there."

She leaned back to look up at Lane. "And I think I made you happy too. Do you know what that meant to me? To know I could make you happy? Me, alone, not my history or reputation? And to know I could be happy with someone else on that level, that was amazing too. Everything with you was incredible."

"Tori."

"Please, let me finish." She took a shaky breath and stepped back. Lane let her arms drop, and Tori clutched at Lane's wrists, her dark eyes intent. "Being with you was such a weight off my shoulders. With you I was just me, and everything was simpler. I know you're hurt that I didn't tell you who I was, but you see, I didn't *need* to. We were enough as we were, without all the politics and science and drama. There were other reasons too, of course. I wanted you to stay safe in your life and your work. I didn't want you brought into my world, to be touched directly by the resistance work; it's so dangerous. Your work was too important to compromise with my association. I think I was too late for that though."

Tori sighed deeply, hands warm on Lane's skin. Her thumb rubbed against the bone of Lane's wrist, and Lane resisted an urge to yank her arm away. She twisted her wrist a little, stalling the action.

Tori frowned but continued. "It was because of me, wasn't it? That Helen was killed? Intelligence found you through me."

Lane's throat was tight. She tried to clear it but failed. She shook her head instead.

Tori frowned. "What? Are you sure?"

It spilled out of her. "It wasn't Parliament operatives that killed Helen."

Tori's expression turned confounded. "Lane. What are you saying?"

Lane shook her head again. "I'm saying the blame for Helen and me, it doesn't rest on you. It doesn't. Okay?"

Tori clearly struggled for words. "I— I see. I assumed when I heard about your lab that . . . You see, after our mission had gone wrong, I went to ground. I thought Ayu and the others were dead and you saw the injuries. I deliberately delayed tapping the network once I was better. So that worked?"

"Yeah."

"I— Good. Good. I'm glad." Tori gave a small, wobbly smile. "I felt so guilty. I wanted you and Helen to be safe, but I also wanted to stay with you, in the new, easier life I could see for myself. It was fake on one level, yes, but it was so good to *not* be involved. To put all the work aside for a little while. It was selfish, but I told myself I deserved it."

Lane snorted. *Selfish*. Yes, exceedingly selfish to want a quiet life out of the line of fire. "You're terrible. Needing recovery after seeing people die. Stars and moons, I can barely look at you."

Tori glanced between her face and hands. "You're right. I could've retreated from the fight, and no one would have blamed me. But I couldn't rest, not when I saw how this Parliament is destroying lives. Do you see now? I thought I'd lost someone I loved. I'd already given up so much to do what I do. I wanted time. And you. I wanted you. I *want* you."

Tori's gaze turned intense. Lane's face grew hot.

"Lane. I don't think I can leave you again." She released Lane's wrists and stepped close, and then she was kissing her, soft lips salty and arms tight around her shoulders.

Lane's breath caught. Here. She was here and alive and still loved Lane. Moons above. Lane closed her eyes. More came back in the press of her mouth: Lavele, their love, the shy confidence Lane had discovered in loving her, the happiness despite everything. All of it was in this kiss and in the places where they touched. In a strange and distant way, this felt and tasted like home.

She'd missed this. But it wasn't the same. It felt out of place. Wrong time, wrong place. Wrong person.

Lane broke the kiss and pulled back.

Tori frowned in confusion. "Lane?"

Lane gently brought Tori's arms down. "I . . ." Her mind was whirling, and she tried to get her thoughts out. "You broke my heart. You did. And— Yeah, what's left of it does love you. In a way. You know, *you know* how I love you and how I am with you. That doesn't just go away. And things are different now. I'm different now, and we can't have what we did. Tori, what do you expect to come from this? What do you think will happen now?"

"I don't know. I truly don't." Tori brushed the backs of her fingers against Lane's cheek. "I never expected to see you again. I thought you were gone for good."

"Didn't you wonder about me and Helen?"

"Only every single day." Tori dropped her hand and crossed her arms. "I left quickly because my network found me. They needed me back. New regulations were coming in, and people were disappearing, and too many people thought I was dead. I needed to raise morale, to show people we *could* still fight, that we still have power. And the network found me through government channels, which meant Intelligence knew where I was. My people planned riots to cover the operation to extract me from Lavele. I *had* to go."

Lane wanted to shake her. "You could've said something. You could've left a tag, a post, a text, a fucking *note*."

Tori looked wretched. "I told myself I was keeping you safe, that you and Helen would be all right. You're both so practical. You'd stay out of trouble."

And that was the ice-cold bucket of reality Lane hadn't realised she'd needed. She took a few steps back. "We weren't and we didn't."

Tori clearly didn't like the change in distance if the way her mouth twisted was any indicator. "I—"

"Look," Lane rushed on, "you've explained what happened, and I'm grateful. I am. But we have to think about now. If you're here and trying to get to Fides, you're in immediate danger. I understand that."

Tori nodded. "Elleul is here for us. I'm certain of it. If there's any choice in the matter, I'd send Ayu. Or you." She seemed sad. "Part of me wants to tell you to take it and go. You deserve to be free too. You know that, right?"

Like she'd dignify that with a response.

When the pause turned into silence, Tori shifted her weight uncertainly. "Why *haven't* you used it? Don't you want to?"

It wasn't an option. "No."

Tori sat back down on the sofa with a sigh. "What a mess."

Lane eyed the gun on the floor, then kicked it away from the sofa before Tori noticed. "Understatement."

"I don't know what the right thing is. You're as necessary as he is. I want all three of us over there in safety."

How optimistic.

Tori smiled, small and sad. "The dreams I've had, about you and me, and me and Ayu, and us three . . . Lane, I've missed you *so much*."

This time, it didn't hurt to hear that. "I missed you too."

"I'm sorry about what happened. I'm sorry about tonight. And I'm sorry about the qubicon."

Lane started. The qubicon. She'd forgotten.

"I know it was wrong to take it," Tori said. "I was so used to having it on me, I didn't even think about it. If I hadn't rushed, I would've left it."

She didn't look guilty at all. Instead of mentioning how leaving things behind was generally easier than not, Lane asked, "It still works?"

"Yes." Tori's smile strengthened. "It still works. I do the upload every morning and evening. You're a genius. You really are."

Lane had never felt less like a genius.

"When Ayumu told me what you said to him, I thought you either hated me or you wanted the qubicon." Tori's gaze was level. "Maybe both?"

Lane moved aside and walked to her bookshelves. The books she'd brought with her, the ones Tori had recognised, sat front and centre. They'd formed one small but integral part of her research. The notes, the models, the code, Helen's prototype and the others she'd been building, she'd destroyed all of that. But not the books. They'd inspired her career. She couldn't remember what she'd left so these could come with her. If Tori had given her qubicon back, Lane would've wrecked it too. No traces left behind. Just the dream of it carried with Lane in her baggage, dried seeds of an idea between dry lines of academic prose.

And if Tori gave it to her now, what would she do with it?

Five years ago it would've been twisted plastic and metal, no question. Now? She was tempted, but she wasn't sure.

The possibilities were overwhelming: Lane could continue her career, could build and create things again. She could work with the body-machine connection once more. She could extend qubyte technology. Frankly, it was incredible that the qubicon still worked. The prototype she'd given Tori had improvements on Helen's, so who knew how well it would work in tests. If her *prototype* was this stable, the implications were immense. The work she could do on entangled quantum molecules, the potential of extending their captured state, stabilising it further—life could be so different.

Having to keep the work away from the Parliament bugs and scanners and netbots would be worth it, but immensely difficult. She'd have a target on her back, one as large as Tori's. Lane wasn't interested in that kind of life. She also wasn't interested in the people who'd see her technology the way Tori did, as a means of furthering their agendas.

Nah, the best thing she could do was what she'd done in the first place: destroy it and make damn sure no one could manipulate her with it ever again.

But the prototype had Tori in its keeping. Having any version of Tori Kusanagi's mind at her disposal wasn't a situation she wanted to handle.

"Lane."

She turned around.

Tori lingered near her, her expression hopeful. "I can bring the qubicon to you if you want. I'll give it back." Tori bit her lip. "You don't need to give me the ticket in exchange."

That cursed ticket. Lane should've tossed Fentiman out on his ass. "That wouldn't be fair. Besides, the qubicon's linked to you. If you leave it with me, the entanglements would eventually collapse. That defeats the purpose of it."

"No. It's your research, your invention. It should be with you. Let my data go; what do I matter in the face of tech like that?" One side of her mouth twitched upwards. "Besides, if Ayu went and I stayed, it would stay too. Maybe I could keep using it. If anything happened to me before I could get out, you'd keep me safe." She reached out and touched Lane's arm. "I trust you with it. With me. You know that, right? If we were here together, we might be able to make amends. Be together. I don't see a downside to this."

Lane couldn't imagine it. There was no sense of permanency in Pann, not even for her and Helen. Tori didn't fit in at all with the smoky streets under the cutting light of the ring. Living here, buying groceries, finding work, bribing people to leave her alone—it didn't fit. Tori Kusanagi stormed into situations, saved lives, and got out before the Parliament caught up. She kept moving. Lane's Yui—idealistic, soft—wouldn't last long in a city like this.

And if Ayumu meant so much to her, Lane doubted she'd be happy here without him. And if Tori kept on helping refugees avoid the trip queue, as Lane suspected she would, Renée might be forced to arrest Tori eventually.

She shook her head. "No. Forget it." She glanced back at the books, then faced Tori. "I'll give you the damn ticket. Use it for yourself or Ayumu. I don't care."

Tori's hopeful expression turned pained, and her hand tightened on Lane's arm. "Was the qubicon all I needed to offer?"

Lane shook her off, then felt bad and patted Tori's shoulder to reassure her. "Nah. You were right. We needed to talk."

"I said more than you did."

That took her back. Tori had always been chattier. She'd used to say Lane had been like a clam in difficult conversations: tight-lipped and hard to prise open.

Lane had never agreed with that. "Tori."

"I'm glad I could finally explain what happened to me, and that we talked this out." Tori's gaze searched hers. "I know we can't be the same as we were, but you haven't changed as much as you think. I know you've been hurt and life here wasn't what you wanted, but you're still the person I remember and love. You help the hackers, you help other people, and now you're helping us." She grasped Lane's hand and heaved a large breath. "You had me worried. I'd heard things about the prefect, about you and her being close."

Renée. Lane didn't want to think of her right now. "That doesn't concern you."

"Lane, she's a textbook corrupt official! I'm amazed you speak to her at all."

"I said, it's none of your business."

"I'll always worry about you." Tori squeezed her hand. She had more calluses than Lane remembered. "You're aware of her background, right? She's Janus through and through—police officer, rich parents, cushy life. Her dismissal was a management reshuffle and she came here to sulk."

"Sulking isn't how I'd describe her."

"Well, from what people here have said to me, she's waiting until she's been forgiven and can return. I don't care what her statistics say, she doesn't care about her job." Tori ran her hand along Lane's arm. "I don't know what's going on between you two, whether it's friendship or something else. But even if you're friends, you have to know she can't be trusted. She won't help you. She won't help us. People on their side never do."

Lane was aware of all that already. Rationally. What had Renée said? Something about people not being logical. Yeah. "Are you done?"

"No. I can tell you're putting on an act for this place, and maybe for her, but you don't have to. Don't limit yourself. You could be so much more. I'm just so glad you're still doing the right thing, still fighting the good fight."

Perhaps there was a universe in which Lane was actually the way Tori saw her. Lane wasn't sure how to tell her there was no act, not for Pann and not for Renée. Maybe she bluffed a little, but she wasn't pretending or lying.

In a way, she wished Renée was here right now. A sharp joke would be welcome, as would a pointed wink and that wordless, mutual understanding.

Nonetheless, it was flattering that Tori could see something good or hopeful in her, even now, after all this. Lane was certain she'd left her better qualities at the bottom of a whisky glass on the trip out of the core. Maybe she hadn't.

Tori hesitated, then came closer, her hand running up Lane's arm to her shoulder. From here, Lane could smell her, a slight tang from the dust and pollution clouding a softer linen. Tori glanced down—at Lane's mouth?—then met her eyes. "I will always be there for you, Lane. Now that I've found you again, I'm not letting you go. No matter what. If I leave, I'll organise a trip for you out of here. If I stay, I'll do that the same. Even if we're separated by a galaxy, by a universe, I'll love you and I'll help you and I'll stay in contact with you. You're not on your own anymore."

The way her words tumbled out of her, over and over, eyes shining as she tried to make sure she was heard, she was *understood*— Lane had forgotten that. There was something beautiful about her unwavering constancy and optimism. Lane's throat went tight and a prickle of discomfort rolled along her back and shoulders. "Tori, you don't have to—"

Tori bent down and kissed Lane's palm. There had been other times when Tori had done that, and while it had never felt amazing, she used to like the affection and romance in the gesture. Now there was calm surprise at the shallowness of the touch. A dry brush of lips on her skin, a warm touch of breath, then the childish urge to pull her hand back and wipe it against her overalls.

Lane resisted, barely. Not the time, not when Tori looked as open as she did. "Don't. Not ... Look, I ..."

Tori rose, face hopeful.

"I need to process all this."

"Yes! Of course. Can I come back later tonight? I have a meeting to attend, but I could bring the qubicon afterwards."

Lane tugged her hand free. "You might want to cool it on those meetings. Salus isn't like the core, but that doesn't mean attending isn't dangerous. Same goes for helping the hackers."

"It's fine. I'll be careful. I'll bring it, and we can talk more."

"Won't Ayumu notice?"

"Yes. Don't worry about him, he'll understand."

That seemed like an overstatement of his generosity, but the nice part about being in her position was that Lane didn't have to give a shit about him. "Sure. Come by. I'll be waiting for you."

Tori's face lit up. She stood and wrapped her arms around Lane, kissing her again. Lane hesitated, let herself have that taste of home again, then ended the kiss. It was too strange now, after all this time. Almost foreign.

She took a step back, Tori watching her with a familiar interest. She ran a hand down Lane's side to her hip. "Lane. We don't have to, but we—we could ... while we're here ..." Her hand pressed in, asking. Again, the way she used to.

Lane hadn't expected this. She never did *expect* this, regardless of partner. That at least hadn't changed. But this felt so off, so forced, especially compared with the ease she had with Renée.

They really had changed.

"I, uh." She backed away, leg bumping into the coffee table.

Tori watched her with a small knowing smile. "See, you're still the same. I don't think I ever told you how much it meant that you trusted me to make it good for you. We have time now, and it's been so long. It's amazing, almost miraculous, to reconnect with you. Do you think you could?"

"No."

"Are you sure? I want to show you we still work together, the way we used to. I know there hasn't been anyone else." Her voice turned a little bitter. "Even if the rumours about you and the prefect are true, I can't see you sleeping with her."

If Renée were here, she'd be so unimpressed. More and more, Lane wished she was—not in her official capacity, obviously, but to help Lane deal with this disaster of a conversation. "I said no. You and I aren't together, and this isn't us anymore."

Tori's face fell.

Lane tried to summon some tact. "We've said a lot tonight and I need some time to think."

"You're right. It's too soon." Tori held her arms out. "I'm glad we found each other again."

Lane hesitated, then hugged her. "Me too."

Tori held her tight, her arms bony but strong. "I'll see you later tonight."

"Sure."

Lane ushered her out the salon and locked the door behind her, breathing a sigh of relief. Salus's ring, that had been a lot. Had Tori always been so intense? So certain of herself? Lane didn't think so, but five years had dulled enough memories that she wasn't sure.

Helen had finished organising the bar and had migrated to a corner where she was busy placing her latest sculpture. Something bulky and big; Lane honestly didn't care. Weak late-afternoon sunlight filtered through the windows; they would open soon. Back to the usual routine of admin, bouncing, and drinking. Lane beelined for the bar and the top shelf. She picked up a bottle of Event Horizon, bit her lip, and began pouring a healthy dose when she heard Helen walk over.

"What did she have to say?" Helen asked.

"Nothing important."

"Sure, sure, nothing important would make you reach for the whisky quicker than normal." Helen paused. "I *think* that's quicker than normal."

Lane placed her glass down and glared at her. "I have needs, you know."

"Out with it. And put that back."

She returned the bottle to the shelf. "She left Lavele because she was needed by the resistance, plus Intelligence was onto her. What happened between us was accidental, but, um, meaningful. She still loves me. She's going to give the qubicon back. Lots of tears about me giving her or Ayumu the stupid ticket, because of freedom, safety, the movement, blah blah blah." Lane gazed at the whisky, wanting the burn. "What *didn't* she say. Excuse me for a few hours."

"No way." Helen came right up to the bar, hand held out. "Give."

"Hell no."

They glared at each other before Lane drank deeply. The sheer *relief* from the burn was both worrying and freeing. "I'm fine."

"You don't seem so, not even by your standards."

Lane sucked in a breath, then let it out. "We worked some things out. We still love each other. But it's not the way it was, and . . . I suppose I wondered if it could be. I'm not sure why. She wants to continue where we left off." She pressed her hand to her eyes. "I need to think this over." Not least because Renée fit in there, and she wasn't sure how.

"Think *what* over?" Helen's sarcasm hadn't changed. So much conveyed in a few choice words. The familiarity was comforting. "I bet Renée would have something to say about that whole love spiel. I've got some thoughts too."

"It's not up to either of you. And we're *not together*."

"You and Tori, or you and Renée?"

Lane was ready to strangle her. "And you wonder why I drink." She had to focus on the bigger issue. "The important thing is she's bringing me the qubicon and I'm giving her the ticket."

Helen's fingers tapped a pattern on the counter. "Just like that?"

"No, not just like that. She's desperate, and so's he, but the ticket's for him. She wants him safe, and said she could be here without him."

Helen shook her head. "It's not logical. I don't believe her."

"You didn't see how she looked."

"I don't care. Her work involves persuading people to her cause. If she loved you so much, she could've found you before now. The system isn't *that* big."

Lane hadn't thought of that.

"And she knew your real name," Helen added. "You didn't know hers."

Once they'd made it to Salus and landed in their apartment, Lane had tried searching for Yui. She'd contacted old friends, tried a few services that specialised in finding people, reached out via the hacking groups in Pann, and once she'd become friends with Renée, had even played with the idea of asking her to try the government databases before deciding it would bring more trouble than it was worth. None of it had led anywhere.

The reason was obvious now, but it wouldn't have been the same for Tori. Lots of people in Lane's position, with a vulnerable family member and a subversive work history, had fled to the edges of the habitable zone—Salus on this side of the system, and the two planets currently orbiting the opposite side of the sun and closer to the other safe star system. People had collected on the habitable zone borders like leaves blocking a gutter. Lane had had certain records wiped, but if Tori had wanted to, really wanted to, she could have found them.

Five *years*.

"Probably," she said, "but she thought it was too dangerous to try."

Helen leaned on the counter. "I was afraid of this. Don't buy whatever she's selling, Lane."

Lane closed her eyes, not wanting to see that expression on this face. "You know what I'm like with people. How hard it is to make a connection like that. I had love with her, and I still do."

Helen was quiet. Then, "Oh, Lane."

Lane opened her eyes to find Helen pensive and unmoving in that eerie synth way. "I know. I can't . . ." She resisted glancing at the music centre, with the damned ticket in the old drive. "Fuck. The past is harder to shake off than I thought. This is bullshit."

"I could've told you that years ago."

Another mouthful of whisky. "I'm going to the office. I need to think."

"We're opening in half an hour."

Lane scoffed. "What do you think I'm going to do in there?"

"Drink your office dry, that's what." Helen straightened. "What about Renée?"

Yes, what *about* her? Lane glared. "She's at work. She wouldn't care anyway. You know what she's like."

"Actually, I think she would." Helen crossed her arms—and that annoyed Lane even more, because it was a fucking gimmick. Helen didn't feel uncomfortable. She didn't *feel* anything. She responded as programmed. "She likes you. She told me so."

"Suddenly you're on her side?"

"I'm not saying that, I'm saying . . ."

Lane poured herself more whisky for the road.

Helen's eyes narrowed. "I'm saying stay sober for once and think about who your real friends are."

Fuck that. Lane retreated to her office.

The gun still lay on the floor. Lane disengaged the battery, then put it on a table by the door; Tori could retrieve it later. The same went for her hoodie. When Lane picked that off the floor, a worse-for-wear bug fell out of the soaked hood. Lane caught it, then held it up and squinted. A tiny red light shone in the crushed, sticky frame.

It still worked. And had been working, sending their conversation straight to whatever feed the shadow had set up in the police intranet.

What was that wonderfully versatile word Renée used for moments like this? *Putain.*

CHAPTER
NINE

The rain started in the late afternoon, drumming softly on the roof of the police station. Renée found the distant patter soothing as she worked at her desk well into the evening. She caught up on ticket approvals and read through more reports and issued several arrest warrants. She managed to read the entire Analytics report on the hackers' accounts and activities, right to the last gif. Amazing what a bad mood could do. Even scrolling through endless surveillance feeds felt productive. Her team monitored quite a number of people; more than Renée had expected, if she was honest. Why Elleul had such a low opinion of them was beyond her.

Everyone on the day shift had left, including Elleul. Lingering was quite unlike her, but then again, nothing had been normal lately, so perhaps it was to be expected. She eventually tired of torturing herself and left her office for a break.

The station was quiet. A skeleton crew worked the night shifts at the station, waiting for callouts, monitoring feeds, writing reports, and patrolling the jail when there were people to watch. No one approached her. The night officers tended to be a silent bunch, though she supposed she could put their current reticence down to surprise at seeing her there. She didn't speak with them, instead striding through the bullpen to the break room.

Mistake. The break room stank of MangeX fish and coffee. Her hangover was gone and she was too worked up for coffee. She moved on to the jail.

Empty for once. She avoided looking at the cell that had been Fentiman's.

Walking around wasn't helping her mood. Leaving perhaps would, but things here felt unfinished for some reason. Home didn't appeal. Neither did the salon.

She stalked down the corridor between the cells and the bullpen. She needed distraction. Talking to her staff would work but be strange. Perhaps she should speak with her people more so it wouldn't be as odd to strike up a conversation with them. If only she was hungry; ordering food and eating it would be a welcome distraction. Anything to avoid acknowledging that she wanted to find Tori Kusanagi and slap her.

That *ridiculous* feed. She should fire the shadow. Whoever had decided eavesdropping on people was a good intelligence strategy should have been shot. Tori hadn't said anything clear about the hacker transports or the refugees or money transfers. Some snippets and words, but nothing substantial. Instead, Renée had the tinniest, crackliest recording of a confession on the planet *and* she'd been subjected to little details of the Kusanagis' love lives.

Ugh. Knowing Tori's idea of relationship bliss was akin to considering Elleul's: unnecessary and awful. If she wanted this kind of nonsense in her life, she'd tune into those dreadful drama serials that had been streaming since the invention of cross-system signal boosters.

If that wasn't enough, hearing the person she wanted kissing someone else had to be on the Parliament's list of acceptable torture methods. If not, they were missing a trick. She'd stopped listening at the kissing part—it had turned staticky anyway—but the feed kept loading into her report while she moved on to other things.

It wasn't that she didn't understand. Of course she did, it was all immensely understandable. Everyone had ex issues. That didn't matter. What mattered was when those ex issues walked through the door as a living, breathing person—and not just any person, one whose name would go down in history—and explained with great eloquence and many tears how they were still in love, and their very real reasons for leaving. Lane was many things, but heartless wasn't one of them.

No one was to blame.

It still hurt.

Times like these, she wished she could call her cousin, Nicolette. Nico was wonderful to rant to. She'd pass out cigarettes and listen and nod, condemn everyone to hell, then somehow find a way to make everything wonderful again. Papa would've made some terrible jokes about having the woman in question hunted down. Maman would hug her and pour a good glass of wine.

Merde, she missed them. What she wouldn't give to be able to talk things through with them.

Thinking of them wasn't helpful.

Not that Renée would have handled the same situation any better, though she'd never know and liked to think she would. None of Renée's exes had been like Tori, still in love yet stolen away by dramatic circumstance. She'd also never been in a relationship involving that kind of intense connection. Not until now, maybe. At least all of Renée's exes and her few Pann flings had done her the service of staying out of contact. If only Tori had done the same.

As for pulling a weapon on Lane—

She came to a standstill in the middle of the bullpen.

Honestly. What theatrics. Pointing a weapon, then crying over love. Most people left that kind of thing behind in their twenties. Someone with Tori Kusanagi's gravitas should be above that. However, now that Renée thought it over, was it *so* strange for a resistance fighter, someone known for violence in the name of her ideology, to do such a thing? Or to be so desperate to leave that she'd try it? She was human too. Then again, most of the refugees on Renée's approvals list didn't feel the need to shake weapons in Renée's face when making their woeful arguments for leaving. Some of them had to be resistance members themselves, and they'd managed to refrain from threats.

And this was the person who Lane had loved. Who supposedly loved her. Who Lane still loved in return, if she'd heard things right.

Renée tried to remember if she'd ever done such a thing to Lane, without a weapon of course. She didn't think so. Her officers sometimes carried weapons, but she limited them to nonlethal arms. The lethal ones used for emergencies were gathering dust in one of the lockers. The weight of her position was threat enough to some, and she didn't throw it around lightly. Lane had never given a damn.

Why Lane? Of all people? Why did Kusanagi have to love *her*?

And why couldn't Lane see what Kusanagi was doing? The position she was putting Lane into? It was abhorrent.

She stalked out of the bullpen back to her office. Nico may not be here to help make things right, but perhaps she could take a stab at it herself. Call Lane, explain herself.

Then she realised this would confirm she'd bugged Kusanagi, and she'd have to admit it to Lane, and argh, the embarrassment.

Her tablet rang. She pulled it out to see Lane's name and photo appear. What a coincidence. She kicked the door shut behind her and answered. "Oui?"

"Please tell me the bug was Elleul's." There was a familiar slur to Lane's voice.

Renée settled on the edge of her desk, tablet to ear. "Alas, my darling, I cannot."

Lane cursed. "Renée!"

"I am what I am, and I must do what I must do."

"Bullshit." There was a *thunk*—maybe a foot on the floor or an elbow on a table. "You could distract him. You could run rings around him if you wanted to. But instead you're doing what he wants and collecting dirt on Tori and me. Aren't you?"

"It's not exactly what he wants." Rain pattered on her window. It was quite soothing. Renée watched the drops streak down the surface of the glass. "What he wants is the ticket and missive in hand, and Kusanagi dead or on a penal ship back to the core. You too, if your abilities are worthwhile to the cause, and we both know they are."

Lane snorted. "What abilities? What is *with* people telling me I'm amazing all of a sudden?"

"Perhaps if you didn't forget yourself in your cups, you would agree with us," Renée said, slightly dismayed at agreeing with Kusanagi on this. "He is a dangerous man and I'm not in a position to *run rings* around him. I'm doing what I can to slow him down."

"Yeah, nah." There were some indistinct sounds, then the clear *glug* of liquid through a bottleneck. "I dunno what game you're playing, but it's doing you no favours."

"For myself or with you?" Renée scowled at the floor. "And it's not as though I'm the only one playing games. Kusanagi is a master at them."

There was a small pause. "Okay, how much of that did you hear?"

"Enough."

Overhead, the patter of rain became deeper thumps.

"'Enough' meaning what, exactly?"

"'Enough' meaning I wonder why you're calling me and not her."

"You're angry." Lane sounded surprised.

"You expect me *not* to be?"

Lane went very quiet, but Renée could still hear the muttered, "I don't fucking know." There was a loud sigh. "Look. I told you already. She and I, we're not together."

"That isn't what I heard. I heard a confession of feelings from both of you and a promise from her to return later tonight."

"I did a number on that bug, huh? Sure. Yeah, we have history and that doesn't just go away, but it doesn't mean anything's happening now. That's what I said to her, by the way."

That was some relief, but not much. "While I'm glad to hear it, that's not my only concern. You're trading the ticket for your amazing technology—don't deny you have it, we both know you do. She expects you to return to her side as part of the resistance, and frankly, given what this tech does, you'd be foolish not to."

Lane drew in a sharp breath. "You know what my invention is?" Her voice went hard. "You've been digging into *me*?"

"Not in the ways I want to, but yes." Renée glanced at one of the tablets on her desk, the one waiting a report from Analytics. "You mentioned it and I looked into it. If my understanding is correct, your invention is game-changing. You had a breakthrough, Kusanagi stole it, and now she's trading it for her ticket out of Janus. It seems relevant."

"I can't believe you're investigating me. What happened to the prefect who avoided her job at all costs?"

Renée tsked. "Lane, that's remarkably unfair. I do a lot of my job."

"And your officers do the rest. Right until your old employer came calling and offered you your old life back, and suddenly you're so very thorough."

"As if you're not tempted by the same thing." Renée stood and began pacing the frayed carpet near the window. "You helped enhanced beings in the past. Your invention could boost quantum tech. With improvements, it could even help synth creation go mainstream. You're funding hacker group portal trips for refugees. You're not fooling anyone—not Kusanagi, not Elleul, and not me."

Lane's silence was damning, with a slight hint of sulkiness.

"If you help her, you'll be a new target for Intelligence and Parliament. If your invention gets leaked, and there's a chance it will given Elleul's interest in you and in Kusanagi, you'll have the Parliament chasing you too."

"You mean the NZC won't protect me? Shocking."

Renée bit back a string of curses. "It can only do so much. *I* can only do so much. Rogue actors can come through at any time, like Elleul or that diplomat."

"You just don't want me to help her."

She exhaled in one long breath. "And *yes*, it frustrates me that you're willing to be in danger for this woman."

"You know what I hear? A Janus officer telling me *not* to help a mod."

Lane wasn't in Janus anymore; she had said that herself often enough. Why this now? Couldn't she see what was happening? "I'm telling you to help *yourself*."

There was a startled pause. "You're saying skip town."

It would be best for Lane. No doubt. Did Renée like the idea? Irrelevant. "As long as you have that ticket, I can't stop you."

"Wow. Wooow. You're saying leave my sister, my salon, and— Well, shit, that's noble of you. Not very law-abiding though. Or patriotic."

"Au contraire, it would be entirely legal. You're a refugee too, and the stipulations of the ticket allow you passage. And if you left before I could arrest you for having stolen goods, it can't be my fault. After all, we didn't find it on you before. How could I know you had it?"

This time the pause felt longer. "I'm surprised."

Renée was too, if she was honest with herself.

"Is that what you want me to do?" Lane's voice had turned calmer.

Yes and no. "I think what I want doesn't matter in light of your safety."

"Stars above," Lane said. "I should be sober for this. You're not fucking around tonight."

No, she supposed not.

"I'll return the favour. If I did leave, that would keep the Kusanagis here long enough. They'd eventually do something you'd catch, and you or your officers would arrest them. Elleul would be happy, you'd get that pardon, and then it's bon voyage Pann and hello Newport." Lane sighed. "Hello home and family who are hopefully still around and haven't pissed off anyone important. The pardon would make everything better. Put things right for you. You don't have tech; you're *unpolluted*. I hope it's worth it, because you'd owe Elleul and Parliament for the rest of your life."

Renée was speechless. It felt very strange.

Then Lane said, "I think you could swing it, you know."

"Oh?" Her voice croaked for some reason.

"Yeah. You could handle it. Fuck, you'd have them eating out of the palm of your hand. You can do anything."

"Is that what you want for me?"

"If that's what you want for yourself." The silence on the line was heavy. "Orion wept. Y'know? All this? Exactly why I never talk politics with you."

Renée smiled despite herself. "And I with you, ma chère."

"You're still an asshole for investigating me. And another thing—" A series of thumps—knocks?—came through the connection. "Shit. Why the fuck did I decide to run a business again? I'll speak to you later. This isn't settled. I think you're an idiot for going along with him."

"Likewise for you with her. Don't make any rash decisions. Bon nuit."

Lane hung up.

The rain was heavy now, sounding like buckets on the roof of the station. Renée was at a loss. She had a terrible feeling in her stomach, yet somehow, that horrible conversation had put a smile on her face. Some of what Lane had said stung, but it was always a joy to speak with her.

Perhaps she should eat something after all.

She went to the kitchen and dug through the staff fridge for food. There was always something forgotten or unlabelled— Ah. Two pork buns, perfect. As she ate, she walked through the building and mulled.

In vino veritas. A type of *veritas*, in any case, as Lane wasn't prone to wine. So she truly didn't think Renée was ineffective. What a pleasant discovery. Renée would argue that, in the face of Elleul, former Intelligence and High Member of Parliament, gentle incompetence was in fact rather a good strategy.

She stopped short, chewing thoughtfully. In his face, yes. But he wasn't always around, and Lane was right that she didn't have to dance to his tune. She wasn't. It might not seem like it to idiot mods who considered anything short of open rebellion total acquiescence, but even if Renée somehow made it home, she could still ensure her officers were free to do their work as required by the committee. She might be Janus born and bred, but unlike Lane's unpatriotic insinuation, that wasn't a bad thing.

"Prefect?"

She turned to the side. One of her officers stood next to her, looking a little worried. "Are you all right?"

She'd stopped in front of the bullpen. The skeleton crew who staffed the station overnight were all watching her.

"Yes. Is there an issue?"

"You're just standing here. Without saying anything. And you've been walking around without saying anything for a while now. With respect, Prefect, it's not like you."

They had a point. She straightened and stuffed the second bun into her pocket. "Ah, true. Well-observed."

"Is it Elleul?"

That question caused all activity to stop. Her colleague was tense, posture tight and defensive, and the staff in the pen all wore worried expressions now.

Okay. No time like the present. "What do you mean? Is he causing problems for the night shift?"

The officer shifted their weight. "To be frank, Prefect, yes. He's causing problems for everyone."

How utterly expected. "Such as?"

"He orders us around, tells us to ignore procedure. He wants us to keep making arrests without warrants. He's got my Intelligence file and, well, he says he can add whatever he wants to it. He"—their voice went lower—"keeps demanding access to our records. Those are NZC records. He doesn't allow us to see what he does in there."

Renée hoped Analytics and Tech had been tracking that. "Noted."

"Is there anything you can do?"

She shrugged. "Until he decides to leave, not much." Not that that would stop her. She had authority here; Elleul did not. Time to remind her staff of their allegiance. "Not much that I may do *openly*."

Her colleague gave a small, hopeful smile.

She gazed around the bullpen. "I remind you—all of you—that you are public servants of the Neutral Zone and are subject to me, to the committee, and to the people of Pann. Not to the Janus Parliament. We can and must help Member Elleul within the fullest extent of our legal reach, but cannot and *should not* go any further. This is Pann. This is *our* jurisdiction. We are in control. Parliament has limited power and reach here, and you must remember that when acting and when following orders, regardless of whatever information and influence he has to hand. Comprenez?"

Her staff nodded. The one in front of her said, "Oui, Préfet. We're with you."

She took them in. She'd inherited a few, but many of these people had signed on under her command. It was probably the emotion of the moment, but she felt very proud of them. At some point, she'd try to memorise their names. "We have means of our own to work around him. I will ensure nothing he says or does will affect you or our operations here. I advise you to *appear* to help him, but you have my permission to take your time, lose files, be slow to respond, and anything else you can think of." Expressions of relief broke out around her. "Get back to your work."

The officer in front of her saluted. How sweet. She patted their shoulder and moved on, heading to the back of the building, where Analytics and Tech were. That had been good. She'd convinced herself at least. Now time to see what Elleul had been doing, and what she could do in return.

She found one person in each department, both diligently scanning images and code on their large screens. She went to Tech first and asked if Tech had been monitoring Elleul's changes to their database and his general tablet activity. She confirmed they had.

Renée told her to continue monitoring and to be ready to change the database back to its original state when instructed.

Then she turned to the Analytics officer, who hid a yawn, then smiled at her. "Excellent timing, Prefect. I have some reports for you."

Reports appeared on her tablet within seconds, and she brought them up.

First was a dedicated report on the vast warren of data feeds into and out of the hacker groups from financial accounts across Salus. Simply looking at it induced a headache, so Renée skipped it.

Second was an extract of the money feeds from notable Pann businesses. Small trickles of money that had combined into significant sources of funding. Not just from Lane, but from local businesses across the city. There was even one from a pastry vendor outside the portal terminal. How wonderful that her officers had already solved the crime Lane had reported earlier that day.

Moons above, it had only been *one* day.

But there was no trace of the Kusanagis in there. None of their known aliases, nothing that was related to them. There were multiple anonymous cash injections into one of the hacker accounts that might prove promising, but Analytics would need more time to break through the encryptions around those.

Elleul wouldn't be pleased. Good thing she didn't have to speak to him until tomorrow.

The third report was brief and referenced a directory location on their server. She clicked into it and found the recovered files from the Lavele hearing aids laboratory.

"We couldn't recover everything," Analytics said, pointing out the directory on his screen. "The virus was amateur. It superficially corrupted 82% of the data with garbage code. Okay to clean up, but 38% of the core data was still irretrievable. However, there're literal petas of data to go through, so there's hope you'll find what you need."

Renée tapped into search, found the researcher node, then navigated to Lane's user directory. *lkovacs*, how original. In it were thousands of files and folders, some clearly labelled and others not. Some folders were empty or corrupted. She sighed at the sight of it.

"Do you know what you're looking for?" Analytics asked.

"Something called a qubicon," Renée said. That was what Tori and Lane had called it.

Analytics ran a search and shook his head. "No. Nothing here under that name."

As though it would be so easy. Knowing Lane, she had assigned some hilarious filename to her project to offset searches like this. "I'll keep looking. Excellent work." Renée glanced over at Tech. "If you haven't already, you and Tech should discuss Elleul's activities. I want whatever changes he's made to be logged and removed once he leaves, whenever that will be."

Analytics straightened, face lighting up. "Three steps ahead of you, Prefect."

"Good. If he sends out requests to the core concerning adjustments to anyone's file, or requests involving any personnel here, I want them blocked. Any information downloaded on his devices shall be stored for later perusal by us."

Tech and Analytics exchanged a glance. She really *should* remember her force's names. Bah. Tomorrow. "This is possible, oui?"

"Bien sûr," Tech replied. "I'm just concerned. He's from the *Parliament*. A lot of his information requests include Intelligence files. I understand they're, well, the classified versions. It's a lot of personal data we're not supposed to hold."

Renée was both impressed and unimpressed, which was an interesting mix of feelings. "What are we, Officer?"

"Uh—"

"Neutral Zone. Most of us come from the core, of course, and some from Fides. But we are not *in* the core, are we? And we are not subject to their laws or influence." Renée bent down. "And I am in charge here. Not him. If those files refer to our personnel, it seems only right that our colleagues decide what to do with their own information. After all, we can delete them whenever necessary. We'd be very happy to comply with Intelligence on this, should they find out. But it seems a little unfair that Elleul knows so much about us, but we don't know what. And I, for one, am tired of his methods of operation. What about you?"

Tech slowly smiled. "Moi aussi, Préfet."

"I gave you an order."

"You did." She beamed now. "Consider his communications limited to our channels, and any adjustments to files blocked from Intelligence channels."

"Excellent. If asked, by the way, I never issued that order."

Analytics cleared his throat. "There's one more thing, Prefect." He glanced around, then pulled out his personal tablet, obvious from the orange stickers plastered on its back. "I found the missive."

The missive? The diplomat's missive? Merde, she'd forgotten.

She sat next to him. Analytics glanced at Tech, then turned to Renée. "Please don't ask me how I know this channel."

She looked him over. He stared back, not one implant or piece of tech visible. Hmm. The presence of the tablet suggested lack of tech too, but it could be a ruse. Some mods didn't do the ocular adjustments and liked having a screen to physically put away. Whatever his modified status, he was either a resistance member himself or he knew someone who was. She could figure out how to exploit this later. "Understood."

He tapped into a non-mainstream text channel, a basic hub that Renée could tell was used for sending short strings of information and not much else. Easy to set up, encrypt, and shut down. Ideal for quick, secret communications. Analytics's hand shook slightly. "This channel is highly encrypted and used by one of the resistance cells on Salus." He tapped in a query, and the channel returned a block of data and metadata. She scanned it to find the pertinent part:

Retrieved 21:34:04.33 from 4522:1125:9384:9472:7544

Search took 0.000000003s

Seller: leechF Source: JP Intelligence

Body:

INSTRUCTIONS Use ticket to travel to C.P. in system Fides. Access refugee centre in C.P. Locate below individuals and terminate them. Remove all evidence. Return to HQ and confirm mission complete.

A list of names followed—including both Kusanagis—then multiple tags for search and later distribution.

She *knew* that diplomat hadn't been a diplomat. She should've bet on it. Alas, too late now. And had Fentiman known what he was doing? Killing her was a stretch—tranqing her and stealing the ticket would have been enough—but he'd prevented a very, very sticky situation between Janus, the Neutral Zone, and Fides.

Most impressive was how this hadn't been blasted across every resistance channel in Janus and leaked to the media. Whatever Salus's activists were up to, it was remarkably restrained.

Renée nodded. "Well done."

Analytics swallowed. "This is a personal account that avoids traces back to us. It means he wouldn't see the data logs."

She honed in on the pertinent detail. "He's monitoring our work devices?"

"Trying to," Tech chimed in.

Renée gave a deep sigh. "I appreciate the risk you've taken to show me this. Thank you." She reflected. "Let our esteemed member think the missive is lost. Leave it. Tell no one. Give him read-only access to our work devices, and make write-access approvable by me."

They both nodded.

"Keep up the excellent work."

She left them to it and returned to her office. The rain had lessened, softening back to a patter. Her stomach still felt empty, so she pulled out the second bun and began eating it.

How much clearer things seemed. An assassin foiled in her mission, *well*. No wonder Parliament had sent Elleul here, and no wonder he was so eager to ensure the entire incident was tied up and cleared away. Renée wondered if the Kusanagis' arrival was coincidence—perhaps the murder was the coincidence—but that would be two birds with one purple-faced stone.

She ought to feel flattered. They could've sent multiple Parliamentarians and some actual military muscle to capture the Kusanagis, and instead they'd relied on Elleul. Strange that one man was considered enough to take care of the situation. Perhaps there was something special about him or his background. Or they'd hoped to also rely on her.

Her and the assumption she wanted to go home. Which, in fairness, she did. If Elleul followed through and didn't find out about what she'd just done, she might yet see her parents again. If Lane took her advice and herself to Fides, that would make leaving easier.

The prospect was dizzying. Her stomach sank under a sudden weight, but it might only be the extra pork bun.

Truly, Parliament's audacity was astounding, as was their attempt at subtlety. One Parliamentarian—one who'd come up the ranks through Intelligence, who knew all of Intelligence's tricks—and a loyal Janus Prefect eager for a second chance, neither of whom would draw attention in any way from Fides. It would annoy the NZC, but everything about the tension between Janus and Fides annoyed them. Remarkable that Parliament wanted to avoid any hint of outright aggression. Who knew they had a line and could stick to it?

She settled on the loveseat to think. How could she use this? What would people do next? In a way, this changed very little. Elleul would operate as he always had, the Kusanagis would try to leave, and Lane would remain a stubborn unknown. The major change was in Renée's information. Information was power.

But she still didn't have all the pieces. Exploring known unknowns was always an interesting ride. Lane had confirmed her suspicions about this invention of hers, but Renée wanted to know exactly what a qubicon did. Something that meant getting it back was worth all this aggravation. Tori had mentioned uploading to it. Helen had described it as a means of preserving data captured in an entangled quantum state, and Helen was only around to share that because of the invention itself. Renée knew what the official synth mind loaders looked like, but she couldn't assume Lane's invention would be the same. Whatever it was, it had to be portable if Tori could carry it around.

And it seemed to hold a great deal of sway over Lane and the Kusanagis. It was the kind of item that made them change their minds. Maybe it could change many things. If it could change their minds, it could influence Parliament. Which meant it was valuable. And right now, Renée needed something valuable. She wanted to see it and understand it.

Her evening had filled itself after all.

When Lane emerged from the bottom of her whisky glass, she found the salon packed. Probably had something to do with the relentless rain outside. For once, she was happy to lose herself in the bar owner routine: she did the usual circuits, turfed out a neolud getting aggressive near the video game room, checked in with Rakesh and Serge, ignored all the leeches and desperate customers, and even downed a few glasses of honest-to-goodness water like a responsible damned adult.

After a few hours, she found herself sizing up Helen's latest clay sculpture in the back corner.

It was a replica of a piano. Compact and with wheels, the kind of cheap piano built for pushing around bars and event venues three or four centuries ago on behalf of an endless parade of ivory-ticklers. Not full-size, perhaps two-thirds. Perfectly detailed and carved, down to the scratches at the foot pedals and smoothed edges of the keys, it was another of Helen's masterpieces. Lane wondered where she'd had it fired.

Helen joined her in gazing at it.

"You like?" Helen asked.

"It's worth the wake-up call."

Helen snorted. "Thanks."

"Next time, do something that adds to the décor. No one here knows what the hell this is."

"This is my place too. I can put in what I want."

Lane remembered Helen—traitorously, the real Helen—as a child, then as an adult playing a modern version of this, expensive warm wood and finest steel wire, fingers dancing over the keys and making them pour out her emotion. She'd practised every afternoon for years. She'd attempted playing once, on a piano for sale in a hawker's stall, and refused to talk further about it. They hadn't bought one here.

Now she did things like this. Sculptures, paintings, graffiti, hair styling, wood carving, and more. All styled and executed as though Helen had studied the medium for decades. She once explained she took patterns and instructions from the net and replicated them, nothing more. Lane was impressed, because she didn't have a single artistic bone in her body, but Helen had seemed disappointed when she'd said it.

"You're right," Lane said.

Helen put one hand on the piano lid, brushing across the smooth ceramic. "It takes a lot of effort to reproduce wood grain in clay. That's why I was mixing up different types of clay in the kitchen. I wanted to get the finish and strength right."

"Why this size?"

"I only had so much clay."

"We could get the real thing."

Helen smacked the lid. "No." She scanned the room and then leaned in. "By the way, I was thinking about what you said earlier about her giving the qubicon back to you. Does she realise what that would do? What that implies about the future of synths?"

"She's one of the mod leaders, Helen. *The* mod leader. Of course she does."

"I disagree. She's human and she assumes the best-case scenario. She needs to know we're not the same." Helen leaned in closer. "I'll speak to her about it tonight."

"If you want."

Lane didn't know what that would accomplish, given how the movement rhapsodised that analogue to data was perfect replication, that synths were humans in another form, that the next human frontier was digital. People were betting on tech improvements; however she'd bet just about anything that Tori was on board regardless of what actual synths said. Helen couldn't be the first synth to speak to her, but if she wanted to try being helpful, Lane wouldn't stop her.

The events of the evening played through her mind as she went through the closing routine. The flashing light on the bug, the subsequent "discussion" with Renée. Stars and moons, that had been something else.

Renée hadn't struck Lane as the jealous type, but hey, everyone had hidden depths. And the day had arrived when Renée and Helen agreed on something, which was unprecedented.

The idea of leaving Pann was almost abhorrent, but they had a point. If news about her invention leaked, if she gave Tori the damned ticket, she'd be on Parliament's target list. That was the last thing she wanted. Leaving Pann was the best outcome for her.

It would screw over the Kusanagis. It would leave Helen to run this place herself—in a safe part of the system, true, but for how long? And if Elleul backed out of his promise to Renée, she'd stay here too.

Nothing about that sat well.

She never should've given a prototype to Tori. She should've stopped her research long before she even met Tori. Playing with illicit technology had been such a rush at the time, but was it worth this headache? These past five years? Helen?

What on all known planets would she say to Tori tonight? Or to Renée tomorrow?

She tried to reflect on possible other outcomes as she cleaned, but her mind kept going in circles. If she left, she'd be safe, but unhappy. If she stayed, she'd have her qubicon and could destroy it—or not.

None of it felt right.

In a way, Tori's proposal was the best: letting Ayumu leave was probably the fairest outcome of all; that way everyone was unhappy. But the idea of him jumping ahead of people who'd waited months, if not years, to leave the system . . . that stuck in her craw.

She was supposed to be done with all this. And that ticket needed to disappear. She'd give it over, get her qubicon back, then see what Tori and Ayumu would do. Perhaps Renée and Elleul would stop them—or not. Talk about betting opportunities.

What she also needed was deniability for the damned ticket. Renée would have to arrest her if evidence showed up connecting her to it. Maybe she should tell Helen to wipe her memory banks of any reference to it.

After closing and helping with clean-up, Helen went upstairs, and Lane settled at a table in the bar with more water. She scrolled through the headlines, played a game for a while, and cleaned her glass. Then she straightened the chairs. She checked the games room and set the automatic vacuum bot to sweep it.

Eventually she had to acknowledge it was the early hours and past reason to wait. Helen had gone to bed—well. "Bed." Slow reboot plus defrag. Serge and Rakesh were long home. The rain was abating. Tori wasn't coming.

Lane had stepped onto the stairs when furious knocking sounded at the front door.

That didn't sound like a prearranged-meeting knock.

She went to the door and eased it open, peering into the street.

Ayumu Kusanagi shoved in and shut the door behind him. "Lock it."

She did. He was panting, water beading over his face. His hair hung in wet tendrils and his clothes were soaked. She stared at him, a sick feeling rising within her. "What's wrong?"

He shook his head, his face falling. "I didn't know where else to go." He bent over to take a breath, drops flying.

"What happened?"

He drew in a harsh breath. "We were at the meeting, both of us. Police raided it, so we ran. I lost Tori, but we have a plan for situations like that, so I didn't worry." He leaned down further, water still dripping. When he spoke again, his voice was strained. "She didn't meet me at our rendezvous."

After watching for a few seconds, she realised the drops weren't excess rainwater.

Oh no.

She crouched down, needing to hear it. "Ayumu."

He screwed up his eyes, but the tears kept coming. One hand clawed open his jacket and shirt to reveal, hanging on a chain around his neck, the small cube Lane had designed so many years ago: the qubicon she'd gifted to Tori. The status bar on its front glowed a dull red.

Tori Kusanagi was dead.

CHAPTER
TEN

Lane backed away from the door as though Tori's killer lurked outside it. Ayumu pulled his sleeve across his eyes as he straightened. "It's been blue for so long," he said. "We didn't know the technicalities of how it worked, but she said if it changed colour, then that was a bad thing."

Yes. It meant the partner data of the qubytes had been deleted, and artificial entanglement was in effect. Her data was held in temporary stasis.

This was Helen again. Without the blood spray and very immediate corpse, but the disbelief and sudden intimacy with the cold edges of reality were familiar.

"Do you know where her body is?" Lane asked.

Ayumu shook his head, tears still brimming. "Does it matter?"

That annoyed her. "Yeah." Squashing it down, she steered him to the bar and poured him something medicinal.

He wiped his face again, then knocked the drink back and held his glass out for another. "I didn't think this would be how it happened," he said in a monotone.

Lane poured. "What, you thought you two would grow old together? Die peacefully in the same bed?"

He scoffed. "Please. We dream, but I'm realistic. I imagined multiple scenarios, but in every one of them, we are—were together." He paused for a moment, his throat working, then he gulped down the alcohol and wiped his lips. "I would see it and know. I'd get revenge."

Lane poured her own, then hesitated. If she was being honest, she wasn't feeling up to booze right now. "Do you know who did it?"

"No." His fingers tightened around his glass. "I have some ideas."

Lane had ideas too.

"We're so careful." His voice thickened. "She's normally five steps ahead of anyone tracking us. We had to leave in a rush though. The net is different here. I lost her . . . I just . . ."

"Guess she got unlucky."

"She must have." He forced a deep breath. "I don't want to return to our hotel. Not tonight."

"You can stay here," she said.

He inclined his head at her, then tapped his glass. She filled it once more. He took off the qubicon and placed it on the counter before drinking half the glass.

Lane couldn't help staring at the qubicon. It was surreal to see it once more, like seeing an old friend—and it still worked after all this time. Unbelievable.

She shouldn't have given up her research. Look at what she was capable of. Look at the thing she had made. Renée and Tori had been right.

"What happens now?" Ayumu asked.

She wrenched her attention back to him. "What?"

"With this." He indicated the qubicon. "Tori said it would hold her for a day, but I didn't believe it. Nothing's ever held this kind of data for that long."

"I did design it to hold the entanglements for a day," Lane said. "Specifically, tests averaged twenty-three hours and seventeen minutes."

He blinked. "And it worked?"

She dug deep through time and brain fog for more details. "Beta tests with large quantities of data worked. I do have a successful test case involving a person, but one result isn't scientifically sound. And I'm still not sure it was actually a success. This prototype is over five years old; it's a miracle it lasted this long and still works." Her fingers itched to reach out and assess its condition.

As if reading her mind, he pulled it close with one hand. "I understand. Tori mentioned you gave one to Helen."

For someone who kept so many secrets, Tori could spill them like a pro to this guy. "I did. She's my sole positive result."

He gave a tentative smile. "It worked on her. Helen's still with you. No difference, right?"

Lane couldn't answer that, not when there was such hope on his face.

After a lengthy pause, he turned a desperate gaze to the qubicon. "You're going to be okay." He said it like a prayer to a higher power, closing his eyes and taking a breath afterwards. "We have a day."

"Less than that," Lane said. "Rounding down, the average was twenty-three hours of holding the entangled data in stasis. Core time."

Ayumu frowned. "So . . ."

"Salus's rotation is slower than the core standard. We have until tomorrow evening—I mean, this evening." She did a quick calculation. "About eighteen hours. How long ago did she . . . did the light change?"

He slumped against the bar. "I noticed it maybe forty minutes ago. I think. I *think*." He ran a thumb along one edge of the qubicon absently.

Something lurking in the depths of Lane's brain surfaced. A memory, a requirement, a design challenge, a late rejigging of the display. She reached out to the cube and pressed the glass surface of the red light. Blue digits flashed back at them: 01:48:21. The seconds ran up to 24 before the numbers faded into the red.

Ayumu sucked in a breath. "Timer counting up?"

"Better for testing purposes." She did another mental calculation, then set several alarms on her internal timer function—one at half time, one at fifteen hours, and a final one at sixteen. "I'm allowing us sixteen Salus hours. That's enough time for a plan with marginal room for error."

Finishing his drink, Ayumu seemed to slump onto the counter. "A plan for what? To get her a body? Are there synth manufacturers in Pann?"

Good question. Lane wasn't sure there were. Synth bodies were definitely available here, but they were few and more expensive than on the core planets, with no guarantee of manufacturing quality. Like Helen, it would be a case of what was available, not what was ideal.

Putting Tori in one here meant she'd never leave Janus. Elleul would continue hunting her and Ayumu. He would stay here until Tori was dead once again or back on a ship to the core.

The empty search input on her internal panel mocked her. What could she search for? What could they do? How was Lane going to fix this?

Her gaze slid back to the qubicon and its dull red light.

Tori's memories and personality and all the incredible brain synapses that this age could capture as storable data were being held in a delicate quantum entangled stasis, ready for download into a synthetic body. The movement she'd spearheaded didn't see any difference between the synapses in a brain and the data as expressed through the programming in a synth body. Humanity, in different packaging. It was all the same.

Only, she wouldn't be the same, just as Helen wasn't the same. Tori—her life force, the unique incidence of her mind and body and indefinable inner being that made up the package of her—was gone. As Lane had known her, Tori was dead.

Maybe this was useless as well as foolish. How would the stress and money involved in finding a synth body be worthwhile when the person they were saving was an echo of the person they'd known? It was better to fully release her. Wait and watch the entanglements collapse, letting what was captured of her degrade and corrupt.

Lane could have done that with Helen. At the time, the idea had been unthinkable. Now, Lane felt the relieving finality of permanent death. Those stubborn neoluds and their insistence on letting nature take its course, on accepting the realities of life and death—the idiots were right, and Lane finally *understood*.

Seeing Ayumu's stony face, the tears still running down it, Lane knew he was in his own hell of hope. Making the suggestion of letting the entanglements collapse would be pointless. Worse than pointless. Spouse, lieutenant, mod; he'd refuse the idea out of principle alone.

But she had to try. "I'm not so sure. There might be a few empty synth bodies here. Is that really the path you want to take?"

He blinked at her. "Excuse me?"

"If this works, she won't be the same." One of Helen's paintings—the phase before sculpture—hung on the wall behind him. It was a perfect re-creation of a famous work currently hanging in the Lavele Historical Art Gallery, down to the brushwork and colour matching. "It might be best to let her go."

His jaw clenched. "How can you *say* that? Surely you know better. Of *all* people, you should know better." He shook his head. "You've gone neolud. I guessed it, but Tori refused to believe me. I shouldn't've come here—"

"Stop. Think." She refilled his glass. "It was a suggestion. Obviously it's up to you. I presume you two planned for this."

He gestured wildly. "It was meant to be a backup plan for the core. We were supposed to be here for less than a day. Fuck!" He dragged his hands through his hair. "We'll find a body. We will." He eyed her. "Maybe in Caeliton."

Oh great. Even *better* plan. She crossed her arms. "I don't know that—"

Heavy knocking at the front door interrupted her. Her internal timestamp said two in the morning. Definitely not anyone who should be there.

"This is the police!" came through, muffled by the door. "Open up!"

Of course it was.

They hammered again at the door. When no one rushed to open it, they went quiet. Ayumu caught her eye and filled his glass. "I think they're here for me."

"No shit. Drink that." She went to her office to retrieve the bug, turning it on as she returned to the bar. She placed it in his hair, near the jack behind his ear. His gaze was wary, but he let her do it. "In case you run into trouble in the jail. They might force your tech to shut down."

He nodded. They picked up their glasses and chinked them in a salute as the police lasered the door lock. It swung open with a thud, and four of Renée's finest strode in and over to the bar, moving a tad slowly—Lane might even call it reluctantly. The leader wore a rumpled uniform and a harsh expression on her face.

Lane sipped, then nodded at them. "Good morning. I hope the force intends to repair that door."

Goon Leader rolled her eyes, then turned to Ayumu. "Monsieur Kusanagi, you are under arrest."

Lane glanced at him. He held his glass in one hand, leaning back against the counter as though they'd been catching up over a casual drink. The qubicon was nowhere in sight. "On what charge?" he asked laconically.

"Prefect Bellevue will discuss that with you in the morning."

Lane knew for a fact that Renée wasn't awake right now and wouldn't order a squad out like this if she was.

Then again, this *was* the Kusanagis.

And Elleul.

Lane wasn't sure of anything anymore.

Ayumu's expression cleared, and he sank the contents of his glass, then set it down on the empty counter. "Thanks for the drink. See you later." He stood and headed for the door, the officers falling into place around him like guard dogs.

Lane watched them exit, then leaned over the counter to check the service side. Nothing.

He'd taken the qubicon with him.

Fuck.

Lane turned her attention to the front door. The salon was hushed as she walked across it. As soon as she was at the door, she wanted to run after the squad. She wanted to wring his neck, then take back her qubicon and put it in the safe. She forced herself to stay in place, stiff fingers tracing the loosened lock. If she didn't move them, they shook ever so slightly. The lock had been lasered out in one clumsy chunk; some glue would hold it until the morning. She retrieved her toolkit and began working the adhesive into the metal.

Maybe Ayumu had a plan. If it involved keeping the qubicon on him while being arrested, that didn't give Lane much hope for the rest of it. What was going through his head? Why wouldn't he leave Tori here? Lane was free to move around and organise; he very much wasn't.

Trust, probably. For *some* reason, he didn't trust her. Maybe she shouldn't have hinted at what would follow if they managed to transfer Tori's data into a body.

What about Tori herself? What would she want? She'd been ready to hand it over. When she'd last uploaded to the qubicon felt important somehow. Would she have memories of this afternoon? Of them making a certain kind of peace? Of her final minutes? She clearly hadn't expected whatever circumstances had led to her death.

Then again, who did? Neither Lane nor Helen had expected the man who'd confronted them in their home that day. Lane had stepped through the door quickly, in a panic because Yui hadn't been answering her messages or calls and the city was going crazy, to see him standing next to Helen with her arms wrenched behind her back and a gun to her head.

"Lane," Helen called.

It sounded as though she'd come downstairs without Lane noticing. Lane startled, but didn't look around. She pressed the lock back in and held it for the two seconds the glue needed to bond, then tested the door. It held. An abrupt wave of exhaustion washed over her.

She turned and saw Helen by the bar. "You rebooted quick."

"My auditory inputs relayed what sounded like an emergency. What happened? Who was here?"

"Ayumu Kusanagi." She was so *tired*. "Tori's dead."

Helen was almost as still as one of her sculptures. "Well. Shit."

That about summed it up. Lane returned to the bar, toolkit in hand. "I don't know what's going to happen. He's been arrested, and he has the qubicon."

"What? Is he crazy? The police will take it— *Shit*." Helen rushed forward and gripped Lane's shoulders. "You have to leave."

"No, what I have to do is sleep or drink, and honestly, I'm leaning towards both."

"Lane, Renée *knows*. She knows about the qubicon. Elleul will be watching this arrest closely. She'll spill, she'll have to. If he knows what it is, and that you made it, you're in as much danger as the Kusanagis. You need to go."

Lane blinked at her, then tilted her head. "And how would *you* know what Renée knows?"

"Because I told her. Obviously. Take the ticket and go to Fides."

Lane yawned. "One: No. Can't. Portal recharges overnight, and I wouldn't risk the qubicon falling into Elleul's clutches. Two: Why would you tell Renée anything about that?"

"Because . . ." Helen's mouth went into a flat angry line. "Look, I didn't tell her much; she figured most of it out herself. I wanted to know how I died. When Yui turned out to be Tori, I thought her and the qubicon had something to do with it."

Lane stared at her in disbelief. "And you asked *Renée* to look into it?!"

"You refuse to tell me what happened!"

"That doesn't mean you go to the Prefect of Police about it! Why not just email Intelligence directly about everything? Save Renée the trouble."

Helen glared. "I trust her."

"You're the only person on the planet who does."

"No, I'm not."

Damn it all, she was right. Lane dumped the two glasses into the sink without care. "You're unbelievable. I'm going to bed."

Helen caught her arm. "No. You're going to tell me what happened. Then you're going to take that ticket, go to the terminal, and get the first portal charge out of here."

Lane struggled, but Helen's grip was iron strong and about as forgiving. She stopped and took a deep breath. Now wasn't the time— preferably she'd never have told Helen this—but she seemed resolute. Lane braced herself. "You're right that it was about the qubicon. But Tori wasn't part of it at all. Your death was my fault."

Renée woke with a jerk. Her tablet vibrated on the coffee table next to her, and she groped for it blindly, causing it to fall on the floor. She blinked at the ceiling, yellow from the sunlight streaming through the window. She'd slept in. At the office. Because she'd been up late for some reason. Research? What had—

The tablet continued vibrating. Damn. She rolled over to see what was so important. Dozens of messages from various people, tens of missed calls—what in the system had happened?

Her spine cracked in multiple places as she sat up. She cast around. Definitely in her office. On her *sofa*. Merde, no wonder her back and neck were killing her. She tapped through the tablet to the last person who called her—Atkins—and put it to her ear, stifling a yawn.

"Prefect!" he answered. "You're awake! Please get to the station as soon as you can."

"Absolutement." She twisted in place, holding in a groan as more things in her body clicked. Youth had never seemed so long ago. "What's going on?"

"Tori Kusanagi is dead. Ayumu Kusanagi is in our cells."

She froze. "Repeat that?"

"Someone killed Madame Kusanagi last night," Atkins explained. "The night shift arrested Monsieur Kusanagi at Lane's Salon around two."

"What a busy night." And she'd missed most of it. That seemed a shame. Who'd ordered the arrest in her place? On what grounds? Because while spouses could and did kill each other, Ayumu Kusanagi didn't strike her as the type. She stretched once more, trying to ease the kinks in her back.

"You must get down here. Monsieur Elleul is in a very good mood."

Oh no. "Please tell me Monsieur Kusanagi is still alive."

"Yes, he is." Atkins lowered his voice. "We're watching the holding cells closely."

"Good. I'll be right there." She pulled the tablet away to check the time. Early. Ugh. "Make me a coffee, would you?"

"Of course. How long will you be?"

"A few minutes."

"What? How—"

She hung up on him and checked her shirt. Wrinkled, but fresh enough. Feet in shoes and she was as ready as she was going to be.

The tension in the station was as palpable as the sunlight streaming through the windows. Her officers seemed shaken up, but they shouldn't be. After all, they had faced worse than a death and a celebrity activist being rounded up. Renée ignored the drawn faces and whispered conversations as she walked through the bullpen and into the kitchen, where Atkins was placing a cup under the machine.

Atkins's jaw dropped when he saw her. "My days, you . . . Madame Prefect, did you *sleep* here?"

She rubbed the crust from her eyes. "Coffee. Now."

"A-at once."

She pulled out her tablet and tried to focus.

The calls she ignored. The messages were more interesting. There was one from Tori's shadow around one in the morning, stating she was going to ground. The last update in the official feed was: *Target shot by electric handgun on the intersection of Bastille and Sydney. Target is confirmed dead. Killer is a notable and recent visitor to Pann.*

What in all known dimensions was that? Was her officer so gutless she couldn't name Elleul? Perhaps she should have saved the inspiring speeches for when the majority of her force were present.

Tori's bug was still active for some reason, its feed spooling into the station's data storage. Renée adamantly didn't want to hear whatever Lane had drunk in her office last night and swiped out of the feeds dashboard.

She moved on to the other messages. Several from reporters, the mayor, and NZC members, requesting confirmation of the death. One from an officer stating receipt of an order from Elleul to arrest Ayumu Kusanagi but without motive or warrant. Another from Analytics asking her for a meeting as soon as possible. Multiple from Atkins requesting her presence as soon as she woke up.

None from Lane.

None from Elleul.

And none from anyone else. It struck her as rather pathetic that she hadn't gone home last night and no one had noticed. She lived alone but her neighbours were proving singularly unobservant. It was a little galling. However, it wasn't the first or last time, and if—when?—she went back to the core, she wouldn't have to worry about that again.

She needed to survive this morning first.

Atkins passed a steaming cup over and Renée drained it. She gestured with the cup at him. "Merci. Now you may explain to me why the world has gone mad this morning."

Her lieutenant stood at attention. "Tori Kusanagi was killed last night."

"Oui, oui, you mentioned. We handle murders all the time, Lieutenant. Let's not be losing our heads just because this one's famous." She waved her tablet. "Who has confirmed this beyond the shadow we placed on her?"

"Good Samaritans carried her body to the hospital. DNA matches, plus someone took photos and leaked them. The press keeps trying to get in here for a statement, physically *and* digitally. The firewall is dealing with ten times the usual hacking attempts." Atkins's eyes were very wide. "What if the core sends other people to check?"

"They won't." Renée put her cup back into the machine and pressed the button for another serving. "Elleul is enough. Where is he, by the way?"

"Speaking to Monsieur Kusanagi."

Of course he was.

"Because Monsieur Kusanagi was arrested after curfew last night," Atkins continued. "Elleul put the order through as from you, but we know it wasn't your order. We're not sure what to do. There's no reason to hold him and no one has done any paperwork for the arrest. We're all very upset."

Her coffee replenished, and she took a desperate gulp. "Noted. Is anyone with Madame Kusanagi's body?"

"Yes, we're collecting evidence and personal effects from the hospital. Prefect, we can't hold Monsieur Kusanagi, but Member Elleul isn't . . . that is, to say, uh, he's put in certain kinds of orders . . . Prefect, I foresee only problems."

Parfait. She hoped the night shift had left notes for the day shift, but if not, managing Elleul and her staff was going to be annoyingly messy. She finished her coffee and placed the cup back in the machine for a third hit. She was going to need it if she wanted to get anywhere with Elleul. "Lieutenant, you follow my orders, not Member Elleul's. You work for the Neutral Zone. Remember that the next time a Janus *guest* decides to convince our colleagues to follow his procedure instead of ours."

Atkins cleared his throat. "By the way, we aren't sure where Elleul was last night."

She resisted the urge to roll her eyes. "We may not be sure, Lieutenant, but we know. I suggest you ensure evidence isn't 'damaged' this time." She held up her tablet. "Get her shadow back in here with a proper report. We had so much surveillance on Kusanagi that there has to be camera evidence of *some* kind somewhere. You handle the Kusanagis. I'll handle Elleul."

He nodded, eyes wide. Her coffee finished pouring, so she took the cup and went to the jail. At the door, she typed a quick message to Lane: *TK dead, chaos here, watch yourself,* ignored the extra five messages that had arrived from NZC members, then went in. Elleul was settled in a chair before the bars of Kusanagi's holding cell, his face mottled with bruises and his lip split. Kusanagi sat cross-legged on his cot on the far side of the cell, arms folded, expression bored. An officer sat nearby, tablet clenched in both hands and eyes darting between the two men.

She drew up a spare chair and sat next to Elleul. "Bonjour à tous."

The two of them glared at her for some reason. The officer stood to leave and Renée pointed at him. "You. Stay." He returned to his seat.

She smiled widely at them. "Please. Member Elleul, Monsieur Kusanagi, enlighten me on what events have led to us enjoying coffee together this morning." She took in Elleul's face, then raised her cup and sipped. "Member, you appear to have had a rough evening."

Kusanagi snorted and looked aside. Elleul huffed. "I've been informing Monsieur Kusanagi of what he can expect when he returns to the core."

"Returns to the core?" Renée turned to Kusanagi. "I thought you planned to stay here or to move on to Fides."

"Those remain my plans," he said, voice tight. He seemed quite angry, though on closer inspection Renée suspected he was also tired and grieving. There were signs of tears on his face.

"I see. Why here?" Renée asked.

Kusanagi frowned. "I don't follow."

"You appear to have been arrested, but I see no official record in my dash." She waved her tablet. "We can have this conversation in my office. It's far more pleasant there."

"Prefect, I can only surmise you're being obtuse on purpose," Elleul said. "Monsieur Kusanagi is under arrest."

She lowered her tablet and made sure her voice went cool. "On whose authority?"

"Mine."

"Who is the prefect of this police service?" There was an uncomfortable silence. "You"—to the nearby officer—"release him."

Elleul leaned back. "I would reconsider that, Prefect." The officer didn't budge.

She met Elleul's gaze. Moons above, she was sick of looking at his smug, self-important face. She needed him out of here. Not just the jail, out of her station entirely. Maybe even off-planet. How to manage that?

A tense silence had settled in the jail while she thought. Elleul's mouth was turned firmly down, the guard looked ready to faint, and even Kusanagi was starting to fidget.

She finished her cup and stood. "My office, Member."

He stood too. "Very well."

Kusanagi watched them, his hands working the fabric of his jacket. Renée handed the guard her cup. "Don't move." Then she and Elleul headed for her office in silence. Atkins passed them in the corridor leading to the jail, his face a nervous grey colour and his gaze firmly forward, away from Elleul's. Renée wished, not for the first time, that Atkins didn't have quite so many tells.

In her office, she shut the door, then turned on Elleul. "Your arrests are forfeit."

He frowned. "What are you talking about?"

"You *cannot* issue an arrest order without a warrant, a charge, or evidence. *You* cannot issue an arrest order, period. That is *my* role, *my* authority. Your arrest is invalidated because *you* abused your guest status here. Member Elleul, I can only cooperate with you within the limits of the law, and the law is very clear on this. The committee will go over this incident with a comb, and it isn't in your interests or mine to cut corners."

Elleul waved this away. "It's fine. He attended a resistance meeting last night."

"That is not a crime on Salus."

"He was out past curfew."

"We'll issue him the standard fine."

Elleul began turning red. "He's the obvious suspect in the murder of his wife."

"I'm certain the current investigation will establish whether it was a murder and the identity of the murderer if so, but arrests happen as a result of the investigation, not before it."

Elleul bit through clenched teeth, "He helped hackers illegally teleport people out of Janus."

Renée raised her eyebrows. "Not sure of the relevance, but proof, Member. Where is the *proof*?"

Elleul gestured. "Check your tablet."

She pulled it out and began flicking through her reports. "Which report should I be examining?"

"Analytics on the hacker feeds. Financial transactions."

She flicked through the headache from last night. After a few minutes, she said, "I should hire some of these people. They're better at making money than we are. I can't say I see the link with the Kusanagis yet."

Elleul, with great flair, produced his own tablet and began scrolling. "Here." Elleul pointed at his screen. The displayed section attributed a large amount to an account owned by the Kusanagis. Renée went to the same point in her report. No such attribution. Analytics had indeed been busy.

"I see," she said. "Look at that."

Elleul seemed to have calmed down. "You see, Prefect, whatever evidence you need can be provided."

She knew that from her previous work. Timestamps could be changed, reports adjusted, arrest orders retrospectively assigned to leadership; all of it airtight. He was following the book, and if she played along, the arrest would be perfectly acceptable to their respective governances.

"And what about to me?"

He frowned. "What?"

Renée steeled herself. "I have done my utmost to help you. May I remind you that you're not in Janus jurisdiction and that the NZC is watching us. We must get it right, because everything we do will be blasted across the system in excruciating detail. Tori Kusanagi is dead in *my* jurisdiction, under *my* watch. If I allow you to undermine my authority and our local procedures in order to jettison him back to the core, I need you to make it acceptable not just to my governance but to *me*."

Elleul seemed unable to speak.

"You made me a promise in exchange for my help. I have helped you. Time for you to fulfil your promise."

He regarded her thoughtfully, then a slow, proud smile crawled across his face. "I knew you were Janus through and through." He lifted his tablet and tapped at it, then showed Renée her Intelligence file. Under the work section were a few new sentences: *Made redundant due to restructuring. Accepted role as Prefect of Pann, Salus.* He saved it, then pulled up his messaging application. "I'm sending this to the heads of Intelligence and the Protection and Order Ministry." He then wrote out a message detailing her work and granting her a full pardon.

Her stomach was in turmoil. Her face felt hot—her whole *body* felt hot. Was this happening? Was this real? It hardly seemed real.

She could go home.

All it would cost her was Kusanagi. Too bad she'd told Atkins to discharge him. Hmm. How could she keep Elleul busy before he realised what was going on? Well, the message was waiting in their system, blocked from Janus by Tech. She could tell Tech to let it through. She *should* tell Tech to let it through. Elleul had kept his promise; it didn't matter what happened now.

He sent the message, then eyed her. "Good enough?"

"Good enough."

"Will you continue to give me trouble about *local procedure*?" He placed his tablet in his jacket pocket and his hand continued to hover there.

He still had that cheap, illegal handgun.

And she'd left her taser on the coffee table near the loveseat. "Of course not," she replied, taking a step towards the table.

Her tablet vibrated in her hand, startling them. Lane's name and photo appeared on the screen, visible to both of them. *What?* The timing of this woman . . .

A strange expression crossed Elleul's face, almost greedy. His hands dropped. "You should answer that, Prefect."

Renée hoped Lane was calling to say she was about to depart for Fides, because otherwise Renée was going to kill her for still being here. She pressed Answer and held her tablet to her ear. "Lane. Now isn't a good time."

"Yeah? You owe me a new front door." There was a short pause, then Lane said softly, "Are you at the station?"

"Oui."

"Alone?"

"Non."

"If Elleul's there, put me on speakerphone."

Quoi? Between the media and NZC circus, Elleul fulfilling a promise, that third cup of coffee and now this wretched woman being *creative*, Renée was ready to quit. Fuck Salus and Janus and this entire system, she would sign off her own ticket request and take immediate holiday in Fides for the next four months.

Watching Elleul, she did as Lane requested. "What is this about?"

"The Kusanagis. Tori's dead, right?" Lane's voice sounded tinny in Renée's office, the speaker quality of her tablet unable to capture the rich tones and gravel so unique to Lane.

"Correct," Renée replied. Elleul smirked.

"She had something of mine, and now Ayumu has it. He's in your jail, therefore my property must be in your keeping."

"Property?" She realised what it had to be as she spoke. This was what had kept Renée up so late: she'd found a folder in Lane's old directory with a ton of files and virtual projections. *Project_Rotwang.* She'd hit one of the virtual projections and the preview showed a diagram of a cube-like thing. It was small, a matter of centimetres along each plane.

She'd only scanned the notes, but they'd confirmed what Helen had said: this was something that held incredible amounts of data in a preserved entangled stasis for longer than anyone else had managed, and she'd performed a series of tests involving iterations of prototypes. This was how Lane had saved and loaded Helen. This was what Tori had taken from her, and what Ayumu had on him. Or, to be strictly accurate, was in his personal effects, confiscated by her officers and being returned to him.

Oh. If Tori had stolen it, then she'd used it. This thing had *Tori* in it. Her heart sank.

"It's a necklace with a cube pendant. I want it back."

Renée made sure her expression was calm. "Can you prove it's yours?"

"You've been investigating me. You have my notes. You tell me."

Elleul had crossed his arms and was concentrating, his gaze on the tablet. Renée tried her hardest not to seem suspicious. "That would be a circumstantial link, given the source, but we can discuss it. I don't advise you visit us today, however. There's a media frenzy outside."

Lane scoffed. "I won't be visiting you at all. You'll bring it to me."

What was she doing? "And why would I do that?"

"Because Elleul was right. Fentiman did give me the ticket and the missive."

Renée was never going home or anywhere else; she was going to expire here, in her dinky unaired office, of a heart attack *right now*.

Elleul's eyes were huge. How strange to share a reaction with him.

"You have what?" Renée managed.

"You heard me. Meet me at the terminal with the necklace in one hour. Any later, I'm jumping system to Fides with the missive."

Her tablet slipped in her fingers, and Renée had to grab at it and put it gently down on her desk. It was one thing to tell her to do it, to imagine her departing in a burst of violet, but it was quite another to hear her say it.

And supposedly with the missive that Renée was certain she didn't have. That made no sense. She knew where it was and it wasn't with Lane. And what did she intend to do with that qubicon if Tori's data was in there? Disappear with it? If Lane were here, she'd shake her. "What are you *thinking*?"

"I want my property and I don't want trouble. You and Elleul get your ticket, your missive, and your little troublemaker in one neat bow. I'm thinking we can help each other."

She actually sounded sober as well. Unbelievable. Perhaps a hangover contributed to this insanity. Renée glanced at Elleul, who nodded at her. He bought this? A pit in her stomach, she answered, "You'll get your—your necklace. I'll be there."

A slight pause, then Lane said, "Good. See you in an hour." She disconnected.

Slow with numbness, Renée noted the time. Merde, she hadn't even eaten yet. Perhaps she could grab a sandwich or something on the way to the terminal. Not that it mattered much because *what was that?* What was Lane doing? She'd known Elleul was listening. Why set up a rendezvous like this?

"I presume this property is the result of Kovacs's research," Elleul said.

Ah. He'd found out about that.

He waved his hand dismissively. "Don't look so surprised. You were adamant your investigation was necessary, therefore I kept track of it."

He'd bugged her somehow. Maybe logged her tablet or strong-armed Tech into handing over information. Well, it *was* how he did things. "I see." No doubt he understood the implications of Lane's research. If he did, Renée doubted he'd let Lane walk from this trade a free woman. "That's quite a demand she's made. I'm appalled she thinks she'll get away with it."

He nodded. "Agreed. Of course we won't let her. You know what has to be done."

Did she? They were supposedly on the same side. If she were in Janus with a known terrorist in custody, a piece of illicit tech in custody, a missing missive and ticket, and some subversive scientist with a history in the black market wanted to trade said illicit tech for said missive and ticket, what was the obvious option? After shooting to the nearest beach and drinking heavily?

She turned off her tablet screen and slid it into her pocket. "Arrest her for carrying stolen property?"

"Yes." He smirked. "Local procedure should allow for that."

"It does." How could this play out for her? For Lane? For Kusanagi? He was free now, and she wasn't going to mention that to Elleul anytime soon, not while he was distracted by this proposed trade. She could keep it quiet until after they'd handled Lane. And Lane wasn't going to be arrested, because she was certain Lane had some ridiculous plan in mind.

"You seem a little ... reluctant, Prefect." He stepped closer. Renée could smell stale sweat, dust and copper on him, and she could gauge exactly how tired he was in the creases around his eyes and mouth. "I don't care what Kovacs said to you, what story she gave, or what promises she made. She is a mod sympathiser and supporter, and she is our enemy. She is not to be trusted. *They* cannot be trusted. Whatever she has told you, forget it."

He tapped his chest. "Remember who I am. Remember who you are. Remember what you stand for. Remember how you got here and how you could go back. Or, perhaps, how you couldn't. I can always rescind that pardon. You will arrest Kovacs, and you will be a hero to the cause."

How charming. She resisted fidgeting, biting her lip, crossing her arms, or in any way conveying how uncomfortable she was. "Understood, Member. I'll collect the necklace from Kusanagi's personal effects and meet you in front of the station in ten minutes."

CHAPTER
ELEVEN

Lane paced near the barrier to the Fides portal. A family stood in front of it, surrounding someone who was leaving. He said multiple goodbyes, hugged them all twice, then scanned his ticket on the barrier and went through into the verification room. The barrier closed, preventing anyone from joining him or seeing him.

In the room, he'd insert the ticket into the scanner, and it would verify his details. All being well, the transfer capsule would open, and he'd step inside. Everything about him would be scanned, analysed, and captured as data. The transfer would begin, energy would bend space, time and matter in a stream of violet. When transfer completed, he'd receive a signal, a door on the other side of the capsule would open, and he'd emerge an entire system away in Caeliton, Fides.

Learning about the advances that heralded intersystem travel had been the highlight of Lane's school science lessons. The physics involved still blew her away, even now, when she was using the details of the mechanics to tamp down her nerves.

Violet light shone through the cracks in the doors and the skylight in the ceiling. The family didn't cheer or clap, simply waited until the light faded, then turned and left the terminal.

There was no line. Whoever was next would show up at their allotted time. While the terminal was a public building, few people ever lingered around this particular gate. If anyone interrupted things, Lane was ready to usher them away with the help of her wand.

That's if Renée and Elleul showed up—*when* they showed up. She was ninety-something percent certain they would. Elleul wanted the ticket and missive back enough. If they didn't, she was going to look damned stupid in front of Helen and Renée.

Helen wasn't happy with the plan, and truthfully, neither was Lane. After talking into the early morning and after a few hours' sleep, she hadn't come up with anything better. She wanted the qubicon and she wanted Elleul off-planet. Forcing a meeting here so she could make him take a portal back to the core was the best she could think of.

The tricky part was the main *how* detail. Ideally, he'd leave when she threatened him, but she had the booster on her wand charged just in case. She wasn't counting on Renée helping her, not when her way home was at stake, but she thought Renée savvy enough to realise what was happening and step aside.

Lots of *ifs* there. Big ones. For the first time, Lane wished Renée had some sort of tech, because if she did, they'd have connected long before now, and she'd have sent a message to her without needing to speak or being overheard. She'd tell her the plan. She'd tell her this felt like the right thing to do. She'd tell her . . . everything she'd realised last night when confronted with the reality of loss and leaving. All the things she'd left unsaid because she'd been uncertain or cynical or apathetic. That hesitance was flat-out stupid now. No wonder Renée struggled. Lane had wasted so much time.

Fuck it all. Her head was fuzzy and her body felt stiff and achey. She wasn't sure if it was nerves, sleep-deprivation, or the lack of booze this morning, but it wasn't helpful. She took in the high ceiling and bowed structure, and appreciated the way sunlight shone through the skylight. It fell onto the mosaic-tiled floor, illuminating the design of a bird in flight. Embedded in one wall was a gigantic universal clock, detailing the local time and the times in major cities on all planets in Janus. As she watched, the hour changed over.

A man entered the building and beelined towards her. Hood up, head down, hands in his pockets. She gripped the handle of the wand in her pocket as he came closer, then let go when she recognised Ayumu Kusanagi.

Huh. Had he broken out somehow?

"Pretty sure you're meant to be in the station," she remarked as he stopped before her.

He scowled. "Your precious prefect released me. Elleul wounded her pride by overriding her authority. Morons."

Unexpected. In a good way. But that made him Lane's immediate problem, which was the last thing she wanted.

"The prefect's lieutenant mentioned she was meeting you here, and I decided I wanted to know why." He reached into the neck of his hoodie and pulled out the qubicon, still on its chain. "You've got the ticket on you, right?"

In her other pocket, yes.

But *Renée* was supposed to bring the qubicon.

Ha. How was she going to handle that? What would she bargain with? Lane seriously wanted to see her try, just for entertainment's sake. Not that anything in this situation should be funny, but that definitely would be.

"Depends," she replied.

He took the qubicon off and held it out to her. "Take her to Fides."

She stared at it. "I— What? No. That's not why I came here. Renée and Elleul will arrive at any moment."

"I mean it."

"Given your history, you'll forgive me for not believing you."

His mouth thinned. "I don't care. She has a better chance there, and you created this thing. If anything goes wrong, you can help."

If anything went wrong? It was amazing the thing worked at all after so long. And taking it through the portal . . . Eh. Risky. Matter transference on something like this was untested. Theoretically, it might work, but it didn't take much to disrupt the entanglements. Transferral by portal might destroy the stasis and, in effect, delete Tori's data. The idea was a total crapshoot.

Yup, too sober for this. She shifted her weight and glanced at the main entrance. "I doubt it. If something goes wrong, no one could help."

He gestured at her. "You're our best option." The dark circles under his eyes turned him pallid and tired. "Elleul won't stop until we're dead. Her, me, and you too if he knows about this tech. Having the ticket is enough to be in deep shit. You know that, right? Two out of three to safety is better than none."

Orion wept, how *noble*. But he had a point. She'd have the qubicon and be out of Janus.

Away from her home. Her business. Her sister.

Renée. Who'd sounded unlike herself and stressed this morning. Hearing the tension in her voice had bolstered Lane's resolve to carry this half-assed plan out.

Ah, fuck. There wasn't really a choice.

"Kovacs." He leaned forward, almost pushing the qubicon at her. "If you love her, you'll take her."

"Oh, shut up." She dug into her pocket and held up the ticket. "Here. Go."

His jaw dropped. "What the . . . Are you serious? What is *wrong* with you? How are you the one person in this place not trying to escape? Why *you*? Just take her and go!"

Orion save her from meat-headed idiots. "Why are you arguing?" She slapped it against his chest. "Take it. Leave. Now."

He stared at her. "You're helping us."

"I'm helping myself."

"I don't understand."

"Nah, you wouldn't."

He hesitantly took the ticket from her. "You're sure? Why? You're— *Kuso.*" He put the qubicon back on and started backing away. Lane turned to see what had made him curse and saw Renée and Elleul in the doorway.

Ah.

Shit indeed.

"Destroy it once she's out," she said to Ayumu.

He frowned but gave a curt nod before sprinting for the barrier.

Elleul's voice rang out in the atrium. "Kovacs! Kusanagi! Stop!"

Lane took her wand out, flicking it open to its full length. People nearby hurried away, clearing the portals area.

Elleul and Renée tore across the terminal. There was a heart-wrenching moment where Lane could see how exhausted Renée looked, even from this distance. Drawn face, stiff movements, a tight mouth; all signs that she needed rest. Lane wanted nothing more than to wrap her up and take her away from this situation.

Then Renée tripped, falling into Elleul and sending them both to the floor.

Behind Lane came a confirmatory ding and the hiss of doors opening. On the floor, Elleul swore and lurched to his feet. "Stop him!"

Lane risked a glance behind her, in time to see Ayumu yank off his hoodie inside the barrier before the doors closed, sealing him in. Their side of the area was clear of other people. Who was Elleul shouting at?

"*Prefect*!"

Oooh, he sounded mad. Lane faced them in time to see Renée get to her feet and stumble a step. "So sorry, Member." She shrugged with almost comical helplessness. "Weak ankles."

His face turned a strange shade, somewhere between red wine and plum, and his hand dug under his jacket. Bad sign. Lane moved forward.

Renée unholstered her neurastim taser and waved it. "Calm now, Member. There's nothing we can do to stop him. Parliamentary order for conditions of use, you know."

Lane stopped a few steps away. He froze, eyes darting between her and Renée, then growled out, "Arrest her and turn off that portal."

No one budged.

"Given he's meant to be in a cell right now, I *strongly suggest* you do it, Prefect." The threat was clear.

"That would kill him," Renée said.

"That's the idea."

The portal hummed and violet light poured through the skylight above them.

"You can arrest me." Lane lowered her wand. "I give myself up."

Renée stared at her, then raised a disbelieving eyebrow. Ha. She could almost hear her in her head: *Vraiment?* Lane nodded. *Yes, really. It's all right.* Still Renée didn't move. Instead, she asked, "Where did you hide the ticket, in the end? My people never found it."

"The music centre."

Renée tsked. "Serves us right for not being antique-lovers."

"It's vintage."

"It's *ancient*."

Elleul swore and pulled out a gun. "Must I do *everything* mys—"

Lane swung at his arm, but Renée was quicker, her taser up and crackling. The air sparked with electricity and Elleul stopped short, body shuddering as though his limbs were attached to strings. The gun dropped. Arcs flashed from wand to gun to his torso, dancing across his skin. He fell to the floor, twitching.

Lane was panting, somehow, though she felt like she'd only taken a few steps. Beside her, Renée whistled, then turned off her taser and pocketed it.

The twitches settled and stopped. He was still. Disturbingly still. Lane checked her wand: the booster wasn't on. Her wand didn't deal lethal damage, and neither did Renée's taser. Even combined, they shouldn't have done more than knock him out for a few seconds and stop him moving. Not unless he had tech that conducted the electricity. Which, of course, *he*—

"As you say, this is a pickle," Renée remarked.

"No shit."

The total collapse of his body was familiar in a sickening way. Lane thought she could smell a hint of singed hair or flesh, and her stomach rolled. The gun lay between him and her, similar to the one Tori had left in the salon. In the corner of her eye, her timer began beeping the half-time warning. She tapped a finger to her temple, the physical cue to disarm it.

The violet faded into the usual pale sunlight.

The change in hue seemed to prompt Renée to action. She crouched next to him and checked his mouth. "Not breathing." She eyed the wand. Lane powered it down and snapped it shut. Renée pressed two fingers against his throat. "No pulse either. Oh dear."

Lane slipped the wand into her pocket as Renée rose, her expression a study in conflicting emotions. "How unexpected this all is. I'm quite delighted by the depths I've discovered in you today."

Lane couldn't seem to stop staring at Elleul's body. "Depths, you say."

"Prefect. Are you all right?" Lieutenant Atkins had approached and was watching them with wary eyes.

Where had he come from? Lane looked around: a small group of officers watched them from a few paces away, expressions nervous and stances uncertain. At the door to the terminal, she could see people craning to look inside.

Had they seen everything? They must have. Fuck. It would be a miracle if Lane got out of this one. But she hadn't planned on toasting the guy! Just . . . persuading him. Off-planet. With the ticket as bait.

Well, there were worse things to be arrested for.

Renée turned serious. "Lieutenant, you made it. Good." She gestured at the body. "As you may have already surmised, Member Elleul has been unfortunately murdered." Lane held her breath. Renée glanced at Lane, at Elleul's corpse, then back at Atkins. "The usual suspects, if you don't mind."

Atkins grinned, wide and relieved. "At once, Prefect."

Unlike the small hill where her salon was, the air by the river was clear with a slight salt tang. The banks in the park were shaded in the afternoon, and Lane breathed in deeply, happy to be out in the open, away from the terminal and people. Above her, the ring soared white and shining through the sky. She couldn't remember the last time she'd sat on the ground like this, surrounded by plants and running water. Whatever else came of this conversation, the start at least was a little piece of calm.

After Lieutenant Atkins had taken over the scene, events were a blur. Renée had led her back to the station and given her something to eat. Someone had spoken to her there, one of the other officers. She couldn't remember what she'd said to them, but she doubted it had been anything particularly clever. At some point, Helen had showed up and then Lane had been back at the salon. She'd sat on her sofa and before she'd known it, the afternoon had grown late and a message from Renée was pinging her awake, wanting to meet by the river in Parc Rouge.

Lane felt wrung out. Her brain seemed to be running at half-speed and the events of the last day were disjointed and difficult to piece together. Somehow the Kusanagis were gone, and Elleul was too, and she was sitting in the leafiest part of the city, sleep-deprived and unarrested and unhurt.

She'd let her qubicon go. Ayumu might destroy it; he might not. He didn't exactly strike her as honest. She hoped he would but she doubted it. The choice was in his hands now. Better his than hers.

And maybe it wouldn't matter if he did do as she asked. Inventions and progress could happen at the same time in multiple places; there was likely some scientist in Fides or Orion or even Janus playing with entanglements and quantum data, and finding what she had. It was a matter of time. She was stupid to think she could make a difference by hiding her work. Stupid, perhaps arrogant.

What had she accomplished, in the end? Elleul was dead, Tori was dead, her tech gone, and Renée's chance to go home ruined. *Inconclusive results* would be an understatement.

Soft footfalls came from the right, and she turned to see Renée approach. She wore a light jacket over her uniform and carried a bag in one hand and a flask in the other. Her expression was sombre, and Lane's stomach sank.

"What a day!" Renée sat next to her and stretched her legs out on the grass. Something heavy *thunk*ed in the bag as she placed it on the ground.

"That's one way to put it." Lane eyed her. "You still employed?"

"Unfortunately, yes." Renée rolled her neck to one side, then the other. "All day, endless calls and messages. The NZC is breathing down my neck for answers about Kusanagi and Elleul, the mayor has told me no less than four times she's going grey because of the questions coming from the Parliament, and my officers are all very nervous for some bizarre reason. And the *paperwork*, merde."

"So what are you doing here?"

Renée gave her a withering look. "Because it's after five. Time to leave work and have apéro." She dug into the bag and pulled out convincing MangeX olives, cheese, a bottle of wine, and a loaf of bread.

"Oh. Yeah. Course." She didn't seem angry or overly upset, but if Lane knew Renée at all, she was just getting started.

Renée arranged the food between them, then pulled out disposable cups and opened the wine. "Was that your plan from the beginning?"

The last thing Lane wanted was wine right now. "No. I didn't intend to off him."

"Oh?"

"I wanted to bargain with him. My arrest for the ticket and him leaving Salus."

"*Why?*"

Lane steeled herself. "He was a problem and needed to go, but you'd get the pardon anyway. Which won't happen now. I'm sorry, Renée."

Renée sighed deeply, then handed her a cup of wine. "My dear Lane. I have the pardon."

What? She put the cup down in surprise.

"Oh, don't look so shocked." Renée sipped her cup and grimaced. "I got it from him before we went to the terminal. I reminded him of how helpful I've been. In fact, I'd had Monsieur Kusanagi released moments before, but he didn't know that."

She had the pardon. She could go home. Lane hadn't wrecked things for her. Good. The relief was bitter, and she fidgeted with the grass, plucking at it.

"He wanted me to arrest you."

"I expected that."

"Clearly. Of course, I wasn't going to."

"I hoped so."

Renée made a confused noise. "Only hoped?"

Lane wasn't sure what to say. Her chest felt tight, and she couldn't seem to stop looking at the grass.

"Today was a gamble," Renée continued. "When you called me this morning, the situation at the station was tense, and I wasn't sure how I was going to resolve things. You distracted him, bought me time. I had a feeling that . . ." Her expression clouded. Something like fear, something like anger. "Hm. Nonetheless, I was furious at you for putting yourself in our way, but I can't deny part of me is very glad you did."

Lane turned that over. Tori's death, the media circus, Ayumu in the jail, Renée releasing him, then having the guts to force Elleul's hand in arranging the pardon. And she'd called in the middle of it, interrupting whatever situation Renée was referring to. It had to have been bad if she was this serious about it.

She reached over the food and took Renée's hand. "Glad I could help."

Renée squeezed it. "I am too. Never do it again."

"No promises." Lane studied their hands, how they fit together and the softness of Renée's palm. It felt good. "Nice of you to release Kusanagi, by the way."

"Bah. Elleul overstepped." Renée let her hand go to tear the bread into chunks. "Putain, I should have brought a knife."

By now Lane had torn up a small pile of grass. She turned her attention to the bread. "One of your officers told him you were going to meet me at the terminal. That you as well?"

"I have no idea what you mean." Renée broke off a slab of cheese, placed it on a strip of bread, and began chewing.

"Just trying to piece this morning together. I didn't expect Ayumu there, *with* the qubicon. What were you going to do, hand over a box on a string?"

Renée shrugged and swallowed her mouthful. "Like you were any better. You don't have the missive at all. Did you have a text file you were going to send to his tablet? A scrap of paper? I figured I'd talk you into using the ticket for yourself, then I'd deal with Elleul."

"Hm. I was going to get Elleul to leave in exchange for the ticket."

"Instead you gave it to Monsieur Kusanagi." Renée shook her head. "You should've gone. But I'm not surprised." She made a sudden shocked noise. "Oh—Lane, your invention! Do you have it?"

"No. He took it with him."

Renée's eyes went wide. "Why?"

"Because he's convinced Tori's preserved in it." The memory of Tori, warm and alive, seared through Lane, and she suspected it always would. Yet another pain to add to the pile.

"No, no, I mean, why did you let him take it? It was so important to you."

Lane met her gaze. "I realised other things were more important."

Renée slowly smiled. "I knew it. You do have a sentimental side."

"Guess so." She exhaled, harsh and drawn out. "Not that it got me very far."

"It was a kind thing to do."

"Now who's being sentimental?"

Renée leaned over and tapped their shoulders together. "Madame Kusanagi was in it, yes?"

In a manner of speaking. Lane nodded.

Renée's smile brightened. "I see. That's a risk, no? It will work the same after a transfer like that?"

"No idea."

"Merde." Renée linked their hands together again. "If it works, they'll talk about it. They'll examine the prototype and use it for their movement. You know that, right?"

"I asked him to get rid of it no matter what happened." The more she thought about it, the less she thought Ayumu would follow through; especially if, by some miracle, the data survived the trip. Another thing she'd find out in time. Renée knew a surprising amount about it— Ah, she'd forgotten exactly *how* Renée knew so much.

Lane nudged her. "Hey. Speaking of. I'm not over you investigating me. Helen told me she asked you."

"Take it up with Helen."

"You're the one who said yes to Helen!"

Renée waved that away. "Of course I did. I like your sister. And if you'd told her what happened years ago, she wouldn't have felt the need to ask me."

"You should've told me."

"I think not. You would've been terribly uncooperative."

Unable to think of a comeback, Lane glared at the olives and picked one up to chew. "You're a menace. How'd you figure it out anyway?"

Renée ran her thumb along Lane's knuckle. "I looked into the laboratory. It was quite a thorough arson attempt, but not thorough enough. The published information didn't add up at all. The enhanced humans think the Parliament did it. Intelligence thinks the enhanced humans did it. Ergo, neither of them did. Someone internal did. The logs from the building show no forced entry, which meant someone faked a pass or actually had one. That pointed at you. The data servers were attacked as well as the building. Despite your proficiency with tech, you were in a hurry and the substandard virus you used reflects that. You ensured the building was ruined enough that the police would struggle to wade through the mess, hiding your work. You were the only employee who left the core within the next two days."

Renée clicked her tongue. "The police reports are farcical in their lack of attention. Perhaps they deliberately didn't want to look, but they could've at least *attempted* a cover up. They attributed it to the rioters and closed the case. Amateurs."

Such a delight to watch Renée work. She was so clever. "Well done."

"You were hiding your technology, and given Helen's condition, I suspected your invention and her death were related. However, that's as far as I got. Am I right?"

Lane nodded. "Remember I supplied the black market? One of the brokers I worked with worked out the details of the qubicon from me. On the day of the riots, I went home early and found him threatening Helen. He wanted it: all my data, the prototypes, notes, everything. Said I had to hand it over to the right side before Intelligence took it from me. Mods needed it, needed better from the world, and this was one vital step towards that."

Renée watched her carefully. "You said no."

"I said no."

Telling Helen last night had been awful. Lane had barely managed to get the words out through her fear. She'd related how he'd threatened, she'd refused, then he'd shot Helen and fled, leaving Lane to wallow in instant regret. It was the wrong choice. She'd made a mistake and she was so sorry.

Helen had heard the story, then said she was glad she knew now. She could fill in a missing gap in her memory banks with information. It helped her understand Lane better and answered a number of persistent questions. Thanked her for telling her. Hugged her and reassured her everything was fine. Somehow, the acceptance, both of the story and of Lane's many apologies, had made everything worse. Because if Helen Kovacs had truly been alive to hear it, Lane wasn't sure she'd have accepted it so calmly.

Telling Renée now brought the old shame and misery back. Not as strong, not as fast, but still there, like an old injury. The regret remained, and Lane didn't think it would ever go away.

"I'm sorry." Renée dropped her hand to wind an arm around her shoulders and hug her close. "That shouldn't have happened."

No. It shouldn't have. Lane closed her eyes and willed herself through. "You see why I'm a little touchy about our past."

"Ma chère, you're touchy about everything." Renée pressed bread into her hand. "Here. Eat."

Lane opened her eyes and obeyed. Amazingly, Renée knew the full story and still seemed happy to be around her. Perhaps that was the proof Lane needed that they were both totally insane. "Thanks."

Renee's arm was against her shoulders and Lane took in the moment. The sun was low in the sky, and the ring was growing brighter. The river flowed fast before them, milky green-grey with salt and minerals from the distant rocky hills. Salus had a particular kind of bird similar to the swallows in Lavele, and Lane watched as several flew out of a nearby tree, diving and twisting around each other over the river.

"What happens now?" Lane asked.

Renée hummed thoughtfully. "We wait. Elleul's body will be examined for cause of death, and I know our lovely NZC judiciary will have some words for you and me."

His body, yes. Something strange had happened there. Had she imagined the arcs of electricity? She hadn't right? That shouldn't have been possible, not if he was a true neolud.

"You think they'll find anything *interesting* about him?"

Renée pursed her lips. "I do."

"Oh." A high-ranking Parliament politician, teched enough to break down under electricity. If it was true, Lane wanted to see that report when it was released. Good, wholesome reading for the masses. "Shocking. What a way to be remembered. Remind me why we're both here and not in your jail for manslaughter?"

Renée tapped Lane's head. "My darling. Use your common sense. What happened this morning was blatant self-defence. You know it, I know it, and the officers who saw us know it."

"Ah. Of course."

"Trust me, my station is very happy that he'll never bother us again." Renée gave her a worried glance. "My officers should've told you so. No charges, pending an investigation into cause of death and questioning of the usual suspects."

"I hardly remember anything afterwards," Lane admitted. "That seems remarkably like you following procedure. You sure you're feeling all right?"

Renée smirked. "I feel better than ever."

Lane caught her gaze again and felt herself heat at the expression on Renée's face. "Y-you know Parliament will send someone to investigate *his* murder now. We might get a repeat of all this. Plus there's a lot of media attention coming your way. Elleul, dead.

The Kusanagis, dead and escaped. You're going to have your hands full." She might lose the pardon.

"Au contraire, because it's all in the open, Parliament will be very careful about what they do." Renée gestured carelessly. "We won't have any issues. If we do, I'm sure Monsieur Kusanagi won't mind being the hero who rid Janus of a loathed politician. He *was* there, after all."

Unbelievable. A rush of affection enveloped Lane. She wondered how awkward it would be to stop this conversation to kiss her. "You're going to give Atkins a heart attack."

Renée gave her a piercing look. "I can't trust him with this. There are pictures, recordings, testimonials. I have to consider how to distribute them with maximum effect, especially to the media. I still need that new carpet for my office."

Lane moved the wine cups so she could lean in. "And that pardon? Will you move back?"

Renée watched her. "No."

Huh? Lane straightened, causing Renée's arm to slip down. "But your family."

Renée dropped her hands into her lap. "I know. However, you were right when you said the pardon would come with strings, and I'm not sure how much it would help me or my family in the end." She exhaled heavily. "My Tech and Analytics officers have backed up every file and data request on Elleul's tablet. He has full Intelligence information in those files, you see, and he's been telling all of us about ourselves, including me. I realised that my file, therefore, will have very good details about my family in it. So you see, I have some information already. I have leads now." She glanced at Lane. "Besides, what would I do back home? If I didn't last back then, I wouldn't last long now, even with a pardon from Elleul. Perhaps it's time to appreciate the home I have."

The relief was like sunshine rolling through her. Lane's face was starting to hurt from her smile. "You sap." She couldn't bear it anymore. She slipped her arms around Renée and pulled her close. "Come here." Lane pressed her forehead into the curve of Renée's neck, against her wrinkled collar. She smelled good there—stale, sweaty, but strongly of herself. Lane closed her eyes in wordless thanks.

Renée pressed a kiss into Lane's hair. "I'm glad you stayed," she said abruptly. "Jealousy is so unbecoming, but alas. When you said you wanted the qubicon, I thought you wanted Tori with you. It was only for a second, but I did think it."

"No. That's over. I'm all yours. You know that, right? I was just focused on getting Elleul off-planet. Away from you." Lane turned her face so that her lips rested on the skin of Renée's neck. As she expected—hoped—a small shudder went through Renée's frame. Reflections off the river sent dancing ripples of light across Renée's hair and skin. Lane thought it suited Renée, being surrounded by light.

"You've made me happy for a long time," Renée said softly. "It's stupid of me not to realise and tell you earlier." She reached up and dusted her fingertips over Lane's cheeks and lips, featherlight touches, before cupping her jaw and kissing her as though there were no tomorrow.

Lane closed her eyes and let herself have this, let herself sink into the feeling of love and being loved. Her heart soared, ending up somewhere in the dust of the ring. She held Renée tighter. It seemed incredible they were here, under the weak sunlight of their world, alive and together.

Ugliness chased them and pressed in from all sides, and the coming days would bring new irritants and problems. They would have to think about the people who'd find out about them, and about her, and maybe about her invention.

But now, here, was good. In this space between them was the start of something honest and real; a universe of their own creation out on the edges of nothingness. They had each other, and that was more than enough.

When Renée broke the kiss for a breath, Lane ran one hand down her back. "Does this mean you're finally going to pay your damn tab?"

Renée rolled her eyes and stroked her thumb along Lane's jaw. "Ma chère, have I ever told you how much I adore your sense of humour?"